The Syndicate:
Carl Weber Presents

The Syndicate:
Carl Weber Presents

Brick & Storm

www.urbanbooks.net

Urban Books, LLC
97 N18th Street
Wyandanch, NY 11798

The Syndicate: Carl Weber Presents
Copyright © 2016 Brick & Storm

ISBN 13: 978-1-62286-987-9
ISBN 10: 1-62286-987-7

First Trade Paperback Printing September 2016
Printed in the United States of America

10 9 8 7 6 5 4 3 2 1

This is a work of fiction. Any references or similarities to actual events, real people, living or dead, or to real locales are intended to give the novel a sense of reality. Any similarity in other names, characters, places, and incidents is entirely coincidental.

Distributed by Kensington Publishing Corp.
Submit orders to:
Customer Service
400 Hahn Road
Westminster, MD 21157-4627
Phone: 1-800-733-3000
Fax: 1-800-659-2436

Prelude

Claudette McPhearson walked out of the Clayton County Juvenile Center with a smile on her beautiful face. At sixty years old, the woman still had a youthful disposition about her. She loved children; more specifically, she loved disadvantaged youth. Claudette had been taking in children since she was thirty years old after her husband died in a suspicious fire. They had never gotten a chance to have kids and, even after that, she never had a chance to have children with anyone else.

"I'll see you all next week," she said to the guards as she waved and walked out into the stifling night's summer heat.

Atlanta's weather can be so muggy and wet, she thought as she looked up to the sky. *Looks like rain,* she thought while waving one more time at the guards. They all loved Ms. Claudette, as they called her. The woman had been a staple in the juvenile facility for many years, often taking in some of the children once they were released by the state.

Claudette stuffed her bag underneath her arm after she pulled her umbrella out just in case. She smiled as her black Mary Janes clacked against the steel gray concrete. Normally she would call a cab or one of her foster sons would pick her up, but Jojo, her youngest, was late that day. He either was always late or couldn't make it. She sent him a text reminding him but decided that she'd just take the bus. It was no big deal to her. She enjoyed the quietness of the bus this time of night. She chuckled thinking that the Lord knew the bus was better than riding with Jojo and listening to some song about a trap queen. *Whatever the hell that is,* she mused.

She stumbled a bit as she walked. Her ankle was killing her. Old age had come calling and she hated it. She was still spry but she couldn't deny that her body was telling her to slow down. She was a buxom woman. Not fat in the least, but definitely not small either. Most people claimed she looked like a plumper version of the model Iman. Age and good eating had added an extra twenty pounds over the years but she didn't have diabetes or high blood pressure, things that plagued most black women her age. For the most part, she had done well for herself. She had eight remaining foster children, the youngest one being seventeen. She had raised them, loved and nurtured them into young adults and she was proud of that. Jojo, Melissa, Shanelle, Inez, Lamont, Naveen, Javon, and Cory were her pride and joy.

Javon and Cory were her oldest. Blood brothers, she took them from a life of crime and now both were upstanding citizens, one working for corporate America and the other a law student. Naveen was good with his hands, always building, fixing, or making something. She'd sent him to a tech school for civil engineering. Lamont, well, Lamont was hood and there was no way around that. The young man just had it in him. He would fight at the drop of a dime, was fiercely overprotective of his brothers and sisters and, no matter how hard Claudette had tried, she still couldn't get him not to fight. The boy was a fighter at heart. So she put him in the ring and had a professional boxer training him for his first fight.

Inez, oh, her beautiful Inez sometimes gave her heart attacks. She, too, had anger issues, but they stemmed from a life of always having to fight to prove her right to be seen as human. Just shy of twenty-one Inez was a pre-med student who was well on her way to becoming a great surgeon. Shanelle was a business woman. She could convince any man or woman to buy anything she had to offer. But she was also good with a gun. With her eyes closed Shanelle could take a deer down even if the deer was running full speed ahead. Yes, yes, Claudette had to hone that craft as well as Shanelle's business savvy.

Melissa was her math guru. The girl could look at any number once, remember it, or solve an equation without so much as blinking an eye. Not to mention she was good with money. The girl could count money quicker than your eye could see and she was also good at saving it. Melissa also had a problem when it came to sex. She couldn't say no. She had been introduced to sex way too early and, as a result, she was hypersexual. Claudette had a long talk with her child about the consequences of her behavior as well as other things that would remain a secret between her and Melissa. However, Melissa's accounting degree would come in handy; yes, it would.

Claudette's smile widened as she thought about her youngest son, Jojo. Her little chemist, she called him. Jojo had been with her since he was eight. He was a precocious child. Throughout the years, he had almost blown up her kitchen mixing chemicals he shouldn't have had. Not to mention he almost killed himself in her bathroom when he decided that closing the door while he was mixing ammonia and bleach was a good thing. Since then, Claudette had found every kind of science program in and out of school she could place him in. From science fairs to chemistry camps, Jojo was always in attendance.

Claudette stopped at the walkway of a four-way intersection. She saw one other person standing at the bus stop, a man. That didn't bother her. The old woman was rarely afraid of anything other than losing her children. The smile as she thought of them was still plastered on her face as a black car slowly turned the corner behind her. Claudette was just about to cross the street when the car sped up a bit. The man at the bus stop looked up and started to walk toward her.

She slid her hand into her purse to grip something that she always kept near and dear to her. While she didn't fear any man on God's green earth, Claudette was no fool either. The man was dressed in all black. The cap on his head hid his face. Claudette kept an unassuming smile on her face as she strutted forward. She knew what was about to happen before the man made up his mind to do it. He bumped into Claudette, grabbed her purse, and tried to shove the old woman to the ground. What he didn't see coming was the slice across his carotid artery. One smooth slice widened his eyes. However, it was the look of unmitigated pleasure in the old woman's eyes that sent him reeling. The man clumsily stumbled back, choking on his own blood while trying to catch his balance.

They hadn't told him the old woman would be armed. Nobody told him to watch her smooth sleight of hand just as no one had told him the real reason they had sent him to kill Claudette McPhearson and to make it look like a robbery. They'd only paid the man ten grand and shown him her picture. As he fell to the ground clutching his throat trying to stop the profusely bleeding wound, Claudette McPhearson stood over the man as if taunting him.

She smiled like she hadn't just sentenced a man to death and said, "You've gotta be quicker than that."

Just as she kneeled to jam another blade the man hadn't seen between his ribs to pierce his heart, the black car increased speed. The first bullet hit her shoulder, knocking her backward. Claudette was nimble for her age. She rolled over onto her shoulder and grabbed the gun that had fallen out of her purse. She fired off a few shots, two of which hit the driver, and rushed to hide behind a parked car on the side of the street. Two more bullets hit her in the back and kidney.

She had known the day would come sooner or later when someone would be bold enough to try to take her out. Claudette had no fear and no qualms about it. It came with the territory, she often told herself. She stayed down as tires squeaked and skidded. She knew they were either turning around or the injuries to the driver had made them come to a screeching halt. She saw no plausible escape route, which meant they had thought their plan out thoroughly. They waited until she had gotten to a spot where there was little chance of escape and a far less chance for her survival.

Her mind was on the eight children she would leave behind if she didn't make it out alive. She'd raised them well. Had taught them all she knew on survival. All the lessons, the talking, and the teachings, honing their crafts. She desperately hoped they understood the method to her madness after all was said and done.

The wound to her shoulder hurt immensely. The injury to her back and kidney were damn near causing her paralysis. It was almost unbearable. She heard when the car stopped. It hovered just beside the car she used to hide. The doors to the black old-school Cutlass Supreme opened. Two different sets of shoes hit the ground. One had a soft thud and the other clacked like the person had on combat boots.

This was the end and she knew it. She wouldn't give them a chance to take her out on her knees though. Claudette stood and faced her adversaries. She'd take one of them with her, she knew that for a fact. So as soon as the first one stepped around the car where she had been hiding, she took aim, but the shock of who the person was stopped her in her tracks. Before her mind could catch up with her reflexes, or before she remembered there was another shooter behind her, a bullet to the back of her head put her to rest.

Her lifeless body hit the ground in a slow thud. Her last thoughts were on the eight children she left behind.

Part 1

In the Beginning . . .
Who the Hell Was This Woman?

Chapter 1

Shanelle

As the heavy rain pelted down on us in Georgia, I couldn't get over the fact that my mother was dead. The only mother I'd ever known, who took a little piece of shit like me and turned me into the young woman I was today, was gone. How did she of all people deserve to be killed in a drive-by shooting? I couldn't wrap my mind around that shit. It ate away at me each day and night.

The way the authorities told the story, Mama just happened to be walking to the same bus stop where a gang member from another area was also waiting. She got caught in the crossfire when rival gang members spotted the boy at the bus stop and opened fire. I always told Mama she needed to drive or be sure one of us could pick her up. I never liked her walking, but the old woman never freaking listened. Never. Now we were left alone.

The wind blew angrily around us, whipping the ends of jackets, sweaters, skirts, and dresses. Many people had to hold down their hats and keep the programs from the funeral at the church held tight. Brown, red, and orange leaves danced around our ankles as trees swayed in the music of the wind.

The eight of us stood silent as the crowd thinned out. Our hands intertwined, grief pulling us closer together.

"Somebody please tell me this is a dream, a horrible fucking nightmare," my sister Melissa begged. She didn't care that tears mixed with snot ran down her

upper lip. Her normally pale face was reddened with
sadness. She was tall, at least five foot ten inches. Most
people would look at her white skin and my black skin
and wonder how we were sisters. It was quite simple.
Mama Claudette was the foster parent to eight of us
children, all different races and ethnic makeup. She
took us in and didn't care one way or the other what
race we were. She loved us. Educated us. She sheltered
and nurtured us when nobody else wanted or cared to.
I glanced to the right of me at the rest of my siblings.
Javon, black like me, my fiancé, stood to the left of me,
hand so tight around mine he was darn near hurting
me, cutting off my circulation.

On my right was Cory, Javon's younger blood brother.
He was black and Filipino. He, too, had my hand in a
death lock. His locs curtained his face as his head hung
low. Next to him was Inez, who was Dominican. Her
head was held high while she tried like hell to cry silently.
As her lips trembled, I knew she was seconds away from
breaking down. Next to Inez was Lamont. He was Native
American. For as long as he had been my brother, I'd
never seen the boy cry. He found other ways to show his
emotions, normally by kicking someone's ass. But today,
today, Lamont shed tears freely. The tall, hulking fighter
looked miniscule against the pain we all felt.

Next to him was Naveen, who was Bangladeshi. His
skin was brown, and his silky auburn hair was pulled
back into a ponytail. He was sniffling as he stared blankly
at the beautiful white and gold coffin. Melissa stood next
to him; the tall blonde looked as if everything on her
body hurt. Then there was our youngest brother, Jojo,
who was black as far as we knew but clearly mixed, we
just didn't know with what. He took Mama's death the
hardest. He was guilt-ridden. He was supposed to pick
Mama up but had been running late. I hadn't seen him

eat or sleep since the call came in that she had been killed.

"It's not a dream, Melissa," Javon said.

My handsome king's voice came out with more confidence than I knew he felt. While his eyes watered, I'd yet to see tears fall. As soon as we had gotten the news, he went into protector mode.

The phone rang out late in the middle of the night Tuesday. I jumped awake, sheets tangled around my waist, as Javon sat at the desk in my room typing away on his laptop. We each had our own places, but often spent the night with one another. We'd been together since I was fifteen and he was seventeen. Had we been through ups and downs? Yes. There had been breakups, other women, and other men, but for the last two years he and I had been on the straight and narrow. No cheating. There was still some cussing and fussing. Javon was a leader, an alpha, and so was I. We butted heads often, but I was learning to let a man be a man. It was hard work, but I was coming around to it.

I'd come to live with Mama Claudette at thirteen and he was the first kid I saw. Tall and lanky, he had a look on his face that said he wasn't to be fucked with. Cory had been twelve at the time. I was scared and angry at the world. Didn't want no woman claiming to care for me then force me to leave. So I came in with the attitude that I was going to raise as much hell as possible since I was going to get tossed out like trash anyway. Javon wasn't having it though. Nobody was going to disrespect his mama Claudette.

"Baby, grab the phone," I said groggily. "And then turn that damn laptop off and get in the bed, Javon," I fussed. "Always working," I mumbled.

He cut his eyes at me, but said nothing. He stood, in only boxer briefs and nothing more, and gallantly walked to the table by the window to answer the phone. The muscles coiled in his thighs with each powerful stride. We agreed that when we were together after the night had wound down that our cells would be left in the kitchen on the counter on silent. That way we wouldn't be distracted when it came time to spend quality time with one another.

The fact that my house phone was ringing told me it was one of the brothers or sisters, or Mama Claudette. She often called when she couldn't locate Jojo. That boy was always into something. Luckily most times it wasn't trouble; but, she had received phone calls from cops in the middle of the night when they would find Jojo out with friends doing things he shouldn't have been.

"Hello," Javon answered, baritone deep. The scent of our lovemaking was still in the air, which made me smile a bit. His voice always did something to me. Deep and molasses thick, it flowed over any woman like molten chocolate.

"Who is it, baby?" I asked.

He was facing the window away from me. He had been relaxed. The muscles in his back tensed as the seconds ticked away.

He ignored me and paid attention to the phone. "This is he," he responded. "Yes," he answered. "Excuse me? Say that again."

The tension in his voice alarmed me. I threw the sheets back and got up to walk over to him. I was worried as I stepped to the side of him and laid a hand on his arm. There was a frown on his face that stopped me in my tracks. "Javon, what is it?" I whispered.

"Are . . . are you sure?" he asked then looked down at me.

My hands gripped his forearms as I studied his face, searching for a clue as to what was happening.

"Yes, yeah. We'll come down," was all he said before hanging up the phone.

Javon stared at me for a long time, then frowned like he was seeing me for the first time. There was no life in his eyes and something akin to shock was registered there. I started to feel dizzy. I knew something was wrong. All of a sudden I wasn't really sure I wanted to know what that phone call had been about. What if one of our brothers or sisters had been hurt? The last thing I needed or wanted to hear was that something had happened to any of them. It would kill Mama. Would crush her soul. She'd rescued all of us, taken us from the brink of nothingness, and breathed life into us. If one of us had suffered the fate of death, it would drain the life from her.

"She's . . . dead," he finally said.

I panicked. "Who? Who's dead?"

"Mama. That was, um, Victor Hill, the sheriff. Mama's dead."

Everything that made me human in that moment ceased to exist. Wait, no. Mama? *Mama was dead. I couldn't have heard him right. There I was worried about what would happen to Mama if one of us had passed and the thought never crossed my mind that someone or something had taken her away from us. Our lives ended and began with Mama. None of us had lived until she had come into our lives.*

My bones felt brittle, like someone had sent a full blast of electrical shock through my system. Mouth went slack. If Javon hadn't caught me, I would have fallen straight to the floor. I hadn't even realized I was screaming until he grabbed me and held me in his arms.

"No, no, no, Javon, stop playing," I pleaded, voice choked with tears.

Water reddened his eyes, but no tears fell. Javon was a natural-born leader, so I knew in his mind he was already piecing together how to handle this with the rest of the family. He was a no-nonsense type of person. Once he calmed me down, we got dressed and he made the calls to gather the rest of us together.

That wasn't an easy feat as the news of her death crushed us.

"We have to get to the house so we can greet the well-wishers," I said, once we'd all gotten into the limo provided by our uncle Snap.

The ride home was quiet. The mood inside of the limo was just as sullen, moody, and dreary as the one outside. We could see people already waiting for us when we got there. Mostly white but there were some brown, black, and yellow faces in the crowd. The front door of the house opened to Freedman Park, the only park in the upscale middle-class neighborhood.

In the springtime, peonies lined the front fence. Come summer, a bright perennial border popped up. The inside of the old Victorian-style home still had some of the original 1900s woodwork. The house boasted ten-foot ceilings, dark wood trim, pocket doors, and heart pine floors, and the original glass and molding. Over the years, Mama had increased the space from 2,000 square feet to 4,000. She said she wanted the house to grow with us and it did. We had no idea how Mama got the money to do those things. We knew she was pawning old jewelry she had, working in other people's homes, babysitting spoiled, rich brats for days on end. If any of the people now here knew Mama had an EBT card she used to feed us, they'd probably have shunned her.

"Come on, let's get this over with," Javon said after we all had exited the limo.

The weather refused to be nice to us. The rain started falling harder. Trees whipped the windows and sides of the house. The wind was rude to everyone who was brave enough to stand outside. The poor old lady from next door was damn near carried away by it.

The smells of different foods—apple pie fought with fried chicken in the air—swept through the house. I was so tired of people asking me how I was doing that I was ready to blow. How the fuck did they think I was feeling? I knew they meant well, but when the last person left and after all the mess had been cleaned and the eight of us were left alone, I was happy.

We sat around the massive front room in silence, Mama's smiling face above the fireplace mantel haunting us. Javon looked at all of us. He had taken off the black jacket that matched his suit. He'd rolled up the sleeves of his white dress shirt up to his elbows. The fabric strained against the muscles of his chest and arms. His slacks hung grown-man low on his hips while his dress shoes knocked against the floor. He had a tumbler with amber brown liquid in it in his hand. I knew he was in pain by that alone. Javon rarely drank alcohol nor did he smoke.

"The easy part is over," he said then finished off the liquor and passed the glass to me. I set it on the mantel above the fireplace. "The hard part starts now. None of us have lived a day without Mama. I know most of us were doing this school shit and working so hard because we wanted to make her proud. We never wanted to let her down. Now that she's gone, we have to go harder."

"I got this fight coming up, bruh, but I don't think I can do it," Lamont said.

"You can and you will. All that damn money Mama put into your training. You get your ass in that ring and beat the shit out that Russian-ass white boy, you feel me?" Cory finally spoke up.

He had been quiet the whole time. Javon was the oldest, with me then Cory bringing up the rear. Mama always looked to us to fill the void of guardian when she wasn't around. That was going to be our duty more now than ever. While Javon spoke with more eloquence and decorum, Cory sometimes let the streets slip through his lips if he didn't catch himself. He was a student of criminal law. He had a bachelor's in criminal justice and was a second-year law student. He could run circles around all of us with the law shit he knew, but sometimes his tongue got the better of him.

"It's so hard to focus knowing she's gone, Cory," Inez said through tears.

"I tell you what, if any of you niggas think about quitting anything now that Mama's gone, we gon' have a problem," Cory promised.

"Cory, you have to cut us some slack," Inez replied.

"Yeah, we're fucking hurting here," Naveen said.

"We should be able to at least take a break, Cory, time to mourn," Melissa added.

"Cory's right," Javon cut in. "None of you had better even broach the subject of quitting a gotdamn thing. We have to see things through and I'm going to be on your ass if you think this means you can quit or slack off for any fucking reason."

There was so much bass in Javon's voice that we all stared at him as if seeing him for the first time. It was rare that Javon cursed and even rarer that he raised his voice. Javon was always in control of everything and that included his emotions.

"Yes, we all need time to grieve, but you better grieve while you work. No slacking. No time off," he continued. "And I mean that shit."

Silence followed his order. Nobody was fool enough to say a word lest Javon jump down their throats.

"I can't do it," Jojo finally spoke up.

We all turned to him. His voice was low and even. The designer gold-trimmed glasses he had on couldn't hide the pain in his eyes. They were red and puffy as he glanced at each of us, eyes stopping on Javon.

"Can't do what?" Naveen asked. "Whatever it is, add it to the list of shit you seem to can't do around here. You can't cook. You can't clean. Mama always did it for you. You can't iron your own fucking clothes. Can't do shit, Jojo. Just like you couldn't pick Mama up like you were supposed to," he spat.

My eyes widened. I was so shocked and dismayed by Naveen's words that when Cory jumped up and shoved him backward, it didn't register.

"Navy, chill out," he barked at Naveen.

Naveen and Jojo were the youngest, Naveen's eighteen to Jojo's seventeen, so they often fought like any true blood brothers would. They tended to be back on good terms by the end of the night, but this time, there was something in Naveen's eyes that told me this wasn't any ordinary fight.

"Naw, don't act as if we all haven't felt the same thing. If he had picked Mom up like he was supposed to, she'd still be here," Naveen yelled. "He's a spoiled little piece of shit who needed Mama to wipe his own ass, but when she needed him most he couldn't be there for her. She wouldn't have even had to be at that bus stop if he had done what he was supposed to!"

Jojo's face did something freaky. He frowned then looked like all the air had been sucked out of his lungs. His lips moved like fish as if he was trying to explain or defend himself but didn't have the words. The pain and hurt from Naveen's words were written all over his face and in his body language. Then his expression changed. The hurt behind his brother's words turned to malice. He leapt from the chair so fast it was like a blur. Jojo shot right past Cory and speared Naveen over the chair that was behind him.

It was like something off of *WWE*. I think what shocked us most was that normally Jojo was cool, calm, and collected. He rarely got in fights or spats outside of sibling rivalry. So for him to go at Naveen shocked all of us.

"Fuck you," Jojo howled and he swung at Naveen. "You always talking shit, coming at me like you stupid."

As he squealed and yelled, Cory and Lamont pulled their little brothers apart. Jojo was still fighting mad as tears rolled down his pecan brown face. Naveen tried to shove past Cory, but couldn't. Lamont had Jojo wrapped in his arms. Normally, Naveen didn't show his temper, but judging by the veins popping out of his forehead, he was visibly angry.

When he saw he couldn't get past Cory, he picked up a bowl of gravy sitting on one of the tables and chucked it at Jojo. The bowl hit him in the head. Gravy and blood spilled down his face. Jojo grunted and his glasses fell to the floor.

Melissa and Inez rushed over to him while cussing at Naveen. "Navy, why you do that?" Inez asked with concern in her voice.

"You're a dickhead, Navy," Melissa chided.

"Are you out of your damned mind?" I screamed at Naveen.

Before I could fix my mouth to verbally assault Naveen further, Javon was across the room. I tried to grab the back of his shirt, but he was too quick. His nostrils were flared. Eyes were cold and flinty. When Javon was angry, everyone gave him wide berth so it was no surprise when Cory moved away from Naveen just as Javon reached him.

"Javon, no," I pleaded, knowing he was seconds away from putting Naveen on his ass.

He grabbed Naveen by the collar of his shirt and slammed him down into the chair behind him. The big, cushioned chair rocked and wobbled from the force of the slam and Naveen's weight. He almost cowered under Javon's anger. I was happy that before Javon could do any real damage, he caught himself.

"You sit your ass in this fucking chair and you stay there," Javon said through gritted teeth. "I don't need this shit from you today, understand?" he asked, a finger pointed sternly in Naveen's face.

"All he had to do was pick her up," Naveen said defiantly, making Javon try to grab at him again.

Cory jumped in front of his brother, and spoke something in Tagalog while trying to stop Javon from laying hands on Naveen. Naveen threw his hands up to try to stop whatever Javon was about to do, but Cory had blocked his brother.

I could tell that Javon was trying to keep his anger in check. He was trying to level out his temper so he could be in control and responsible for what he was about to do. But Naveen's actions had pushed him to the edge and Javon was struggling not to fall over. Naveen's chest rose up and down slowly as he bit into his bottom lip, water rapidly leaking from his eyes. Fresh tears rolled down my face as I knew all of this stemmed from the fact that Mama was gone. My sisters and I were used to this. Growing up in a houseful of boys, we'd seen our share of dick measuring contests, but this was different.

"All he had to do was pick her up, Von," Naveen pleaded his case while looking up at Javon. Still crying he said, "That was it. That's all she ever asked him to do and he couldn't do it."

I ran a hand over my eyes to stop the tears. I glanced around the room and it was easy to see that Naveen was right. Most if not all of us had that same thought process at one time or another since Mama's death. I was guilty of it myself. My first thoughts asked why she was at a bus stop when it was Jojo's job to pick her up. She'd taken money from her savings to buy him the car he wanted on his sixteenth birthday and all she'd asked was that he pick her up from the juvenile center three days a week. Jojo had been half-assing the job since he'd gotten his whip. But Mama never made a big fuss about it. Jojo was spoiled. Naveen was right about that, too.

Jojo must have sensed it as well. As gravy and blood slid down his face, he studied all of us. When his eyes landed on me, I dropped my eyes out of guilt. When I looked back at him, he had a pleading look in his eyes as he looked at Javon and Cory. He found no reprieve there either.

"I . . . I was coming. But she said . . . She sent me . . . She texted and . . ." he stammered; but he couldn't finish whatever it was he was about to say.

The glass tumbler that I had placed on the mantel of the fireplace fell to the floor with a hard crash, startling all of us. Mama's picture seemed to be glaring down at us. That calmed down all the anger in the room.

Jojo pulled away from Lamont and ran up the stairs. Javon ordered Naveen to go outside and cool off before he stormed out of the room himself. Cory and Lamont soon left too, leaving me, Melissa, and Inez alone.

Chapter 2

Javon

The woman I felt was my true mother was gone. The only woman who stepped up to the plate in my and my baby brother's lives was gone. Mama Claudette was gone from me. *Fuck!* The image of her sweet, warm nut brown face gazing down at all of us in regard as if telling us to pay her attention back in the house flashed in my mind. I could hear her now: *"Quit with all that discord and sassing. Y'all are family and this right here is not acceptable at all. It makes no type of sense to waste that type of energy on everyone here, because they love you and would not do harm on ya soul. Not purposely and mean it."*

Naveen's words rang true in my mind. I hated that it was there, hated that I agreed. As the eldest of this family, shit, I was supposed to be the logical and clear-thinking one; but I couldn't see past the pain in my heart. Love him like my own blood I did, but Jojo had made a deadly mistake. Part of me wanted to know what the fuck had kept him from keeping his promise to her and picking her up, but another part of me just didn't give a damn in the moment. Kid or not, his immaturity in this one thing had assisted in Mama Claudette's death.

A numbness spread through me. My rising hurt was mixing into a rage that I might not be able to contain. I was known to be a silent killer with my temper. Stone-faced, locked jaw, usually it took nothing for someone to understand not to mess with me, or know that if they did not heed my one-worded warning life would become very difficult from that day on. The way I emoted my feelings started long ago.

From where I stood outside of the house, I could see the parlor where we all once stood. People had entered and exited our childhood home as the wake finally ended. I could smell food resting in warmers from the kitchen. Greens with neck bones and ham hocks, sweet potato casserole, sweet cornbread cake, fried turkey, mashed garlic potatoes, seasoned green beans with potatoes, fried fish of every type: our home had turned into a prime soul food restaurant. All in the memory of our foster mother Claudette.

Looking toward Shanelle through the window I watched her jet forward to frantically pick up the tumbler. Glistening tears spilled over her apple cheeks, as her amber brown skin had reddened. I saw myself going to her in two strides had I been back in the parlor. Saw my other self kneeling down to help her, then pull her into my arms as she held me and cried. But, none of that was going down. I stood with my hands in the pockets of my black slacks staring at my foster mother's garden. It seemed, even as I was a grown man, Shanelle's presence could keep my anger in check, and only two other people could be that type of anchor for me. One was my blood brother and the other was dead.

My first memory of Mama Claudette was simple: she was my aunt. Not by blood though. How my mother, Toya, explained it was that back where she grew up, every kid in the hood called her Auntie, so that's how. Every day it seemed my mom would drop Cory and me on her doorstep, even if my aunt wasn't home. Toya would simply unlock the door, push us inside, and tell us not to get in trouble. See, the woman who pushed my brother and me from her twat was a manipulative leech and gold-digger.

Whenever there was some old head who had money who lost a wife, she'd find her way near him in our neighborhood and live there until she got kicked out because a family member ended up learning that she was there. All of this while Cory and I ran the streets just to get out of the house from her tricking off old men. Nine times out of ten our mother kicked them out and it was on to the next one though. People in our hood always gossiped about how money ended up "missing" whenever Toya got involved.

Twice Toya had been married. Her first husband, my father, was a terminally ill seventy-year-old man who was a war vet, surviving 'Nam. Dude got mad checks, one for being a war vet, and another for serving in 'Nam and having been sprayed with Agent Orange. When he died, my mom moved on, and a fat amount of money mysteriously disappeared with her. Everyone in the neighborhood spoke about that shit until she linked up with Cory's father six months later.

Cory's father was a retired sixty-year-old Filipino who lived in our hood. He used to run several liquor and grocery shops in our area. Toya stayed with him the longest. I remember how he always was handing her ducats. She never took anything from him lower than $2,000.

Toya and him would break up then get back together. He'd always give her money. Cory and I learned Tagalog and Spanish from him and Toya's off-and-on boyfriend in between Cory's pops. Eventually Toya's running in and out of our lives and other niggas' lives settled down when she went back to Cory's father. Years later, after they divorced because she didn't want to move to the Philippines, she collected money for Cory until his father died when he was ten.

After that, she died six months later from being shot by the kid of one of the men she was trying to take money from, leaving me and Cory homeless and in the system. We were in Ohio then. I remember running away with Cory after I pulled a gun on an old, racist couple we were fostered with. Bastards would religiously take a broom and beat me and Cory with it until it left welts on us because we were the beasts from the wild.

We tried to suck it up, because we needed shelter. But when Mr. Wilks broke a broom on Cory's back then turned and whacked me with it, leaving me with a bloody face and a cut down my chest, I knew we had to run to survive. For months we took a little coin here and there, until we had enough for bus fare. We took the Greyhound to Atlanta and a taxi, ending up at Auntie Claudette's house. Once there we had no idea what we were going to do next. She wasn't home. We had no key, we had nothing, so we hid on the side of her house waiting.

"I ain't going back to that fucking place, Von! Where's Auntie? I'm hungry," Cory harshly said in between rocking back and forth on the ground with his knees pressed against his chest.

My tiny shoulders shook in exhaustion as I stood over my brother keeping him protected. Digging in my backpack, I pulled out my last PB&J sandwich. It was just a corner piece that we both had been nibbling on during the trip here. There were three chips left and only a splash of water in a Big Gulp cup I took from the trash, cleaned in the bathroom, and filled with water.

"I don't know where she at. But I know if she comes home she'll take care of us. She has to." Looking at the gun I had in my backpack, I glanced back at my brother with a frown. "Ain't no bitch putting their gotdamn hands on us again a'ight? So don't worry 'bout it. I'll keep us safe for now."

In our talking and cussing in English and Tagalog, we didn't hear when our aunt showed up. "Who're these foulmouthed children hiding beside my house huh?"

Quickly turning, I moved by Cory, who stood up and dropped his sandwich. Both of us stared up at our aunt with our dirty faces, ratty, disheveled hair, and torn clothes. She stood over us in a light yellow, almost white, sleeveless dress and a big, floppy hat. In her one hand was a blue Mason glass with clear liquid in it, and in the other was a fan with a handkerchief. She stood in an odd way with it, holding it toward us and closely studying us.

"I know these aren't my little boys talking like that. Bitch what? You say that, boy?"

Ashamed, I quickly held my hands up. "No, ma'am. Who said dat? I don't know who would say something like dat."

Claudette gave us a once-over. She slowly dropped a lid on the top of the Mason jar and sealed it tight while holding the handkerchief. "Was that you, little boy?" she asked motioning toward Cory.

"Nah-on. No, ma'am. I wouldn't say nothing like dat either," Cory said. "I don't want a whooping, so I wouldn't say nothing like that. I know better."

"Good, because I know I taught y'all about not having a foul little mouth. My little boys don't do that," she said still eying us.

Behind her was our uncle Snap. He stood, legs akimbo, with a smile on his face and his arms crossed over his broad chest. I didn't know what day it was, but he was dressed in slacks, suspenders, and a white crisp shirt, with wingtip shoes.

"Y'all lucky she didn't light your asses with a king switch," Snap said in amusement. "Or hit you with that acid moonshine of hers in that glass."

Claudette turned to chuckle at Snap and hand him the glass. "I know my boys. I wouldn't do that. But yes, they are lucky. If they were any other heathens, it would have been on. Would have taken it old school and threw it right at'cha feet."

I glanced at Cory, who stood watching with big eyes and his hands up. "Oh no! I don't want a whooping now. We'll be good."

"Can we get some of those cinnamon pancakes you make?" I added feeling my stomach tightening in pain.

Uncle Snap chuckled then walked ahead of us some. "I'll head out and bring back some clothes and things. And put this back," he added sloshing the liquid around while holding it up in the sunshine.

Dancing beams of light flickered from that blue Mason glass to swirl around our faces, our feet, our hands, and the area. I kept my gaze on my uncle, watching him walk away and noticing the gun tucked behind his back. Uncle Snap, from what I heard Toya used to say, was a protective man but also a mysterious man. When she was a kid, she almost was raped by an old goon in the street everyone knew back in Augusta. Supposedly, Claudette learned of it and went through the neighborhood to find the old hood at a local bar hiding from her. From what I heard from Toya and when the other old ladies who visited Claudette said when we were around, my aunt almost cut that man from his throat to his asshole.

But it was Uncle Snap who stopped her. He told her something like, "Sista, I got this." Then he took his blade, cut the man's clothes and ear, and then dragged him out never to be seen until a week later when his body was found by some local police, bloated and laid out on the train tracks. The old goon's body was laid out in the baking sun disemboweled by being run over by a train.

When the police came in that old neighborhood—and by "come" it meant they took bullhorns and announced themselves because that old Augusta community, Creek Town, used to scare even the hardest racists and Klan men from coming into that area—everyone acted like they knew nothing.

All of that knowledge played in my young mind. I knew never to get on either one's bad side and knew that if anything happened to us they'd protect us.

Sucking her teeth, Claudette gave us a stern look then motioned to us. "Come on out from behind my house. Where's your mother? I haven't see you two in years."

Relief filled me up as we followed the woman who, whenever we were around her, would clean us up, buy us fresh clothes, feed us until our bellies stuck out from being full, and who gave us a clean bed to sleep in. As we stepped in her home, all of that emotion overcame me until I blacked out on her floor.

I woke up literally hours later, hearing her curse out a caseworker in Ohio. I wasn't sure how she figured it out that we ran away and from where, but she did. Claudette battled for us, and Cory and I ended up being the first fosters in the house.

That memory was always with me. As I thought about it now, I gathered she learned everything from the ticket stubs in our backpacks. The gun I had disappeared that day as well.

This house held a lot of good memories. My fingers ranover the banister that carried the carved names of every kid who came through Claudette's house. Back then, that was when we stopped calling her Auntie and began calling her Mama. For Cory and me, from that moment on, Toya was just a female who pushed us from her vagina. When she died, we were sad, but that lasted only a day. We were raised by the streets, and eventually educated by Mama Claudette.

My world wasn't making sense right now. I had to get it together.

"Remember when she chased us around the house for stealing her purse?" I heard at my side.

A light chuckle came from me matching my baby brother's and I gave a nod reliving it, seeing the image of two little boys running from an older lady, quick as hell, across the front lawn.

"Yeah, and we weren't even trying to steal it," I said with a weak smile.

"Nope, we weren't. We were putting in some money we made in the streets, selling old books and things we found in the trash," Cory explained.

My baby brother stood at my side. His long locs were pulled back and he leaned a fisted hand against the beam that attached to the banister. The smile at the memories of us growing up here slowly disappeared and was replaced with sadness and pain.

"What are we going to do with this place? What are we going to do now?" he asked in concern and grief. "My heart hurts."

Rubbing the front of my shirt, I felt that same sharp pain. "Mine too."

I wasn't sure what we all were going to do. For now, I was reacting and in my pain, but with the memory of that glass falling underneath Mama's picture, I realized that we as the remaining family had to heal.

"Let's go back inside and get us kids back in check," I gently said, reaching out to clap a hand on my brother's shoulder and squeeze.

"Uncle Snap is—"

Interrupting I gave a nod. "I know. I know."

Seeing the devastation on our uncle's face was another reminder about our mother. Since the repast began, he had been in the kitchen sitting at the little table there, smoking and cradling a bottle of White Henny, pouring it in a blue Mason glass. The man lost a piece of himself and it was apparent from the slump in his back and how his head hung low.

As the eldest, it was my responsibility to keep us all in line. Uncle Snap was a part I'd have to work on after this. Back inside, Cory went to bring back Naveen and Jojo. As he handled that, I saw that Shanelle was still cleaning while Inez and Melissa watched her in concern. She mindlessly searched around for more broken glass, kneeling in the process. There was nothing there. I knew it was her working through her emotions.

Taking several strides her way, I kneeled down by her side. "Baby, I think you cleaned up very well. Thank you for that," I gently said staring into her eyes.

It was that fight and softness in her amber eyes that first drew me to her as kids. At first, it was nothing but a friendship thing. Eventually, we fell into the sloppiness that was adolescent teen lust and experiencing love, the type of thing that carried on into our young adulthood. Through it all looking out for Shanelle was my priority. A lot of us kids in Mama Claudette's home related and linked together like family because we came from abusive situations. I think that Shanelle and I connected in an intimate way because of that too.

Because of how I felt about how Toya raised me and Cory as children, I was always angry about that. Angry about scrapping in the streets. Angry about all the fights I had to endure to protect myself and my brother. Angry that he had to do the same in order to protect me. Angry about the many nights we went hungry and couldn't get new clothes because Toya only used money on herself. I grew up suppressing and managing my anger in a quiet, white hot way.

Shanelle understood it in some crazy way and I always respected that in her.

Helping Shanelle stand, I used the pad of my thumb to wipe her tears away.

"I hate that we're fighting like this," she whispered where only I could hear her. "But . . . but, Navy is right."

My inner thoughts agreed, but the way my stomach clenched, I knew that I had to be the bigger man and not allow the family to dump on Jojo.

Stepping back, I guided Shanelle's hand to put the broken tumbler in the trash. "I know, baby, but we're wrong too. Thank you for fixing Mama's picture, too."

"I had to, but you're welcome," she said with a sullen tone. "It's still a little crooked."

Our eyes locked on one another as we spoke with no words at that point. She softly exhaled and she moved behind me as Naveen and Jojo walked in with Cory.

Neither would look at the other.

Jojo kept his gaze on his feet and Naveen looked everywhere but at my face. It was wild but it was like seeing myself and Cory when we were their age. In my mind, I could hear Mama Claudette whispering that, though she was gone, everything still was the same and we had to protect each other at all cost.

We were family. I had to do this. So, I swallowed my own disappointment and need to blame Jojo for her death; then I addressed the family. "We all are going through it. We all feel some type of anger, disappointment, and remorse through our shared pain. Yeah, we know Jojo didn't step up to his responsibilities; but, if he had, we don't know what could have happened, family. Think on it.

"They still could have gotten hit in passing. We just don't know. That type of street life we can't control, so we can't dump our angst on Jojo like this. He needs us. We all need each other," I said spreading my hands out as I spoke. "Mama wouldn't want us to be this way, and we all know it. Am I wrong?"

Lamont, who came from the kitchen with Uncle Snap, dropped to take a seat in an old wooden chair, his long legs stretching out as he stared up at the picture of our mother. Melissa, who could sometimes be like a little mother bear, next to Shanelle, stepped up to Jojo and wrapped her arms around him sniffling as she hugged him.

"No," Inez said walking up to Lamont and holding his hand.

I watched Cory throw his arm around Naveen and we all stood glancing at each other, with Shanelle sliding next to me to hold my hand.

"We're all we got. So if we break up, then we really lose," I said staring at every one of my family.

"I . . . I didn't mean to leave her like that. It wasn't on purpose," Jojo said finally speaking up. He stepped forward, then tripped on the corner of a side table where he stood. As he did so, Shanelle rushed forward.

The picture of Mama Claudette shifted again then fell forward causing me to turn and catch it. As I did so, my hand flew to the mantel of the fireplace it hung over it. A sound like a latch clicking drew our attention. Behind Lamont, an old bookshelf that held all our childhood accomplishments/awards, books, and other trinkets pushed open.

Every one of us stood confused and baffled looking sidelong at the bookshelf. Because a good portion of us grew up black, and in the black culture, no one made a move forward at first. We all just stood, looking like a congregation who just witnessed the pastor being caught with his hand in a cookie jar; then we glanced at each other. I mean, our mouths were agape, and our eyes wide in shock about the *Tomb Raider*–like secret lever or whatever it was that just opened up before us.

Shanelle helped Jojo up, who wiped at his glasses and wet eyes. I put the picture back in place, then Cory with Lamont walked toward the bookshelf.

"What is that?" I asked at the same time as Inez.

It wasn't a literal question that I was asking everyone, because I knew that none of us knew what it was; however, anxiousness hit me at what could be in front of us.

"Go look, Jojo. You did it," Inez said backing up.

One of us laughed and my brother Lamont gave a shrug then pushed at the bookshelf. He was always the type to explore dumb crap for fun. It was in his nature not to be afraid of the small stuff. From our view, it slid out and to the side. There was nothing there but a wall, or so we thought. When Cory knocked on it, nothing out of the ordinary happened.

"It's just a wall," he said looking back our way.

But it was Naveen's sharp eyes and mind for mechanics that sorted it out. "That's a trick. The door is right here," he said pointing to where Jojo had fallen.

In front of the fireplace, a panel of wood sank into the floor. Inspecting it, Naveen pushed at it and watched it slide to reveal spiral wooden stairs as if a wine cellar could be below. Whatever was there, Naveen's also fearless personality took the lead before I could.

"If something comes out of that place and tries to kills us. I'm beating everyone here asses for being stupid right now," Shanelle said behind us, yet she was inching closer in curiosity.

Shaking my head, I quickly followed Naveen. I glanced at Cory in a way only he and I got as brothers, and he moved to close off the room by pulling out the pocket doors, and locking them just in case. Once Cory headed down, Melissa followed. Inez ended up being the last to go with her scary ass, so that she could close the door that led to the kitchen in order to give Uncle Snap privacy and keep what we were doing on the low.

One by one, we made our way below. At first, everything did appear to be an old wine cellar with various books and things as if Mama Claudette had just finished Bible Study or tutoring classes. But, as I glanced around the dark place, finding a light switch, I saw that Naveen was gone. Panicked, I moved around until I found a hallway. To the right was a fancy shower and, as I kept going, another wall popped up with a bookshelf that was slid to the left.

Following it, I heard the others behind me.

"What the hell is this," I heard Melissa say. "Is this some type of maze?"

"Feels like it," I heard Shanelle say. "At least it's clean. It seems as if this has been used regularly. What was Mama doing?"

"Thank God Mama was a clean freak. If one spider or mouse jumped out, every last one of y'all would be kissing my ass, because I'm out! *Dios!*"

Shanelle's solemn chuckle filled the tunnel as she sharply whispered, "Shut up, Inez."

Ignoring them, I cupped my hand to my mouth and shouted, "Naveen! Where the hell are you, man?"

Moving quickly the deeper we went, I stopped when I saw light. Making a quick left, I was surprised yet again when I stumbled into a massive chamber. The place was so big that it looked like a condo apartment. I mean it had everything. A modern chef's kitchen, fancy furniture, a sky light, expensive art, and in the middle Naveen stood with wide eyes. Turning to where he looked, I saw on a wall a glass marker board with pictures, red Xs, addresses, money amounts, and next to it, on a pop-out wall, guns, stacks of cash, and bags of various types of drugs.

"Fuck out of here," I muttered, walking into the place. "Why the hell would Mama have this place . . . and this shit?"

I stood next to a large flat-screen television that turned on showing us the inside of Mama Claudette's house, outside of her house, the neighborhood, several other areas where we lived, and areas I couldn't place.

"Because, Claudette was murdered. She was one of the biggest queen pins in Atlanta, and all of you she chose to groom to take over her empire; and one of you to take her place in the Syndicate."

Shanelle and Inez's, "Oh, hell no!" basically summed up everything we all were thinking.

Looking around as one, we saw Uncle Snap standing in the tunnel entryway where we all had come from. Straight up, I was tripping on how casually he moved around the place as if this was nothing brand new to him. In his hands were his bottle of Henny, and that Mason glass. The old man took slovenly sips, then moved to a pillar in the room. With a deep grunt, he slapped this palm against the pillar, revealing a side panel that brought the rest of the chamber alive all around us. All the sadness in his eyes seemed to partially melt away as a stern seriousness replaced it.

The old man moved away from the pillar, walked in front of a large black reclining chair then dropped down in it. Taking a seat in front of us as if he were a king, our uncle stretched his legs out, took another deep swig from his jar then watched us as if waiting for us to respond.

Honestly, from that moment on, I had nothing to say because a brotha's mind was on lockdown. I stood with my siblings staring in utter disbelief. What the hell was this?

Chapter 3

Shanelle

"Wait, wait, wait," I yelled. "Slow down. Say that again," I said to Uncle Snap.

"I guess you all know her secret now," he replied while looking at all of us. "Your mother was many things. She was a chameleon. She could blend in wherever she went, which made her the best at what she did." Uncle Snap stood, never letting that Mason jar leave his hand.

"What the hell are you talking about?" Javon asked, the frown on his face matching mine.

"Look at this," Naveen said. In his hands was a gray and black lockbox.

Javon took the lockbox and flipped it from side to side. "Something's in here but there is no key to open it," he said.

"Sure there is," Uncle Snap chimed. He pointed to the necklace I had on, then to Inez and Melissa. "All three of you have one of the keys that will open that there box. One can't open it without the other two."

Inez's hand slapped against her chest. "She said she gave this to me because I'd always have one of the keys to her heart," she said.

"She told me mine was because I would always have the key connected to her mind," Melissa said quietly as she fingered her key like seeing it for the first time.

I placed a hand on my key, and glanced down at it then back at my sisters. "Mama said this key was mine because I opened her heart, her mind, and her soul. I was her first daughter."

"Heart, mind, and soul," Cory said aloud. I looked over at him. "That's what's written on the bottom of this lockbox," he said.

Uncle Snap nodded. "Open it," he said.

Inez and Melissa looked at me as if they were waiting to see what I would do. While I had a thousand and one questions, I knew the key to some of those answers would be in that box. I asked both of them for their keys, took the box from Naveen's hand, and studied the keyhole. One hole was in the middle with two smaller holes outside of it. I placed the keys in each one and watched in awe as the locks clicked, clacked, and turned on their own. The lid popped open.

We all crowded around. Inside were more keys and tiny notebooks. Being the leader he was, Javon picked up the keys and small tablets.

"What's in it?" Jojo asked. Melissa had bandaged the cut on his head. It wasn't serious enough for worry.

There was a serious scowl on Javon's face. It was the look he got when he was working and something was perplexing his mind. "Some kind of codes and monetary figures," he answered absentmindedly. "Melissa, take a look at this," he said, passing her one of the tablets that had money marked in it.

The girl's eyes roamed like marbles back and forth across the pads. "Holy shit, this page alone has at least half a mil on it. Seems as if Fridays and Sundays are the days most money rolls in from whatever it was she was doing," she said while flipping through the pages. "Holy shit," she said looking at Uncle Snap. "Is this all Mama's money?"

"All her money and all her drugs, too. Mama ran the Syndicate," he answered.

"The what?" we all asked collectively.

"The Syndicate. It's a criminal enterprise that traffics in millions of dollars of drugs throughout the United States yearly. From the Port of Miami to the border of Canada, the Syndicate is a force to be reckoned with. Your mother, Claudette, ran all of that. She's been in charge for years. The only woman with enough balls and heart to do so."

"So, wait, let me get this straight," Javon cut in. "Mama was a drug dealer?"

Uncle Snap tilted his head from side to side. "Among other things. All this money you see, all these drugs, it belongs to y'all now. One of you gotta step up and take this thing over or all she built will be pillaged and stolen in the blink of an eye."

"So this whole gotdamned time Mama has been preaching to us about staying out the streets, she was running the motherfucking streets?" Cory snapped.

"She owns these motherfucking streets and managed to take care of all you."

"She was a hypocrite," Javon added.

Uncle Snap snapped his attention over to Javon. His brows furrowed and the veins in his neck popped out. "You better watch your damn mouth," he warned.

Javon squared his shoulders, not out of defiance, but because it was just who he was. He was never one to back down from anybody, unless it was Mama. "Or what, Uncle Snap? Huh? You gone lay hands on me because I'm speaking the truth?"

"Yo, li'l nigga, how the hell you think your mama managed to keep y'all in this uppity-ass neighborhood? How you think she was able to take care of y'all so damn well? Send y'all to that fancy-ass private school? You think them damn food stamps she was getting was cutting it? That damn sorry-ass piece of welfare check? You really think kissing those white folks' asses was getting her by? No, nigga! She was out here, hustling, putting niggas in the ground who dared disrespect her. Claudette was out here in the streets while you li'l motherfuckers lay comfortably every night!" Uncle Snap roared.

Javon fired back, "Look at this shit! Look at all this shit! The money, the drugs. We're standing in an underground bunker! For years we've thought Mama to be like Mother Teresa or somebody only to find out she is the thing that goes bump in the motherfucking night?" he spat. "And we're supposed to be okay with this shit?"

"Javon, calm down," I said.

"Calm down? Calm down?" he repeated while glaring at me. "Am I the only one feeling like I didn't know the woman I thought I knew?"

"I'm not saying that, baby. I'm saying, can we try to go through all of this, whatever this is, before we pass judgment on Mama? For all we know, she did all of this to protect us."

"Protect us from what exactly? The people she did business with? Her?"

"Baby, Javon, please. I'm not saying whatever this is she had going on was, is, right. I'm saying, let Uncle Snap tell us what she had going on in detail before we condemn her."

"I'm not condemning her. I'm questioning who the fuck she was. Was she sweet little old Mama Claudette or was she something more sinister? Did you not hear Uncle Snap say she was murdered? Someone killed her because of all this shit, Nelle. And I'm just supposed to calm down?"

Javon's legs were planted wide. He kept moving his hands in repetitive sharp gestures. He glanced around the room at all of us. I guess he was looking for one of us to do more than just stare at him. I knew he was hurting. Finding out Mama was a queen pin put the nails in our proverbial coffins. It was soul crushing to find out the woman who had nurtured us and taken all of us in off the street turned out to be the very thing she preached to us about staying away from.

When he didn't get the response he wanted from the rest of us, he laughed with a hard edge, crossed his arms over his chest, and took the seat that Uncle Snap had vacated. He shrugged. "A'ight," he said deploying sarcasm. "Fuck it. I'll be quiet since I'm clearly the odd man out."

"Javon—" I called out, but he cut me off.

"Nah. I'm cool. Y'all seem happy and content with it. I'll shut the fuck up." His body was so tense, he looked like a damn stone gargoyle.

Uncle Snap moved around the room. He grabbed a DVD case and shook it at us. "Y'all need to see this," he said. "Javon, I know you're mad and you got a right to be, but at least look at this video first."

Javon didn't move. He didn't nod or acknowledge that he had even heard Uncle Snap. Once Snap had put the DVD into the player, we all stood around anxiously, eager to see what was on it. After a few seconds of a blue screen, Mama's smiling face popped up.

Inez gasped and threw a hand over her mouth like seeing Mama alive again was too much for her.

"Hello, my beautiful children," Mama's motherly voice said. "If you're watching this video then, unfortunately, I'm dead. And that also means my death was brought on by the hands of my enemies. By now I know Raphael, which is your Uncle Snap's real name, has told y'all who I was underneath this façade of Mama Claudette. Don't get me wrong, I'm still your Mama Claudette, but I'm so much more than that. I was about thirty or so when this life was passed down to me when my husband died. I took the hand life dealt me and I made it work. I had already been pushing dope since the age of fourteen. I could flip a brick in a matter of hours. My daddy taught me all there was to know. I won't give you a history lesson right now though. Just know that I love you all and Uncle Snap is the only person you can trust right now," she explained.

Mama stopped talking for a few minutes. She looked away from the camera and when she looked back, she was crying.

"I never thought I'd see the day someone would take me away from my babies. The eight of you changed my life in ways you'll never know. Because I love you so, I zoned in on each of your better skills and I nurtured them because I knew this day would come. I run a whole empire, babies. As the young folk say, my name rings bells around every state in the U.S. and even internationally. I put in work and it all came back to me tenfold. We're not poor. We never have been, but I needed to teach you all how to remain humble. So I made sure we lived levels and levels below our means. Is all the money legal? Hell no, but for the most part, I made sure all the legal businesses could never be touched or connected to the Syndicate. That brings me to my next subject."

I listened, slack jawed, as Mama told us about the gas stations, clothing stores, houses and property, and car dealerships we now owned in the wake of her death. Some of the keys we had found were to safe deposit boxes in banks around the state, out of state, and even internationally.

Mama cleared her throat then stood. "Javon, I know you," she said. "You're probably standing around with your chest puffed out, pissed off that Mama has lied to you."

She was right about everything but the standing part.

"You're pissed because everything you thought you once knew has come undone." She chuckled. "That's because you're a natural-born leader who, much like me, hates to be sideswiped by anything or anyone no matter who they are. You hate to be caught off guard, which is why you're so good at always being in control. That's all well and good because it's you who I choose to take my place. I knew you were a leader from the moment I found out you had safely brought your little brother across state lines to the one place you knew you both would be safe."

We all looked at Javon whose eyes were dead and flat as he looked at the screen. He shook his head and muttered something unintelligible. He uncrossed his arms and rolled his shoulders as if his shirt was creating discomfort.

"No one can run the Syndicate but you, Javon. You have to take up this mantel. At this point it should be four days after my death. That means you only have six more to decide what to do. I'm assuming that my death has only been mentioned maybe once or twice on the news. I had it set it up that way as I have friends in high and low places. In the case of my untimely death, I didn't want too much media attention to come my way. I know you're probably wondering why. Well, son, if the people in the Syndicate found out I was dead with no heir to take the throne, they'd run over metro Atlanta and we can't have that. But, most importantly, they'll come after my kids to make sure none of you got the idea to try to come for them. I'm already gone. I don't want to lose Snap or any of you. Look in the lockbox, learn the numbers system I have going on. Look at the money I have coming in. Call a meeting of the Syndicate and let them know with my fall comes your rise to the head of the table. And these are some very powerful people, baby. As you rise, take your brothers and sisters with you. Make the Syndicate respect your conglomerate."

She stopped again as if trying to get her words together before continuing.

"I've been training all of you for this. Javon, you have the business mind. Shanelle, you were obviously born with business savvy. You have the gift of the gab and your gun skills can't be matched. You're Javon's backbone and you have been since you walked into this house. No matter what you two have been through, you both are the definition of ride or die. He's going to need that more so than ever now.

"Cory, you're the lawyer. You're street smart with the book-learnt sense to match. You can do what nobody else can and that's legally defend your brothers and sisters. Melissa is the accountant and not to mention she can use her talent to get what she needs as well. She knows what I'm talking about, too. Inez, you're important. As the doctor and surgeon, if something ever happens to one of them they can come to you without having to need a hospital. Shit like that is very important. Trust me. As a doctor you can provide much needed medical attention if needed. Naveen, you're a mastermind when it comes to engineering. The safe houses you can build can save your lives. Lamont, you are the muscle. Nobody packs a punch like you. I've seen what you can do and I know you'll put any man on his ass quick. And, Jojo . . ." Mama stopped. Her eyes twinkled when she mentioned his name.

"Jojo, you're my baby. And I really didn't want to involve you in this. It's Javon's call whether he will let you at the table. But you're a chemist at heart. You have the power to create product that can go unmatched. Your talent can and will, one day if Javon decides, take us to the next level in the drug game. Javon, you have the whole team you need, people you trust. You run the Syndicate with an iron fist with your conglomerate right behind you. I have to go now, but take heed to all I've said. Listen to your uncle. He won't steer you wrong. I love all of you; and note that nothing and nobody in this world has ever meant more to me than the eight of you."

Once the video was done, we all simply stared at one another. The silence in the room was deafening.

"So this isn't a joke?" Cory asked, still in obvious disbelief.

"This is legit, nephew," Uncle Snap answered. "It's not a joke. I'm sorry you all had to find out this way, but here it is now. Out in the open. So the question remains, Javon, are you in or are you out? Without you, this shit is doomed."

Javon didn't say one word. He stood and left the room. I knew he was on his way back to the main house. I rushed behind him. I had no idea what to say to him. The revelation that had just been laid at our feet was mind blowing.

"Javon, wait," I said as he walked up the final stair to come back out through the fireplace.

He turned and took my hand to help me out then glanced down at me.

"What's on your mind?" I asked him.

"Nothing," he answered.

"You're lying, Javon. After all of that you just heard, you expect me to believe nothing is on your mind?" I asked.

He looked away and then shook his head. "Am I the only one put off by all of this? I mean, our whole lives was a lie, a big-ass façade. We put in all this work, going to school, getting upstanding jobs in the community, trying to make Mama proud and for what? For what, Nelle? Just so we could become the very things she always told us not to become? Fucking statistics? This life only leads to two places, Nelle, jail or hell, and I for one am not going to be the one to take us there," he said with finality them stormed away.

He was headed upstairs to his old room. I fell in line behind him. The room still looked the same. The full-sized bed was made up with a black comforter. Falcons memorabilia was strategically placed about. That was about it. He had always been a simple kind of man when it came to things like this.

"Even so, baby, you can't just walk away like that. The rest of them are waiting for you to say something. They're waiting for you to tell them where to go, what to do. They look up to you and you know that," I said, resting a calming hand on his back. "I . . . I don't know what to think right now. We need time to process this, I know, but not if somebody is going to be trying to kill us. Not if Uncle Snap's life is in danger. We have to do something."

"So what you saying, Nelle? You want me to leave behind everything I worked so hard to become, and become the leader of a drug syndicate? A crime family is what you want us to become? Cocaine cowboys? Here we are thinking Mama was a saint and she was really the black version of Griselda Blanco. I can't"—he stopped then took a deep inhale like it pained him to breathe—"I can't willingly lead my family into this lifestyle."

I moved to the front of him then kissed his lips.

He placed his hands on my hips and pulled me closer. "We already lost Mama," he said, lips brushing against mine. "I can't afford to lose any more of you. We'll figure something out but, right now, I can't make this decision, baby. I can't."

Over the next few days, the tension was thick around the family. Javon and Cory were on everyone's ass to get up and get to classes or to work. My mind was all over the place. I honestly didn't know what to do or what to think. I'd been searching Mama's room left and right trying to find anything else that would tell us who she really was. Melissa estimated that there was close to $10 million in the underground bunker alone. She and Inez traveled to banks all over Georgia with Lamont in tow, opening deposit boxes and getting a tally on things. Naveen had gone through the house and found four more hidden entries and exits.

Cory had jumped head first into his legal studies. If shit so happened that we were going to become this conglomerate Mama wanted, Cory said he needed to know the ins and outs of the criminal justice system more so now than before. Jojo pretty much kept to himself or he was in the basement doing whatever it was he did in his chemistry lab Mama had made for him down there. He and Naveen weren't fighting, but they kept their distance from one another.

While Javon and I worked for Reed and Haswell, a top-level financial advising firm, my mind was on the many times Mama had taken me to the gun range. There I was thinking she was training me to defend myself and in the end she was training me for something more ominous. Uncle Snap presented us with pictures of the people of the Syndicate. Twelve of them including Mama were all gathered around a long, rectangular table like the twelve tribes of Israel. Mama was the only black woman in the crowd. Two white women and an Asian woman were the only women besides Mama. I had to admit that Mama's power was impressive.

Three days turned into four then four into seven and Javon still hadn't said a word about what Mama had wanted him to do. Uncle Snap didn't push him either. He said he would let nature take its course. I had no idea what he meant by that at the time, but we soon found out.

Another Saturday had rolled around and Javon and I were coming out of Scales 925 after having lunch when a black Hummer rolled up and stopped us from crossing the street. Instinctively Javon pushed me behind him and I stuck my hand inside of my purse. The last week had been tense. We had been walking on eggshells the whole time, always looking over our shoulders to make sure nothing popped off.

When the door opened and three Italian men dressed in black suits stepped out, my heart rate sped up. "Baby," I said low so only Javon could hear me. I had to admit, I got scared. I wasn't used to this kind of fanfare.

"Shh," he said without turning to look at me. "I got you," was all he said to me.

"You're Javon McPhearson, Claudette's oldest son, right?" one of the men asked.

"Who wants to know?" Javon asked off the cuff.

The three men fanned out as if they were about to attack us. People looked on, silently wondering what was going on, but went about their day while casting curious glances over their shoulders. The weather was the nicest it had been in days. The sun was shining, birds were chirping. The smell of grilled steak and other spices filled the air around us. I clicked the safety off the gun in my purse and gripped my gun.

"We don't want any trouble, but the Syndicate would like to meet with you," the man answered.

Javon stiffened, his head tilted to the side as if he was in deep thought. I hadn't told any of the others, but the past few days with Javon had been hell. He was moody. He snapped at me if I said the wrong things and God forbid I mention Mama or the Syndicate at all. He wasn't trying to hear it. The man I loved was all fucked up. One night he didn't come to my place like he said he would and I got a sinking feeling in the pit of my stomach. When I asked him where he had been and why he didn't show up like he said he would, his only answer was that he needed some space. I said nothing. I respected it and left him to his own devices. Javon was a ticking time bomb and I knew once he was detonated we were all in trouble.

"Let me get this straight," he said as he set his briefcase down then opened his suit jacket.

I saw one of the men push the ends of his blazer back revealing that he was armed. I was sure the other men were as well. While I was confident I could take them all out, I didn't want to do it in public. "Javon, baby," I said, trying to get his attention.

"These people in the Syndicate sent for me like what? I'm supposed to be at their beck and call?" he asked, ignoring me.

"You can come peacefully or we can force you to come," the man responded.

"Is that right?" Javon asked then chuckled.

I prayed to Mama and God that none of those men was foolish enough to try to force Javon to do anything. Once turned up, there was no turning him down. The next few seconds were a blur. Shit happened so fast I didn't really have time to blink or think. To the left of me, I saw Lamont rush in. One punch to one of the men's jaw sent him to the concrete. He was out cold. While the other two were distracted and going for their weapons, Cory came around the side of the Hummer, snatched the other man's gun away then whacked him across the head with it. That left the leader who had been talking. He drew his gun on Javon and I aimed mine at the man's head so quickly, my nervousness and fear no longer mattered.

"She doesn't miss," Javon warned the man.

"I said we didn't come for trouble," the man spat, face reddened.

"That's too damn bad. You tell me you're going to force me to do anything and it's trouble. You run up on me and my girl while coming from lunch and that's looking for trouble. Tell those motherfuckers don't send for me unless I call first," Javon snapped.

He picked up his briefcase then swung it, knocking the man back up against the Hummer. Blood flew from the man's mouth and nose as he went down. Javon then glanced around. I had no idea where Lamont or Cory had come from, but I was damn glad they were there.

"Put it away, baby," Javon told me.

I knew he was talking about my gun. I slipped it back in my purse and followed my brothers as we made haste to get the hell out of dodge.

Chapter 4

Javon

It took years of dedicated work for my MBA while taking a dual degree route. I graduated not only on time but a year early from the University of Georgia's School of Business at the top of my class. On top of that, I ended up securing a job with Atlanta's top financial advising firm, Reed and Haswell, as an information security analyst, and now it was boiling down to not meaning a gotdamn thing? It had taken everything I'd worked for to get out of the streets and gutter and to not be looked at as that foster kid; to now have it all thrown by the wayside thanks to the truth behind who my foster mother was?

Silently watching the road in front of me as I drove Shanelle and me away from the supposed Syndicate, I was heavy in my thoughts as I chuckled to myself. *On top of that, my professional business reputation is now cast aside in public thanks to being approached by motherfuckers who shouldn't even know who the hell I am? What fuck shit is this huh?*

Yeah, suffice to say I was pissed the hell off.

Since learning the truth about Claudette, the disrespect seemed to only have gotten worse and piled up on my shoulders. All around me, everyone watched me waiting for me to tell them what to do and where to go in all of this bullshit. The audacity to accept stepping into a criminal world was in everyone's eyes except for my own. How could my family be so brainwashed to even entertain the thought of being a part of some illegal shit? For the life of me I couldn't understand it. Which was why these past weeks had been the hardest on me.

Now, the pressure had been amplified and I was being forced to meet with people I'd rather have nothing to do with or entertain by speaking with them. However, with Cory and Lamont appearing like smoke in the wind and going toe to toe, along with Shanelle pulling out her gun, I had more shit on my lap to deal with now. Gripping the steering wheel to the point of my knuckles turning white, I realized that Shanelle had been talking to me.

When she touched my hand, her words seemed to seep through the roaring of my thoughts. "Javon, slow the car down, baby," she urged.

My jaw clenched tight, the nerve in it bounced, and I whipped the car off the highway until pulling into an empty parking lot. "What the fuck was that?" I shouted turning in the driver's seat.

"Baby, what was what? They were about to hurt you, and us," Shanelle said wide-eyed leaning back from me while looking around. I guess it was to make sure we hadn't been trailed. I knew we hadn't though; that was my own paranoia seeping through my anger. From the corner of my eye, I saw Cory's ride reach us and park beside us. Both of my brothers climbed out and I followed suit, glaring.

"So we all don't know what it is to be normal anymore? You all are now eager to live a criminal life and brandishing guns and shit like bustin' heads open is an everyday thing for us?" I shouted at my family.

"Von, we were covering your back," I heard Lamont say as he pushed back his hoodie.

Wide-eyed, I shook my head at his tone. "Nigga, you're only eighteen years old! You graduated high school last fucking year and your life has been about fighting in the ring. Now you're good on turning into the real Rick Ross? Monty, you should be at the gym right now working on getting that belt!"

I was so angry that I pulled off my jacket. I stepped to the car seeing Shanelle exit it and then threw it in my black Lexus. Turning back to everyone, I glared at my family and pushed up the sleeves of my black button-down shirt just to try to rein in my devastation. Yeah, I was wrecked. Broken by what just went down and I didn't have the words to communicate that I was legit scared for my family at this point.

My brother dropped his head as I stared at him with my arm out pointing. I could see Lamont was conflicted too but he didn't back down.

"I wasn't about to let no nigga take you out, not by just sitting there doing nothing when I know that I can fight. Yeah, I graduated last year but I've always been in the streets, you know that. Handling those bitches wasn't nothing for me because it's what I do and how I'm wired, brah. So yeah, I guess I am ready to be on some G shit if that means protecting you and protecting family, man," he said pounding his fist against his chest.

Anguish cut across my heart. I lived my life up to the point of living with Mama Claudette by crafting a survival plan for my little brother and me. It was easier back then. All I had to protect was me and him. This shit was different. I wasn't an innocent child making threats just because someone got in my face and was trying to harm me or take from me.

Now, I was a grown-ass man, making threats that I had to follow through on to keep my family alive. I had to become the streets I was born into. I had to become that nigga I hated. A nigga who killed and took with no remorse because his dick got off on the power of eliciting fear in others. Or, because he was just too fucking dumb and lazy to even be able to think that he could do more than fuck up a community and kill people for his own gain. I had to become that.

Naw, I was now being forced to become that and it was driving me crazy. Mama Claudette had rewired my mind to see that I could do more than be the streets, and now I had to flip that switch back? Everyone around me was looking to me to do that?

Fuck.

My life wasn't my own.

Stepping up to me Cory locked eyes on me but kept his distance. "What we did ain't nothing new, Von. There was no way that we wouldn't watch your back."

"Why were y'all there? That's what I don't understand. Why were y'all there? I asked, incredulous.

My little brother blew out steam, looked around then slid his hands in the pockets of his jeans before addressing me. "First off, none of us want this life either, Von," Cory said with a gentle touch in his voice; but there was something off about him. I couldn't place my finger on it just yet and my mind was still trying to process all that had gone down anyway. "But it's falling in on us. We came to talk to you about it since you haven't been answering our phone calls."

I shook my head cutting my eyes as I thumbed my nose. "So you're not in front of me right now to plead your case of why I should be accepting of all this bullshit? You're not trying to live the grandiose life and kick it like Tony Montana huh?" The last of what I said was spit out in sarcastic Spanish.

Mimicking my sarcastic laugh, Cory glanced briefly at Shanelle then Lamont before sighing. "Nah, but we need you to be." Walking up on me Cory pointed back with urgency at where we came from. "*Hermano,* did you not see how those fuckers were? They were testing you and ready to take you out in one blow because you are a threat to them. We are a threat to them. Clear your mind. None of us wants this shit, none of us, but we got it. We inherited it and now we have to follow through with it or we'll all be lying right next to Mama."

Turning from them my head spun out of control with everything that was being said. A closed-off part of me that remembered what it was like to be in the streets whispered in my mind. It was a part that I allowed to disappear after feeling safe and secure at Mama Claudette's. It was the forgotten part of me that only Cory knew and from the look in his brownish-gray eyes, I knew it was that part of me he spoke to.

"Nigga, don't act like you never almost killed for us," his unspoken words in Tagalog and Spanish said. *"Don't act like you forgot about one of Toya's boyfriends and how two of those niggas came up with a cut throat and a gunshot wound when at one time both separately tried to beat then rape you and me."*

The stern look on his golden brown face and his gaze reminded me of everything I did to protect us both, as my conscience whispered to me. *Don't forget what y'all did. Don't forget the feel of that gun and blade in your hands, or the blood. Don't forget he took them from you and helped take those niggas down as well. Don't forget family loyalty.*

"Cory's right, Von." Shanelle's soft voice interrupted the silent fight between my brother and me. "Pulling my gun on them was scary but I'll do it again if they ever come in our face again; and next time, if I have to, I'll pull that trigger. We have to think like that now if we're going to survive."

Everything they were saying was irrational to me except the part about survival. "What do we know of shipping product, running that shit? Fighting is easy, simple. But then after that we have killing and micro-managing, basically. We know nothing," I added trying to keep out of my voice the need to plead and stop where we were going.

"Not true," Cory said watching me. "Every one of us has been around the drug game enough to pick up some things. I know we did."

"Still . . ." I started to say then shut up. "I need to think."

"Mama said trust in each other. That's all you got to do, Von. Don't you trust us?" Shanelle gently stated while walking with me as I went back to my ride.

Looking down at her I sighed. "That's the thing. I do and all I'm trying to do is be the real constant that keeps us on the right path."

"Sometimes, shit doesn't go the way you try, big bro," Lamont said with a sullen expression still standing near Cory's ride.

"And sometimes, no matter how much you try, your plans don't mean a thing when a gun is locked and loaded on your skull." Pointing at his temple, Cory mimed a gun with his hand then dropped it. "I don't want this, Von, but I'm going to learn everything I can to cover our backs, know that."

"Even doing time or death?" I added in retort then slammed the side of my door not wanting to keep this conversation going.

The ride home was silent even though I felt Shanelle's searching eyes. My own stayed shuttered and focused on the road while making sure that we weren't followed. I figured that since the men who were part of the Syndicate knew where we were this afternoon they definitely knew where we all lived as well. The very thought of that made my blood boil.

Climbing out of the car, I grabbed my things, moved to open Shanelle's door, then waited until she got out. We were in the garage of our apartment complex when my cell phone rang off the hook. I hit the alarm then we headed up in the elevator as I sent Cory's calls to voice-mail. I had nothing else to say on the matter, which was why I was ignoring my brother's calls. Luckily, Shanelle didn't press me about it either. I ended up listening to her speak about work and other random things to distract me. The sentiment, among others, was appreciated.

One of those other things was the fact that she walked around in one of my shirts. This one was my gray college T-shirt. My gaze was locked on the lobes of her caramel brown ass as it jiggled when she walked back and forth in the kitchen making us spaghetti, garlic cheese bread, and a mixed salad. Today was her turn to cook. Watching her on the low, I checked her appearance. Shanelle wore hip-hugging black silk and lace boy shorts with knee-high black socks. Though her ass wasn't *Magic City* huge, it was naturally large enough to swallow those puppies and it helped distract me from my thoughts. Though for some reason, I wanted to ask her why she was so willing to accept our foster mother's arrangement.

Sticking my fork into the plate of food she set in front of me, I picked at it and frowned in thought. "Why are you willing to risk your life and the life of our family to go with Mama's fucked-up scheme?" I asked speaking to the plate. Bright red smeared around on the plate mixing with the yellowish-white strings of noodles and rounded chunks of cheese-covered meatballs.

Shanelle's quietness was ticking at my nerves. I knew that she was trying to carefully form her words and opinion and I didn't want that. I wanted the real, 100 percent truth from her.

Cutting into the meatball, I continued my poking at the plate, twirling it in the sauce. "Be one hundred with me."

"I always am, Von. To protect family, I do whatever need be," she said sitting next to me. "But, to answer you, I'm not willingly going with Mama's scheme. Who logically would place themselves in harm just to sling some dope and dodge bullets when they are in a position where they don't have to?"

Annoyed, I grabbed the garlic bread and dipped it into the sauce. "I'm not feeling that, because you were one of the main ones ready to put those killer dope girl gloves on."

Pushing back from the table Shanelle didn't even touch her food. She just squared her eyes on me then frowned. "It's not even like that. I say again, my choice in this is one thing: survival, baby. If someone is going to gun for me and mine because of our mother's choices, then guess what? I'm going to strap up and buck the fuck up a'ight? Understand me on that please, baby."

Sometimes, I just needed her blunt realness. Everyone around me had me feeling as if I were in a tunnel. Their eyes begged me to step up. I didn't want to. I still was thinking, but my main constant was Shanelle. Naw, I didn't rely on her too much because I made my own choices. But, like any sane man, if you have an intelligent woman by your side then you make her your equal. That's how it was in the old days of Africa and that's how it would be with me and Shanelle.

Which was why I exhaled and backed up from the table.

"You have to make a choice. We're all waiting on you, Von," she said following me.

"No, I don't, and I'm not telling you all to wait on me. Make your own choices. If you y'all want to die, then go do that. I'm not about to shoulder that because

Mama is dictating this shit. She specifically chose us for this. Do you understand that? We were her pawns and nothing more," I said pulling my arm from her hold and walking away.

"Von, you have to confront this," Shanelle pleaded. "What she did I want to say is wrong, but I . . . I just can't. She took us out of crappy, sometimes horrific situations and gave us peace and sanctity. I can't . . . I just can't hate her for that part of it."

I could hear in Shanelle's voice her tears choking up her speech. "But what about this part of it huh?" I asked reaching out to wipe at her tears. "I'm scared for the family. You don't understand that if I accept this, we won't be the same."

The softness of Shanelle's body pressed against the front of me. Licking my lips, I dropped my head to press it against the crown of her soft hair. For now, I conceded. For the past week I had ignored Shanelle's touches. Right now, I needed them to take the edge off and focus. Lifting her around my waist, I took her mouth and allowed our tongues to dance. I was tired of my own complaints and just wanted to forget the bullshit.

"I miss her," I muttered against Shanelle's lips.

Shanelle's light moan sent a rush of desire through me, especially with the feel of her haven pressing against my swelling hardness.

I was about to say, "Damn," but she interrupted me before I could.

"We all miss her. I miss her so much, baby. I feel like this is the only way I can be close to her now," she said lightly massaging the back of my neck. "We need you, baby."

Groaning low in my throat, my head dropped back against the hallway wall we stood in. She had her hand against my hardness, creating a heady massage that had me eager to fill her up. It was crazy. I knew that she was trying to use her body to coax me into a choice but my base desires had me ignoring that for a quick hit of her sweet kitty.

When it came to sex between us, Shanelle and I were always compatible with our libidos. If we needed each other, we always got down to business, no qualms about it, even when angry with each other. It was how we communicated sometimes and, right now, our bodies were doing the talking. I watched Shanelle pull off my black beater. She slid her palms over the ridges of my amber brown toned abs. I enjoyed how she seemed to get off with just touching me and seeing me with no shirt on.

The tips of her fingers traced the indent of my hips. They leisurely found their way over the light trail of hair running from my belly button and disappearing into my slightly sagging drawstring pants. It was then that a husky groan slipped from me as she pressed her velvety lips against my bare chest. A part of me wanted to still battle her, have her on my side and mindset with this all, but when she worked my pants down and allowed my manhood to spring free directly into her mouth, a nigga was undone.

Shanelle had the reins in this and the moist sucking of her kisses were sweet music to my ears. Head dropped back against the wall, I watched her work and cater to me as if this wasn't about my pleasure but about hers. Honestly, if it were, I couldn't care less. My fiancée's mouth was a prize to be celebrated and I was enjoying the moment. Intrigued by the magnificent and enchanting way she was able to swirl and snake her tongue around my tip before sucking me like a Blow Pop, I pulled back, reached down, and traded places with her.

Now it was my time to admire her like the artwork she was. Dropping to one knee, I lifted Shanelle on my shoulders, leaning back to see her alluring curves. On her hip, lining it was a line of stars ending in an ankh. I allowed the tip of my tongue to taste the sweetness of her skin against my taste buds. As my hands trailed under her shirt, my palms found their way to the plush, malleable mounds of her melon-sized breasts. Like cantaloupes really. I enjoyed how she arched into them. The hardness of her nipples playing against my hands adding to the desire between.

A slick smile played across my face. My tongue found its way against the silky slit of her womanhood to be rewarded with the opening of her petals and the slow reveal of her pussy's bud. Suddenly hungrier than a motherfucker, I dived in and drank her like rain. She let those thick thighs clamp against my ears as her fingers ran over the clean line part on the right side of my hair then through the soft, kinky curls of my afro fade. Egged on, my hands slipped under her cushy ass. I palmed and massaged her until I had her bouncing against me and struggling to hold on as she said my name.

Shanelle was a sweet distraction. Too bad that ended at the sound of the house phone ringing. We both tried to ignore it. My baby was begging me to give her the D, but the phone kept ringing. We both knew that when that happened it could only mean an emergency.

Angst made my stomach clench as I rushed to the phone with her by my side. I picked up and the first thing I heard was my brother rapidly speaking in panicked Spanish and Tagalog.

"Von! Nigga, you should have answered your cell phone, the both of you. This isn't the time for a blackout, man," he said in my ear.

Putting him on speaker, I put the cordless down then crossed my arms in worry. "What's going down? Were y'all followed?"

"Shit, yeah! We need you at Mama's. Jojo and Melissa got snatched!" Cory said, emotion making the phone shake on his end.

A stone cold shot froze me in place. If it weren't for Shanelle, I wouldn't have heard what happened.

"Are you serious, Cory?" she said in frantic panic. "How? Where? Who saw it?"

Rattling started on Cory's side of the line then he spoke up. "Fuck, man. Shit. A'ight. Lamont is talking to Inez. She said Jojo was going to pick Melissa up from her classes. Her car broke down remember? So, he was going to pick her up and get some shit from the store from Inez. As he was pulling up to Melissa, a black truck got in the way and someone snatched her. Jojo was on the phone with Inez when this was going down, so he was relaying everything he saw. Everything."

As I listened, I backed up and quickly got my shit and got dressed as Shanelle followed me with the cordless phone.

"Jojo . . ." Cory paused then he continued. "Jojo hopped out his car and ran after them only to be snatched too. We found his cell in front of the student and faculty parking lot. We need you down here, Von. We need you both. We can't lose them too."

Blind, hot anger raged through me. I already knew what I had to do. Everything Mama said and Uncle Snap said was going to happen was in progress, all because they wanted to disrespect her memory and press my family. *A'ight.* See, when backed in a corner, no one was ever safe from me when I was pinned down and when I broke free.

Glancing at Shanelle as she quickly dressed, I stepped to the door. "Let's go. We're on our way, baby bro."

Don't fuck with mine. That's all I have to say.

Chapter 5

Shanelle

"Take me to them," Javon said as soon as he walked through the doors of Mama's house.

Uncle Snap was already there, strapped up like he was five-o or somebody. Dressed in navy blue slacks held up by suspenders and a white dress shirt with a black tie, he looked like the age-old detective he wasn't.

"You need to think about this, nephew," Uncle Snap said, holding his hand out to Javon.

"I said take me to them," Javon repeated.

I was nervous, but I was ready for war. Thoughts of Melissa and Jojo being kidnapped in broad daylight made me anxious, my trigger finger itchy. It reminded me of the days we all used to fight in the neighborhood. If one of us fought we all did, but that was normally because kids knew there were eight of us and they normally came ready to jump us.

"First you wanted him to suit up and become the leader and now you want him to think about it?" I asked Uncle Snap. "Think about what exactly?"

Inez's face was set in stone as she looked between us and our uncle. Monty and Cory stood posted like they were down to do whatever needed to be done. Naveen's eyes conveyed the worry he felt.

"What are you going to do, nephew, run up on a collective of the kings and queens of the underworld? And do what exactly?" Uncle Snap asked.

Javon stepped face to face with our uncle and stared him down. "Old man, you take me to these motherfuckers who snatched my family or you're the enemy to me at this point. Make a choice, Uncle. Make a choice and know this is the last option you get to make," Javon said.

His tone was so cold and malicious that it made my flesh crawl. I hadn't expected Javon to go there. Clearly Uncle Snap hadn't either as his shoulders straightened, his spine stiffened, and he took a step back. "That's how you feel, Javon?" he asked.

"That's how the fuck I feel. Now, what are you going to do about it? Take me to them or cross the line to the other side," Javon snarled.

"You ain't got no plan. Ain't got no fucking weapons. Haven't sat down with these people, but you want me to just lead you into the lion's den?" Uncle Snapped asked incredulously. "Ha. Okay, li'l nigga. Since you got balls of brass. A'ight."

I could see Uncle was hurt behind Javon's words, but I could also see Javon's eyes had glossed over and he was no longer operating on respect and rules of the game. He was operating on instinct and the need to protect.

Uncle Snap snatched up a set of keys and we followed him to his truck. Cory hopped up front while the rest of us jumped in the back. The truck was so eerily quiet not even the radio seemed to drown it out. Javon's jaw was set in stone. His thigh rapidly brushed against my thigh as it bounced up and down. I had no idea what he was thinking or what was on his mind. All I knew was I didn't want to be on the other end of his wrath in the moment.

It took us about thirty minutes to get to a nondescript warehouse in the middle of nowhere. "The Syndicate normally meets here to discuss numbers and products that have been shipped in," Uncle Snap said after we had all exited the truck. "When Claudette didn't show up last Saturday people started talking. It's my guess that Melissa and Jojo are in there somewhere."

Javon didn't respond. He marched forward, with determination in each powerful stride he took. Before he could reach the door, Uncle Snap reached out to grab his arm.

Javon looked at Uncle Snap's hand then up to the man's eyes. "Listen to me, nephew, a'ight? I know you're angry and you got all right to be, but try some decorum when you come face to face with these people okay?"

"Anyone of them got something to do with Mama being dead?" Javon asked.

"They very well could."

"And they took Melissa and Jojo?"

"One of them did, I'm sure."

"Then fuck decorum."

Uncle Snap sighed. "Nephew, remember Mama's words? You can trust me. I ain't the enemy. Been with your mama for years. I love . . . loved her. She was all I had. Rescued me the same as she did all of you, but in a different way, you feel me? Understand what I'm saying?"

Something unspoken passed between Uncle Snap and Javon in that moment. I didn't know what it was, but Javon's stand softened in a way only I, Cory, and maybe Uncle Snap could see.

"Understand me, nephew. I got you, no matter what. But in order for any of this shit to go down smoothly, please just listen to me," Uncle Snap pleaded.

Javon didn't say anything. He gave one head nod and that was all that was needed between the two alpha males before me.

"One more thing, Javon. The Syndicate, they're the governing body of all the top crime families in the U.S. They rival what was once known as the Commission up North. So this ain't some silly street turf shit. This is the real deal. The big kahuna so to say. If someone put a hit out on Claudette, these are the people who approved it. These are the people who divide up turf and give it to the different drug dealers all over the U.S. This shit is bigger than some petty drug lord getting a crew and naming it the Cartel who runs one city or some shit. The Syndicate could go up against the cartel of Mexico if they so chose. That's how big this thing is you're walking into. This is what your mama ran for over twenty-five years. Do you know how hard that was to do as a black woman? That means she bodied many a nigga and did some shit that would make you all cringe, for over thirty fucking years!"

The reality of Uncle's words settled among us. Cory looked at me. Monty and Inez looked at Uncle in awe while Naveen stood unmoved.

"When you walk in here, nephew, if you about to say fuck all I just said, then you let these niggas know you ain't coming to play no games. Mama had to become a monster to demand their respect. You're going to become something worse. So before you walk in here, that devil that dances on your shoulder . . ." Uncle said as he used two fingers to poke the area over Javon's heart. "And don't deny it, Javon, I've seen that thang in you for years. Seen you fight to keep it under control. I know it when I see it because I loved it and encompassed it when I decided to love yo' mama. So that devil and that God that battle for dominance in you, need to become one."

As soon as Uncle finished his last sentence, the door to the warehouse came open. Men heavily armed and dressed in black fatigues ushered us inside the building. While the outside wasn't anything to write home about, the inside was another story. We were led down a long, dark hall until we came to intricately carved double doors. Before they let us in, we were patted down and stripped of our weapons. A move that left me feeling like we all had targets on our backs.

Once that was done, two of the guards pushed the doors open to a room that was so immaculately decorated it looked as if we had just walked into a mansion in heaven. Gold carved lions sat regally in two corners of the room as lights that looked like torches lined the walls. In the middle of the room was a long table just like the one Uncle had shown us in the picture before. Above it was a low-hanging golden chandelier. Empty place settings of dishes sat before each person as if dinner was normally served at these meetings. All the chairs at the table had been filled except the one that sat off in a dark corner of the room.

My heart sank knowing that had been Mama's chair. The rest of my siblings must have felt the same as all their eyes turned to the chair then back to the table. All eyes were on us. There was a white man who sat at the head of the table, which made Javon tilt his head. Anytime his head tilted I knew something bothered him to the point of anger.

"Good afternoon," Javon greeted him, which surprised me. "I'm not sure if you know me, but we're just going to assume you do since you sent for me earlier today. I'm Javon McPhearson. My mother used to run this here Syndicate I'm told."

"'Used to' being the operative words," the white man sitting at the head of the table said.

"Please don't interrupt me again when I'm speaking," Javon said. "You sent for me. I refused your invitation. You proceeded to kidnap my little brother and my sister as if . . . as if that was okay. Miguel," Javon called, "how would you feel if I went and snatched your daughter from that private school in East Hampton, New York?" he asked.

I, along with all my other siblings, stepped back and looked at Javon like he was someone we hadn't seen before. How the hell did he know these people by name?

"What about you, Ming Lee? Your twin daughters are nestled away in London at a private academy. And you, Rusev? Your son is in hiding in Cali, blending in with the surfers and preppy rich kids. I was under the impression that children and women were off-limits," Javon said.

Uncle Snap was wide-eyed for a few minutes then he chuckled and mumbled, "I should have known."

I wanted to ask what he should have known, but I was smart enough to keep my mouth closed. I knew each of the people he called by the way their eyes widened.

"I had nothing to do with any of your siblings being taken, Javon," the one named Miguel spoke up. He was a Latino male with a close crop of curly hair atop his head. He carried a stern look about him as he sat with his hands clasped in front of him. Just as Javon had studied them, it seemed as if they had studied up on him as well.

"Neither did I," Rusev added, his accent not thick enough to impede his English.

"I would never sanction such a call, Mr. McPhearson," the woman named Ming Lee answered. She was younger than she looked in the picture I'd seen of her before. Her long hair fell into a silky wave over her eye. The side was held back by a floral hairpin nestled in the side of her hair. Her eyes lured you in, but clearly she wasn't to be taken lightly. She too was dressed in a black suit, like the men at the table. As they spoke, Javon walked closer to the table. I looked to the left and right of me and decided to stay where I was. Cory and Uncle Snap flanked Javon. The tension in the room was thick.

"Cormac, you're sitting at the head of the table as if you've been voted to take the place left vacant by my mother."

Cormac's hair was pulled back into a ponytail. Catlike gray eyes followed Javon's every move. His pale skin needed a tan, but his arrogance was on a hundred as he eyeballed Javon.

"The rules of the Syndicate dictate that someone step up in the interim in case the boss of the bosses vacates their seat. I stepped in because I've been with the Syndicate just as long if not longer than your mother has . . . well, was," Cormac said.

My eyes turned to slits at the way he said "was." I didn't even know the man and wanted to kill him on the strength of the fact that I thought he was making fun of Mama's demise.

Javon walked around the table and touched each man and woman on their right shoulder. Some nodded as a show of respect, others bristled. I had no idea what he was doing, but I trusted his logic and instinct. "Cory, bring me Mama's chair," Javon said.

I watched on silently along with Naveen, Monty, and Inez. Once Cory brought Javon the chair, Javon set it next to where Cormac was, then stood behind the man.

"Did you take my sister and my brother?" Javon asked calmly.

Cormac's face reddened when Javon laid a hand on each of the man's shoulders. My fingers moved on their own out of nervousness. I started to feel antsy.

Cormac signaled one of the guards. They left the room and came back seconds later with a distraught Melissa and visibly shaken Jojo. Our little brother didn't have his glasses on so I knew he couldn't see two paces before him. Melissa's right eye was bruised, which angered me.

Cormac chuckled and tried to look behind him. "I, ah, I simply wanted to get your attention, lad. It's been seven or so days and you haven't reached out to us. I know Raphael has told you the way things are done by now. Your mother was a smart lady. I know she left provisions in place."

Javon did something I didn't expect. He laughed. It was almost maniacal in nature. "Oh is that it?" Javon asked as he patted the man's shoulders and then looked around the table. "Oh well then, it's no big deal, none at all. He just wanted to get my attention. Ha, ha. I respect that. I respect it," Javon said, almost as if he was rambling.

Then he stopped laughing and talking. His upper lip twitched in the left corner. His sleight of hand was baffling to the eyes. He snatched up a long fork and before anyone could react, he jammed the fork in Cormac's neck over and over and over again. Each stab was harder than the one before. People at the table sat unmoved as if they were used to seeing people killed in such a violent manner. Blood spurted and spewed all over the place. Javon's teeth were bared as he did so. He'd snapped. Cormac gargled blood as he struggled to breathe. Futilely, he tried to grab behind him to claw at Javon.

The guard next to me was occupied with the scene before him, and shocked. I snatched the handgun on his hip, popped the safety and, before he could raise the gun in his hands, I'd blown his brains clear across the room. Taking out the guards in the back of the room was easy. One shot. Two shots. Three shots. Four. They all went down like dominoes. Monty's meaty fist pounded another guard until he was laid out in a bloody pulp. Inez had jumped on the back of one while Naveen sliced the man's stomach open. When they took the weapons from us, they never paid attention to Naveen's belt. He'd made it himself. When not used for a belt, it effectively turned into a sword. I wouldn't know when or how the boy made it, but he had. That came from growing up in a place where he had to learn to fight for survival, food, and his manhood.

I looked back up just in time to see Javon shoving Cormac's head down into the gold bowl before him. I swore it looked like Javon was foaming out the mouth and had gone mad.

"Anybody else want to get my fucking attention?" he yelled, spit flying from his mouth as he jabbed the fork in the air pointing at the other men and women around the table. "Anybody else wanna get my fucking attention! Don't ever, as long as the day we're out of commission, come for my family. Ever! You want to get my attention, huh? You niggas got my undivided fucking attention now."

An hour later, we all sat in Mama's house, stunned to silence behind all that had happened. After ensuring that Melissa and Jojo were okay. Javon refused to talk about the murder he had just committed.

"I'm sorry," Javon eventually said. He was still in bloody clothes. That same maddening look was still in his eyes. He sat with one hand up to his face with his thumb and pointer finger in the shape of an L. "I haven't been all that honest with you guys. For the last week, after learning all we had about Mama, I would come here several times a day, while everybody was away, and sit in that damn underground bunker and go through all the shit that was left down there. Went through all the videos, all the files. Learned the identities of those in the Syndicate. You can say I did my homework. I didn't know why then. I just knew my instincts told me to and I followed them."

"Good thing you did," Uncle Snap spoke up. "It gave you an advantage."

"I got a meeting with these folks again in two days. I still have to figure out which one of them killed Mama. I know Cormac probably had something to do with it, but more than him had to make the call. I don't know what

I'm going to do. Don't know what I'm going to say, but I know this: once we step into this game, we ain't gon' be playing marbles while these niggas playing chess. If I'm to run this shit, it's going to be my way, my rules. Jojo, let's get this out the way; you're not at this table. You're too young."

Jojo frowned. "Come on, Von. Y'all always leaving me out of stuff."

"Jojo, I said no. That's the end of it. My heart was almost ripped from my chest when I got that phone call that you and Melissa had been taken. I couldn't bear the thought of anything happening to any of you, but to have something happen to you, Jojo? I can't have that. It's no secret that you were Mama's favorite. Something happening to you would be like losing her all over again and none of us want that. The answer is no."

Jojo sank back in the chair he was sitting in and looked dejected.

I had questions for Javon. I wanted to know why he didn't clue me in on what he had been doing. It was nothing more than my feelings had been hurt because the only reason I hadn't gone back to the bunker was because I wanted to do so with him.

"What you did, nephew, shows why Mama picked you to be the leader. Nobody else would have been wise enough to study these people like you did before you even decided to step into this game," Uncle Snap praised Javon.

Javon stood. "Yeah. I'm going to go take a shower. We got work to do." He looked as if he had aged ten years in less than three hours.

I could tell the pressure on him was almost unbearable. I decided against bringing my feelings to Javon. He had enough on his shoulders. I knew he didn't need to add my hurt feelings to the mixture. So I kept it to myself. This was bigger than me and my feelings.

Over the next few days shit was hectic. We had all pretty much been staying at Mama's house. Every night at six, Javon expected everyone to be home and gathered in the front room or around the dinner table so we could talk. It was a Thursday, three days after Javon had gone back to sit with the Syndicate. He had only taken Uncle Snap and, when he came home, he was hush mouth about what had gone on in the meeting.

"Cory, I need you to look up some shit called the Foreign Narcotics Kingpin Designation Act, also known as the Kingpin Act. See what that shit entails so you can be prepared just in case some shit goes down. Also, the RICO act and all that shit. See if you can get more hours at that law office you're interning at and, also, it would be a good idea to see if you can get an internship at the district attorney's office, feel me?" Javon asked him.

Cory nodded as he tore into his steak.

"Melissa, you and Inez finished going to all the banks yet?" he asked my sisters.

They both nodded eagerly. Melissa said, "Von, there is so much money, big bro. My pussy is wet just thinking about it."

Uncle Snap choked on his coffee. Jojo's eyes widened. Cory frowned. Naveen and Monty chuckled, but never stopped eating while Inez cackled. I shook my head. Melissa had a sex problem. She was addicted to it. Most people would call her a whore, but we didn't. Mama taught us better than that.

"I mean just from the safe deposit boxes alone, we're set for life. Our kids' kids' kids are set. Not to mention we're splitting Mama's insurance policy, which gives us all a little over sixty-two thousand dollars each. We got this house and the equity in it. Mama's jewelry. Shit, the businesses. So much money coming from everywhere, big bro. It's almost maddening," she said.

"How much of the money in the bank is clean money?"

"As far as I can tell, all of it."

"Claudette was good at keeping clean money clean and dirty money dirty. You don't last in the game over thirty years by making mistakes like mixing money," Uncle Snap said.

Javon nodded. "Inez, keep working with Melissa, but also remember what we talked about. Monty, focus on your fight coming up. That's all I want from you for now. Naveen, once dinner is over, show me the ins and outs of the secret trap doors in this house. We have to get these drugs out of here."

"Speaking of which, there is a shipment supposed to be coming in at midnight at Dekalb-Peachtree Airport tonight. You need to be there. Also you need to meet the supplier who will be there in the morning," Uncle Snap told Javon.

"Okay," he answered.

"And have you decided who's going to take Cormac's seat yet?"

"I have. I want to reach out to Lucky in New York. Mama spoke fondly of him in her notes. I want to meet him."

"Good call," Uncle Snap said.

I watched as Javon gave orders. He sat at the head of the table like he had been born to be a leader. The dress shirt and dress slacks he had on were in vast contrast to the baggy shirt and jeans I'd met him in. Javon asked everyone to leave the table but me and Uncle. I ate quietly while Uncle Snap told Javon to pay attention to how things would change around him now. He wanted to him to take special note of the way people in high places would regard him with much more respect now.

"There're levels to this shit," Uncle declared. "And Claudette paved the way so you could step in at the highest."

Uncle finally left after a few more words between him and Javon. Silence engulfed the room when it was just me and Javon alone. My fork hitting my plate and Javon gulping down his drink were the only noises in the dining room.

"You mad at me?" he asked me.

"No," I answered without looking up from my steak.

"Okay."

There was silence between us again before he spoke up. "I need you," he said.

I slowly looked over at him. "I know you do."

"You have to keep me humble. Have to keep me on my toes."

I nodded. "I know."

"You see, it's in us, baby. In all of us. It's just been lying dormant. Mama must have known that. The lives we thought we left behind, we didn't. We just put it to bed. When the time called for it, we all stepped up to the plate. That innate ability to survive at all costs kicked in and all it took was the right button to be pushed."

I kept eating as I listened. I chewed my steak slowly.

"I'm sorry," he said then grabbed my hand. "Keeping you in the dark while I was researching all Mama's shit seemed like the right thing to do that time."

I looked at him. "I'm not questioning that. But, we've always been honest with one another."

"I didn't lie, Nelle."

"You told me you needed space."

"And I did. That wasn't a lie. I needed space to look into shit. I had to figure shit out, baby, and I had to do it without distraction."

"I'm a distraction now?"

"Yes," he answered honestly. "You've always been, baby. I can be mad as fuck. Ready to kill a nigga; but if you say my name, I falter a bit. Now that Mama is gone, Cory is the only other person who can do that, but you? You, Shanelle, have power that no one else has. That's why you've got the most important job of us all."

"Which is?"

"Keeping me grounded. I'm no fool. I know with this life comes great power and I know what power does to a man."

He squeezed my hand then stood, pulling me up with him. I walked into his embrace without him having to pull me closer. I laid my head on his chest and listened to his heartbeat.

"Hold me accountable, baby. In all this shit, hold me accountable when I'm fucking up. Make me remember this moment because, after this, life as we once knew it is over."

Part 2

Things Will Never Be the Same

Chapter 6

Javon

I played into everything that I wasn't trying to be, everything that Mama Claudette needed me to be, and it was playing over and over in my mind on rewind while I sat at work staring at the cursor on my screen. Cormac was my first true kill done maliciously. My conscience wanted to play it as self-preservation for my family but, honestly, another part of me called that bluff. There were other ways that I could have taken care of Cormac. Yet, I chose to kill and my family followed suit behind me.

Running my palms over my face then lacing my fingers to comb through my hair, I exhaled slowly and bowed my head. I was on the path of being a monster, all in the name of family and Mama Claudette. The type of man I was, was vastly shifting. Coffee cup in my hand, I stared at the latest viruses and security breaches to look out for. I also was adding the knowledge to the security compliance policy forms I had drafted. Combing over them, tweaking them here and there, I took a sip of my strong drink and thumbed my nose. To the left of me was my cell phone lighting up for my attention.

Various texts from the family drew my attention. Inez sent me a message excited about achieving an internship at Emory Hospital. A wide smile spread across my face. I quickly sent her a text back telling her how proud I was of her. With her working at the hospital I summed up that she'd be out of the picture of our new family business.

I had given her a side plan that I knew would satisfy
Mama's plans of her working for the Syndicate, while
also keeping her safe in her personal life and her goals.

"Heading out?"

Briefcase in my hand, I gave a nod to my coworker
Everett. Peeking from her computer was our other
coworker, Gloria. We were the only black folk in our
department. Let me note, I say black because we all look
it, even though Everett is East Indian from Harlem, NYC.
Funny, but not funny enough, we all worked together. All
of us were working our way up to become supervisors
and heads of our department. As of now, because of my
effective style of working, I was ahead of all of them.

"Yeah, my mind is elsewhere," I said heading to the
door.

"I told Everett to take some slack off of you considering
your loss," Gloria said in concern.

My gaze focused on Gloria's caring smile. "Thank you
for that, but everything is done on my end."

"Oh, man! Even with a loss, you're steps ahead,"
Everett said with a chuckle and clap of his hands. "High-
achieving ass."

I gave an amused chuckle. Both of them reminded me
of an episode of *Parks and Recreation* in personalities,
and their friendship with one another. Though it was
policy not to date within the same department of the
company, Everett and Gloria kept things secret. All
friendly competition between us all stayed civil, because
we were the only people of color in our hood, as we
called it. None of us was going to block another or step
on another, was our secret code. The goal was to knock
out those who didn't support us, and do our thing. Funny
enough, I was living that code with my new role.

"What's that saying, Everett man? We always have to
work twice as hard to gain what they get with a cough and
a sneeze?"

Both Everett and Gloria laughed. My assistant and fellow coworker who was close with us, Danny Ito, came from behind me, chuckling having heard me, and handed me folders.

"Thanks for these, Dan. All right, everyone, have a good evening. I'll see you all later."

"If you do decide to take that personal leave let us know," Everett said behind me.

"NA," I said, which was code for "nigga ass," "you're not getting my position."

Chucking the deuces, I headed out, stopped at Shanelle's department to leave her a note; then I went to my ride. Driving off, I made sure to watch my surroundings while keeping myself active through the rest of the workday. It was a means to an end, to bide my time until what I had to do at midnight. The second text I received was from Cory and Uncle Snap. It was a message telling me to check my inbox. I knew from them using that term that it was code for me to use my blackout cell phone. Taking the highway and exiting near the airport, I parked in a quiet area and sat listening to messages on my blackout phone.

"Everything was cleared. Luck is on your side." After that, I counted what was said then dropped my head back against my seat with a sigh.

Lucky was flying in at five in the morning, which meant meeting him at a set of modern condos that our mother and Uncle Snap owned. After everything, it was Shanelle's responsibility to oversee the real estate. I had explained to her that I needed her to be my conscience, but I knew she could do more than that, which she was.

The sound of my car alarm chipped behind me. I moved to the back of my Lexus, popped the trunk then pulled out a change of clothes. Tossing everything in it, I stood in nothing but black leather gloves, my boxers, and a tank in an empty car garage. Behind me was a truck. I walked to it, unlocked the back, and climbed in. Closing the doors, I looked around the tight quarters noting freshly pressed dark jeans, black dress boots with rubber bottoms so that I could move in them effectively, a black designer button-down shirt, and black suspenders.

Hurriedly putting everything on, I kept the top of my shirt unbuttoned then rolled up the sleeves of my shirt, showing off the tattoos on my forearms. I reached for a fitted gray houndstooth trench coat. Attached to it was a hoodie. When I pulled the coat on, I reached up and pulled the hood over my head. Keys sat in the driver's seat with directions from Uncle Snap to where I needed to go to swap out the van.

I drove in silence until I made it to my switch-off point. Parking, I hopped out and headed toward the waiting Benz. Hands in my pockets, I dropped my hoodie by tilting my head back, hit the unlock button on the keys I had in my pocket then slid into my ride.

My current location was deliberately close to the meeting spot. I sat back and watched planes lift in the air while others smoothly landed on the runway. Darkness cloaked the sky while I sat in wait. With a quick glance to my black Rolex, I checked the time. Currently it was eleven.

Allow me to break down what I was doing. One, I was exchanging supplies. Two, I was meeting the supplier. My mind was going a mile a minute causing me to shake my leg in my seat while in wait. Mama's notes were clean and to the point about what I needed to learn in shipping kilos. Because of her death, this meeting was important. I already knew that, after this, I would not meet a supplier in person again. This shit was for my extended cohorts to handle, which was why I was anxious.

Eyes were everywhere and with any whisper that product was flying in from somewhere or being delivered, problems could go down. Having my cover busted just because I was stepping in as the leader could work in favor of the Syndicate. They could gain from me being caught my first time out and I didn't need or want that. So, I was anxious.

My eyes darted back and forth as I watched people appear. With them was Uncle Snap and Cory. The side of my door opened and I didn't have to look to see who it was. Long legs pushed the passenger seat back, a small bag dropped between them, and the door closed.

"In the future, since you're my shadow now, you'll have to work with Shanelle to get cleaner with your gun aim. I'm glad you're with me though," I said keeping my gaze ahead.

Rifling through the back, gloved hands checked a handgun, added a silencer extension, and then strapped up on his body wearing all black. My brother had a serious expression on his face, but a smile spread across it as he turned my way. "No one can touch how she handles a Glock, man," Lamont said laughing.

I nodded in agreement with a slight chuckle. "You're right, which is why I said what did. From the fact that your face isn't blistered blue, I take it you won the practice round?"

Lamont flashed his purely whites in excitement. "Hell yeah, I did. Nigga went down before the one, two, three."

Proud, I reached out and squeezed the back of his neck. "Good look. That means you have all eyes on you now for that belt, you know?"

"Yup, and I aim to get it. In the meantime, though, you good on everything?"

Mont watched me, concern in his eyes. I knew since killing Cormac that everyone was looking at me differ-

ently. Including myself. "As good as I'll ever be. You?" I
asked, tilting my head to get a better look at him.

He pulled his seat belt on and looked around the car in
awe, running his gloved hands over the surface of everything. "Yeah, yeah. Never thought I'd see you handle a
nigga like you did. It changed the game and I appreciate
it, I mean, what you're doing for us."

"Family comes first. So it's nothing." Shifting my focus
ahead of me, I kept my inner thoughts locked.

Bags of building material, concrete, wood, barrels,
and then some, were loaded in my van while other vans
pulled up next to it. I focused ahead as Uncle Snap
looked my way. Waving with two fingers out, he gave
me a head nod and I pulled off through the gates of the
large holding facility as he handled business. A long
limo appeared at my side while I drove, following me
in tandem. We drove through the streets around the
airport while attempting to stay unassuming.

Whoever was driving the limo amused me. If I sped
up, he or she would match my patterns, which had
me grinning. I shifted gears, made a sharp right, and
then pulled into a shielded empty parking lot. As I
waited, the limo pulled up close to the car, both of
our windows rolled down, and I kept my cool. Plumes
of smoke rolled away with the wind as a hand with a
well-manicured French tip appeared in view.

"Driver, pull up please. I wish to see our new friend's
full body," I heard commanded in a light feminine voice.

Just chilling where I was, the limo did as ordered.
Stepping from the car were several meaty men. Each
one wore glasses and pristine suits. From the way they
moved, it was apparent that they were carrying heavy
weight.

"You ready for this?" I asked undoing my seat belt.

"Been born ready," Lamont said with a leering grin.

Lamont and I both climbed out of the car. I noticed my brother wore sagging black jeans with black Jordans. For a change, he too wore a button-down shirt that he wore out of his jeans. On his head was a snapback that he wore low over his eyes. While we stepped forward, we both kept our heads down. I kept my gaze on the limo door before me.

As the door opened by one of the big-ass security guards, my eyebrow quirked when a sparkling red Louboutin made contact with the pavement. Honey brown shapely legs had my attention as the body they were attached to stepped from the limo. In my mind, my mouth dropped. A beauty with plump red lips flashed a smile at me then reached behind her. Mama was lethal sexy and she knew it by the way she moved.

My connect wore a thigh-length white bandage dress that pushed up small but plump breasts and showed off a narrow waist with a lush backside. The wind whipped her large, natural sandy red afro that was braided on the side.

I watched, then glanced quickly at Lamont as her twin stepped out with her. This one wore a matching red dress as she waved sparkling red fingernails that matched her shoes.

"Bonjour," the first twin said as her gray eyes shifted between Lamont and me.

Stepping forward, I gave a respectful nod. "Bonjour, Gemini. Welcome to Atlanta. I hope that by the reports sent to Paris, you know that I am Claudette's replacement."

"Ah yes, we know all about you. However, what is your code name?" the second twin asked. The one in red kept her arms around her sister's waist as she rested her chin on the woman's shoulder.

"Call me Leo," I said since their code name represented the zodiac.

Seductively giggling, both glanced up and down at me then flashed seductive grins. "Yes, that fits you," both said then began making kissy sounds as they frowned and reached for me. "We are so sorry for your loss. Claudette was a beautiful old woman. So commanding and so knowledgeable."

The twins covered my cheeks with kisses. Aurelia and Arielle were our French/Canadian connects. Both women were of French Creole descent with family and drug ties from Paris, Turkey, Israel, Cambodia, the Caribbean, and South Africa. From my research they were also working on having a larger pull in Germany and the UK as well. Heroin, and other popular Euro club drugs, were their specialty. From my mother's notes, it was our obligation to keep the pipeline flowing through the U.S. club ring and entertainment world with their product. Our links internationally also were required to distribute.

Our exchange was simple: we did for them, they did for us, needing our sourcing more than we needed their product. Knowing this, I flashed my own flirtatious smile as they hugged me. Stepping back, I took both women's hands and flipped them to kiss their tattooed wrists.

"Oh," I heard one twin say as she whispered in French that she'd fuck me right where I stood.

Chuckling, I practiced the art of seduction as I locked my eyes on them and stepped back. "I'm glad you both approve and sincerely I thank you. I hope to keep her legacy strong."

"*Oui.* Let us commence in our business shall we, in her honor?" the one in red, Arielle, said gazing at me, then Lamont.

Keeping at my side, my brother watched by rubbing his chin and licking his lips in the process. Both twins seemed to feed from his interest. They both stepped forward and moved to rest their arms over our biceps.

"From my understanding, distribution has not broken even with Claudette's departure," I explained going straight to business. "The Canadian pipeline in my opinion can only do better and that's where you both come in."

"Tell us why, Leo, hmm? As you've just explained that everything is still, as you all say, chill. How can it only do better?" Aurelia asked.

Smiling, I reached out and plucked her chin. "I'd like to show you. Since I am now head of Claudette's circuit, I think that we should celebrate. What do you think?"

"*Oui,* let's!" both women said in unison

"Follow us then." Helping them back in their limo, I had Lamont give the address and we rode out.

Leading them away from the drop-off point and guiding them through Atlanta was nothing. Driving them to Buckhead, we pulled up. I threw Lamont my jacket as he frowned.

"Man, I can't go in like this for real?" he fussed.

"You know you can't. All eyes are on us, and you know how they do us, man," I explained.

Monty sucked his teeth and scrunched his face with a light chuckle and bob of his head. "Yeah, yeah, ya right. Give me that weak-ass jacket, man."

Tossing it to him, he pulled off the sweatshirt jacket he wore, threw it behind him then slid into my jacket. Once settled, we got out, and introduced the twins to Atlanta nightlife with ease. Since the women were used to European clubs, I made sure to take them to a club that had a mixed environment and played a variety of music. The place was hot, and I had to thank Shanelle for suggesting this club. We could kill two birds with one stone this way.

Bodies swayed around us and surrounded us like a herd of animals as I led them to VIP. Both twins held my hands looking around in awe and bopping to the music. Once in our private area overlooking the club, Cory stood up to greet them with Shanelle by his side. She stood with her arm casually resting on his shoulder in a bad-ass slit dress that showed nothing but her thick thighs and bare hips. To the untrained eye, it appeared she had no panties on, but I knew she did. *Or she better have.* Anyway, the two of them locked eyes on me, and I gave them a nod as I introduced them.

"Gemini, meet the rest of my team if you will. We have gifts for you both," I said reaching for a small box and handing it to them.

Considerately, Aurelia reached in and pulled out a mahogany-lined cigar with a glowing teal tip. She twisted it between her fingers then glanced my way. "An electric cigarette?" she asked raising an eyebrow.

I gave a nod with an amused smile while I reached out and pushed a button on the side for her. A light swirl of smoke with the scent of vanilla and strawberries wafted between us.

"Something like that. Take a puff and tell me what you think. Don't be cautious; trust me, you'll enjoy the experience," I coaxed.

Flicking the tip of her pink tongue over her lips, she gave me a haughty smile. I watched her seductively inhale and hold it to allow the smoke to playful roll in her mouth. Studying me through her hooded gaze, she gave me a sexy-ass smile then snatched me by the back of my neck to kiss me. My eyebrow rose in amusement and I felt her skillfully blow the smoke out between us.

When she stepped back watching me, I gave a slick smirk while using the pad of my thumb to wipe her lipstick away with a sly chuckle. My lips were closed when she kissed me, but she didn't know that as I flashed my teeth grinning.

"So, tell me. How do you feel, Aurelia?" I asked in French.

Wide-eyed, Aurelia and Arielle both giggled, then Aurelia spoke up. "Oh, my! You're sneaky, *oui?* I feel . . . I feel . . ." Softly moaning, her head dropped back while she slowly closed her eyes.

Music vibrated up through everyone's bodies. The rhythmic beat pumped into us and created an urgency for everyone to dance. I quickly glanced at Shanelle who narrowed her eyes but kept a clean poker face. I knew that she was going to get in my ass later. But business was business. I didn't see that kiss coming and, again, I kept my lips closed. Never try your own product, that's number one in the game.

"Mmm." Aurelia muttered some raunchy words in French then stepped to me. "Give me more. Right now. This feels like raw sex. A sweet, orgasmic rush. What is this?"

"Arielle," I said offering her the other cigarette. "We call it Mist, and it is our prototype for the next move in our pipeline. If you continue to be good to us, Gemini, we might be pressed to arrange a unique deal with you."

Taking a deep drag of the cigarette, Arielle's eyes glossed over. She moaned in ecstasy. Biting her lower lip in the sexiest of ways as she reached out for Lamont then moved against him fluidly dancing. As they connected with the music and he guided her to his groove, Arielle lustfully slid her hand down his body, cupped his junk then groped him.

"Yes, this is liquid sex," she said, then glanced my way. "Let us think about this. For now, we dance and enjoy this amazing gift of yours."

Arielle then stepped away from Lamont to grab her twin's hand only to grab him again. They continued their seductive movements then melded into the bodies of dancing people around us with Lamont in between the pair. Entertained, I calmly stood back with my arms crossed over my chest, legs in an akimbo stance, while bobbing my head to the thumping tempo.

"Tell Jojo that his intuitive mind is crazy with it," I said speaking while keeping my gaze on the women before us. "Thank him for creating such a banging product, and let him know that this still doesn't prove a thing." Mind calculating and planning, I paused in my wording then sighed. "Tell him to focus on his studies and continue crafting Mist for us. That's as deep in this that I want him to go."

At my side, Cory chuckled. "He said you'd let him in after testing this."

"Whatever. He's not smart," I said swallowing my grin.

Since the first meeting with the Syndicate, after his kidnapping, Jojo had locked himself in the lab Mama had made for him. Whenever any of us tried to get him to leave, he'd ignore us and keep the door locked. After maybe a couple of days later, he came out with Mist, explaining that he was reading the product notes Mama had left him in a diary. In it were specifics on ideas she had over the years on what type of drugs might keep the pipeline profiting. Being the type of thinker he was, Jojo did his research and figured by crafting a drug that mimicked an electric cigarette it would be easy to distribute and easier to cause a dependency on when smoked.

Having tested it on one of his friends who was into club drugs, he watched the effects and handed us the box, telling us that he was still tweaking it, but would be safe to use for now. Having now seen it in action, I was blown away that he was able to craft something like that so fast and effectively. My baby brother was sick with it and had me reevaluating my plans.

"They look happy."

Looking at my side, I gave Shanelle an observing nod. She sidled herself up against me, pressing her soft curves against my side, then rested her hand against my arm. "Yes, they do. I think we've secured their loyalty; what you think?"

"I think you need to wash your mouth out," she said with a slight tone to her voice. "Did you inhale?

"No, I didn't inhale, and give me a glass of ice water and I'll do just that." Looking down at her, I took in her beauty. I allowed my hand to land against the small of her back, hovering over her round ass. "Cory, I need you and Lamont to keep them entertained. After you get them hooked on everything, hit me up. Shanelle and I will be meeting up with Snap to pick up Lucky around five."

"I don't have a problem with that one," Cory said stepping out of VIP to walk toward the twins.

Everything was in motion. The next steps in my plans were just beginning.

Chapter 7

Shanelle

All is fair in the name of the game. Besides, I'd been through the fire of Javon cheating on me. Just as he'd experienced me cheating on him. After suffering a miscarriage because I got into a fistfight in the middle of the street with one of the hood bitches he was cheating on me with, I no longer felt the need to go that route again. She'd shown up at Mama's house wanting to fight and I was itching to give her the beat down she deserved.

I was too damn young and immature to care about the baby inside of me. Let me rephrase that: I cared about my child. But the need to beat that ho into the ground was greater. I'd embarrassed Mama that day in front of the whole neighborhood. In the end I got what I wanted. I stomped that broad into the ground. I won that battle but lost the war. I thought she would go running to her car to go home after getting that ass beat, but no. She went for the box cutter she had hidden on her. I still had the keloid across my back from the affront. Once I'd fallen to the ground, she gave a running punt kick to my stomach to seal the deal.

That took both Javon and me down a few notches. I think it actually matured us a bit. We hadn't cheated on one another since. Which was why I bristled when he kissed one of those twins.

Seeing him kiss another woman took me back to an old head space. I got the urge to drag that pretty bitch through the club while beating her face. But I was beyond that now. I calmed my nerves and exhaled. This was business and I had to leave all that petty shit behind. Javon just secured a major deal. Getting a supplier like Gemini to keep in business with him after Mama died was huge. It would look favorably on us with other dealers as well.

Furthermore, I was annoyed because I was still horny. We still hadn't finished what we started when Melissa and Jojo got taken. As a woman there were only certain men who knew how to sex you into oblivion and Javon did that for me. No matter how many men I'd had sex with after him, nobody was able to do to me what Javon could. Sometimes I hated that because he knew what he was capable of, which was probably why he knew he could calm me down with sex as well. When women hollered that the dick was too bomb, Javon was the prototype.

As the music blasted through the club, I stood around and took in the scenery. Since Javon had walked in, people gave him wide berth. Javon always walked like he commanded attention, but since this newfound power he walked with even greater determination. It was crazy how fast word spread in the underworld about him. And when the owner of the club walked over to personally thank Javon for gracing his club, I knew we were in the big leagues.

"Please, come to my office so we can discuss a few things," the older black man said. "Ms. Claudette and I had a system set in place and I would like to know if I'm still in your good graces."

The man looked like he could be a school principal instead of a club owner. Silver and black hair graced his head in a faded fro. His veneers seemed to be a bit too big for his mouth, but he was dressed *GQ* fresh. Short and stumpy. Even though he looked clean cut, I could tell he was a slime ball.

Javon nodded as he glanced at his watch. "I have a few minutes to spare, but only a few minutes."

"I'm Bruce Saunders. Everyone calls me Mr. Saunders," the old man said.

"Okay, Bruce. Lead the way to your office."

I could tell that Javon calling the man by his first name riled him. It was clear he thought he was important, a big shot. "Ah, okay then." Bruce reached behind him to usher the half-naked girls he had with him to the front. They were of all ethnicities in various thongs, no bras, and the tallest heels I'd ever seen. "I brought you some refreshments," Bruce said.

Javon frowned as if he was offended. "Your first mistake is ignoring the fact that you see a lady already here with me. Your second mistake is assuming that pussy moves me. I'm not some fool-ass nigga who gets excited at the sight of pussy. I've had pussy. All kinds of pussy. Don't ever disrespect my manhood again by assuming, because I'm young, I don't know how to control my dick."

I bit back a smile as Bruce and the women seemed taken aback by Javon's blunt assertiveness. Yes, there had been a time when Javon probably would have bagged and tagged a few of the girls, but I was happy to see that those times were behind him still.

"This is my fiancée, Shanelle," Javon said, taking my hand and pulling me next to him. "When you see her, respect her like she is me. Don't ever offer me pussy in her presence or when she isn't around. Understand, Bruce?"

Bruce's eyes widened as he took me in. Standing at five foot seven, I had to look down at the man.

"Ye . . . yeah. Yeah, man. Sure, my bad. My bad," Bruce replied nervously then chuckled. He started shoving the girls away as he made his way to his office. "Go on. Go somewhere and do something," he ordered them.

We headed up the stairs to the third floor then down a long hallway until we made it to Bruce's office. My nose crinkled immediately. For this to be an upscale club, Bruce's housekeeping skills in his office were lacking. Food containers were all over the floor. Liquor bottles were all over his desk. I thought I actually saw women's thongs lying about, which may have told why it smelled like musty pussy in his office. I cringed.

"You're fired," I said to Bruce.

"Wha . . . Wait. What?" he stuttered.

"You're fired. Any man who keeps an office looking like this isn't worthy of having an office let alone a club. Not to mention you've been stealing from Mama for years. She bailed you out when your club was going under. You defaulted on your loans to her and, to top it off, I say again you were stealing from her," I said as I slipped my hand in my purse. "We came up here to talk to try to see if you would tell us the truth, but I no longer give a shit. My sister Melissa will be taking over the club," I said as a matter of fact.

Bruce looked at Javon who stood at the door like a guard. I could tell that he wasn't impressed with the place himself. Javon shrugged. "She's talking to you. Not me," was all he said.

"This club brings in close to fifteen thousand dollars a night on Mondays and Tuesdays, the slow days. On Wednesdays and Thursdays it brings in close to twenty-five grand a night. On the weekends, including Sundays, this club should be grossing at least seventy-five grand a night and that's without all the celebrities who roll through. Yet, you only turned in seventy grand a week to Mama."

"What? I never stole from that old woman! Never!" Bruce declared. "I . . . I may have kept a few dollars for the maintenance of the place. You can't just come in here and snatch my club from underneath me like this." Bruce was talking with his hands. His slight New York accent annoyed me. His eyes darted around the room like he was looking for a place to run and hide.

"You're lying," I said. "I hate to be lied to. Furthermore, the club is no longer yours. You defaulted on your loans two years ago, I say yet again."

"Mama knew you were stealing from her, Bruce. She'd been documenting it for a while, but because she and your wife were best friends, she let you slide," Javon added. "Lucky you, she died before she could kill you."

Bruce's eyes widened.

"Javon left the decision in my hands whether to fire you or kill you. I chose to fire you."

After Javon and I talked in the kitchen, I decided to take his lead and study the things myself that Mama had left behind. Real estate was my thing so I decided to look into all of the properties and businesses we owned. If we were going to be this force that she had envisioned, we had to come in strong. Not just for the sake of us, but because the rest of the Syndicate would see that Javon meant business. Although I was pretty sure after seeing him murder Cormac with a fork they knew he wasn't anything to play with.

"Mama loved your wife as a sister so as a way to respect their friendship, I won't riddle your body with bullets, but once the night is over, you will be escorted from the premises," I said.

"And don't do anything stupid like empty the safes or take anything that doesn't belong to you. If you do, I'll find you and I will kill you," Javon added.

I chuckled inwardly. It was crazy how effortlessly Javon stepped into his role. While he may have had some convictions about it, he couldn't deny that being a leader in the underworld came naturally for him. It was as if he had been born to do it.

Putting Melissa over the club had been my idea and I was glad Javon agreed. With the bulk of the money we had to turn legit, running the club would help Melissa to do it as well as keep a steady supply of club drugs moving throughout. Melissa was anxious to leave her piece of shit job anyway. She only stayed so Mama would see her put her accounting degree to use.

Javon and I had exited the club and I was in the middle of trying to convince him to give me a quickie when his cell rang. "Oh for the love of God," I squealed. "What's a girl gotta do to get some dick around here?"

Javon chuckled but answered his cell anyway as we hopped into his truck. We had to go meet Lucky at five in the morning. According to Mama's notes he was a part of the Luciano bloodline. Supposedly he was the bastard son of a mobster in Lucky Luciano's bloodline. Javon said a few words in Tagalog, which let me know he was speaking to Cory; then he hung up the phone. I noticed the cars that followed us anywhere we went as well as the men in black, as I called them.

"Who are those people?" I asked Javon. Since he was already looking through the rearview mirror, I was sure he knew as well.

"Mama called them Forty Thieves," he answered. "According to her notes, in the event of her death, she said, they would show up."

"For what?" I asked.

"Protection. I'm the new head nigga in charge of a national crime syndicate. In her notes she said it would be foolish of me to trust any member off the bat."

I nodded as I knew what he was saying to be true. As we pulled into traffic, I had things on my mind that I wanted to speak to him about, but I didn't want to seem out of place. I decided to keep my thoughts to myself for the time being.

"Inez got the internship at Emory," Javon said after we got on the expressway.

I frowned. "Emory? Thought she was setting her sights on Atlanta Medical or Grady since they're level one trauma centers. When did she change her mind? Mama's notes says Inez told her she was trying for Grady."

Javon creased his eyes a bit then shifted in his seat before glancing at me. "I don't know. Maybe she couldn't get the one at Grady?"

"Hmm," was all I said.

My sisters and I hadn't spent a lot of time together since Mama had died and that was my fault. I'd been so busy trying to keep Javon at ease that I'd neglected my sisterly duties. Yes, we'd spoken in passing when Javon was giving out orders or when Melissa and I discussed her running the club, but that was business. I needed to sit and speak with them on personal matters. I made a note of it as Javon got off the exit going toward Mama's neighborhood.

"I'm going to drop you off and then come back. I need to meet with Snap about a few things before we meet Lucky in a few," Javon said as he parked the car in Mama's front yard, looking at his watch.

I noticed Inez's car in the front yard. Melissa's was still in the shop. I didn't see Jojo's car, which made me wonder where the fuck he was this time of night. I turned to look at Javon. "Is this what we're going to become now?" I asked him.

"Not sure what you mean, baby," he said.

I smiled a bit. "You're going to turn into one of those drug lords who's never around for family unless it's business. Always dropping me off and then running off to handle the next task? Kissing other women?"

Javon threw his head back and chuckled. "I'm probably going to become all those things," he said as he looked at me, a smirk on his lips. "But I'll never become a man who doesn't know where home is. My dick and my heart belong to one woman," he said as he hooked his pointer finger then lifted my chin so my eyes could meet his. "I'm yours and yours alone. The Syndicate and all this other shit is my mistress, but my future wife will always come first. That's what makes me different from the rest of them."

When he leaned over to kiss me, I smiled against his lips. I trusted him and I believed in him. I just hoped that with all the power that had been laid in his lap he would be able to keep his word.

Chapter 8

Uncle Snap

"So, the Irish want to meet with you. Cormac was their man at the table. They'd like to be a part of the next meeting in hopes they can talk about replacing one of their people at the table," I said to Javon.

Quiet as kept, this old man was glad the young'un stepped up to the plate. This game, this lifestyle was all I knew. When me and Mama officially met, I was twenty. She was ten years older than me, but the woman had a walk on her that would make Jesus sin. I knew I shouldn't have been sniffing after Kingston's old lady, but the woman was beautiful. Once Kingston died in that fire, I moved in where his loss left a void. Took me another five years to get her to look at me as more than her henchman.

I chuckled inwardly thinking of the times she and I shared. I was going to miss that woman. Couldn't get her to give me a child nor her hand in marriage, but she gave me everything else I asked of her. I was working for her husband when we met. I was one of his hit men. Started running errands for him when I was fifteen. Not much mattered to me back then other than staying off the street and having money to eat. At fifteen I would have robbed my mother and grandmother if that meant I could keep food in my mouth.

I wasn't a good kid. I wouldn't make no bones about
it. A li'l nigga like me only had two things on my mind:
money and who I had to hurt to get it. I grew up in the
most fucked up of situations down in Mississippi. So
when Mama—I called Claudette Mama from the time I
met her—started taking in orphans after Kingston died,
I was all for it. A lot of the youngsters reminded me of
myself.

But it wasn't until Javon and Cory showed up that I
knew Mama would be doing more than just fostering
kids and then letting the state come in to take them
when they felt the children's time was up. Cory and
Javon started the cycle of Mama legally adopting kids.

"I'll meet with them out of respect, but my decision has
been made," he said as he poured himself more Jamaican
rum. "How the hell did Mama get this much power, Unc?"

"I'ma tell you, be lucky you knew Mama the saint
because Mama the crime lord was a ruthless individual.
I've seen her fillet grown men. Seen her slice off dicks, kill
women, kidnap children when she had to back in the day.
She is one of the reasons the rule about leaving women
and children out of the business was made." I chuckled at
the look on Javon's face. "Ya mama was nothing to play
with. When Kingston died, she knew she had a right to sit
at that table. The same shit she doing for y'all, King did
it for her. Left her pristine notes on what was what. Told
her who to trust and who not to trust."

He sat there for a minute like he was letting it all sink
in. Shit, over the years, it surprised and impressed me
that Mama was able to lead a double life so effortlessly.

"A black woman from the South commanded the
respect of an entire syndicate of drug lords. This isn't just
some run-of-the-mill shit, Unc. I walked into a room and
stuck a fork in the neck of one of the leading members
because he said he was trying to get my attention. I know
I've walked into some shit I'm not sure I'm ready for,"

Javon confessed. "But to think Mama wielded so much power?" He shook his head like he still couldn't believe it.

"Yeah, but you in it now, nephew. You made your mark. Young, intelligent black man walked into a roomful of the top criminals in the underworld and shut shit down. Not to mention at the second meeting you showed respect to each and every man and woman at that table. You asked their thoughts. You asked their apprehensions about you taking over and then you laid down your plans for the future. Hell, I gotta admit, shit even I was impressed."

"I don't know, Unc," he said shaking his head. "I did all that shit because Mama wanted me to. I read her notes, took notes on my own, and then walked into that room like I knew what the fuck I was talking about."

I chuckled and took a sip of moonshine from the blue Mason jar in front of me. "That's the thing, li'l nigga, you did know what you were talking about," I told him.

After killing Cormac, Javon scheduled another meeting at the table. These old heads couldn't stay around too long, especially not in one place, so for them to agree to meet with Javon a second time shocked the shit outta me.

"Most niggas gotta work damn near they whole lives to get what you got right now, nephew, to get where you at. You got Mama to thank for that. There're levels to this shit and rules that say that if the head of the Syndicate is taken out, the right to their seat goes to their heir unless otherwise delegated. Mama gave you a running head start."

"Which makes me a fucking target, too."

I nodded. "Oh, yeah, don't get me wrong, a few of the motherfuckers at that table probably coming up with ways to lay you down."

"And these are the men and women I'm supposed to trust?"

I threw my head back and laughed, the powerful liquor making me feel better about the void in my heart. "You'd be a fool to, nephew," I said.

Javon chuckled with me then got quiet. I could tell where his mind was. "How long you been in love with Mama, Unc?" he asked me.

That question sobered me a bit. "Practically since the first day I laid eyes on her. Shit, but she didn't give a li'l cocky nigga like me no play until five years after her husband died." I smiled at the memory. "Shit, best night of my life was when she was in my small-ass apartment waiting on me when I got home. Boy, y'all's mama was a bad-ass woman back then. I mean she was still bad until the day she died, but back then? Whew. I came home and she was sitting in my recliner with nothing on and some sexy heels."

"Come on, Uncle Snap, I didn't need to hear all that," Javon said with a disgusted frown on his face.

"Boy, looka here, I'm trying to tell you. I think I died and went to heaven a few times that night. Never had no woman work me over like that," I said with a grin, just fucking with him at this point.

Javon stood and shoved my shoulder. "Uncle, chill on all that shit right there, a'ight?" he said then chuckled.

"A'ight, a'ight. You got that. But back to business; what about the Irish?"

"Like I said, I'll meet them, but I already picked a replacement. Also, I think a lot more people in the Syndicate about to be pissed off at the new plans I'm proposing."

I took a long swallow of the moonshine then set the glass back down on the table. "Wha'chu mean?" I asked him.

"The Syndicate has had the same women and men for over fifty years in some seats. It's time for change,

Unc. If I'm going to run this joint, then I'm going to run it my way."

Something told me that what he was about to say I wasn't gon' agree with. "Say what's on your mind, son."

"I'm removing six seats from the Syndicate. Once those six are gone, I'm replacing six of the old with six new."

I shook my head, already seeing that he was about to create enemies he wasn't ready to deal with. The shit storm he was about to cause could mean blood would be raining on over Atlanta for years to come. "Whoa, Javon, wait a minute. You trying to commit suicide? These men and women been running the Syndicate and the trade for decades and you think you gon' just come in and tell folk they can't eat no more?" I asked him, still shaking my head.

"This ain't about telling them they can't eat or making folk starve. This is about evolving with the times, Unc. We need fresh thoughts, new ideas. New product. Jojo can make any damn thing he puts his mind to. He went in that basement and in less than a few weeks presented me with new products. Now I know Naveen helped him with the mechanics of the electric cigarette, but Jojo's chemist mind made the liquid shit that goes inside of it. The old heads still think the only way to make money in the drug trade is coke, crack, and heroin. I'm young. I know how to compound on what we already have. I know how to make it ten times better. The money that could be made on club drugs alone, we're losing it to the rich white college kid drug dealers because the old heads won't see the value in it."

"I mean the coke, the kind we bring in, is the best in the South. We got that on lock," I reminded him.

"That's the thing, Unc, we have to expand. Broaden our horizons. Not to mention, Mama was saying the same thing in her notes. Before I even read that part, my mind was ticking away about what I could change to make it better."

"Yeah, but," I started, then blew out air like steam was coming from my mouth, "you're ruffling feathers here, Javon, and I don't see how this shit gon' work out for you."

"I got it, Uncle Snap. Trust me."

"Trust you?" I repeated then chuckled although I found nothing funny. "You're the same man who just last week wanted nothing to do with this shit and now you want me to trust you?" I stood and moved closer to Javon so we could be face to face. "What you're about to do will change everything and though Mama put you in this place of power, don't think these old-world gangsters won't take you out; and then they'll take out your family. These same men and women had something to do with Mama being murdered."

Javon stood, shoulders squared, head held high. "I know, which is why I'm surprised you wouldn't be more supportive of me getting rid of the people who may have put a hit out on her."

"I'm not saying that, son. What I'm saying is you need to ease into this thang. You can't just walk into the Syndicate and push all those people out. There will be backlash."

"Backlash that I'm prepared for, but the threat of it isn't going to stop me."

I was sure my face carried the angst I felt. God knew I didn't want anything to happen to this boy, but if he was willing to put his damn life on the line just so he could prove to the Syndicate how big his dick was then so be it. Mama would kick my ass once I got to wherever she was one day, but as long as she knew I tried to keep him from signing his own death warrant then I'd take it.

Chapter 9

Shanelle

Lucky wasn't what I was expecting. I thought some smooth Italian dude was going to open the door to the condo to meet us. I mean, Lucky was Italian, he was just Italian and black. Tall, maybe an inch or so taller than Javon. The suit he had on had been tailored to fit his broad shoulders and athletic physique. I couldn't see his eyes that well in the morning dawn until he flipped on a light switch, but the way the man moved reminded me of the alpha in Javon. I shifted my weight from one foot to the other. I was tired and hadn't slept.

The fight between Inez and me once I had gotten to Mama's house still weighed on me. The girl had a bruise on the left of her face the size of Texas. I'd walked in the house to her on the phone apologizing to some nigga. She was begging him to come see her and apologized for making him hit her. I'd never been so angry in my life. Inez could never seem to find a man who didn't like putting his foot in her ass. I didn't know why she always attracted the worst of the worst kind of man.

"You okay?" Javon asked me for the second time since we had left the house.

I knew he was looking down at me, but I was staring straight ahead. I nodded. "Yeah, just tired," I said.

"You sure?"

I glanced over at him. "Yes, I'm sure."

I didn't want to bog him down with female bullshit. I still couldn't help but think back on what had gone down. Melissa had walked in on Inez and me about to come to blows.

"Don't fucking act like you care now, Nelle, don't," Inez barked at me.

"What? Act like I care? I do care! Why do you think I'm in your face now?" I shouted at her.

"Because you like to be in control of shit. That's why. You come in here now acting like you care about what's happening with me when all you do is sniff up behind Javon's ass. You and Javon, Mr. and Mrs. Perfect. Well forgive the fuck out of me for loving a flawed nigga, okay? Not everybody can be as perfect as Javon."

I frowned and swallowed the bile that had risen in my throat. Where was all of this coming from? "What are you talking about?" I asked her.

She had on biker shorts with a red sports bra. Her light brown skin had ruddy undertones while her kinky natural hair swayed about her shoulders anytime she moved. "I'm saying that you don't give a shit about nothing unless you can be in control of it or unless Javon approves. Since he's been in charge of this newfangled shit, you been his fucking shadow. Where he goes, you go. Lucky us got to go to one damn thing and that's when he went to get Melissa and Jojo back. Everything else we get the back end of it."

I was confused as fuck. "How did we go from talking about a nigga beating your ass to you talking about Javon and me at meetings? For your information, that was the only meeting that I got to be a part of as well," I defended.

Inez closed her eyes tight and shook her head as she paced the kitchen floor. If I didn't know any better I'd

*say she was on drugs. She screamed a bit as she pulled
at her hair. She was about to say something else until
Melissa walked in.*

*"Oh gotdamn, Inez, what happened to your face?" she
asked.*

*"None of your damn business. Leave me alone. Both of
you just leave me alone," Inez said.*

*She tried to walk from the kitchen, but I blocked her.
"No, not until you tell me what the hell is going on."*

*"Ain't nothing to tell. I got into a fight with my boy-
friend. End of story."*

*Melissa walked over. "Looks like you were the only
one in the fight, Inez. We're doing this again? Shanelle
is just trying to help. We don't want to see you go down
this road again."*

*"Oh here you go," Inez said. "I guess since you're going
to be running the club, Shanelle is your best friend now?"*

*Melissa's face turned red, which made me question
what wasn't being said. "What?" Melissa asked.*

*"Guess you ain't so pissed she snatched Javon from
your fingertips no more?"*

*"Oh my God, Inez. Cut it out," Melissa said. "What I
said . . . That was a long time ago."*

*"What was a long time ago? What the hell are you two
talking about?" I asked.*

*"The fact that you knew Melissa liked Javon, but
didn't give a shit and got into a relationship with him
anyway," Inez answered.*

"What?"

*"Whatever, Shanelle. Play dumb and be the perfect
daughter Mama thought you were. Run off, marry
Javon, and you and he be the king and queen of the
underworld. The rest of us be damned," she declared
sarcastically then shoved past me out of the kitchen.*

I was so confused, it was frightening. Apparently there had been conversations going on that Javon and I didn't know about. Was that what they all thought of me and Javon? They thought we were perfect? Did Inez and Melissa feel Mama thought I was better than they were? When Javon and I made it known we were a couple, Mama was happy about it and nobody else had made a big deal about it, or so we thought.

I turned to Melissa, who walked back over to the counter and started putting the groceries away she had brought in. "What is she talking about?" I asked her.

She turned to me and smiled a bit. "Don't worry about it, big sis. Stuff I said awhile ago is all."

"Yeah, but tell me. I want to know."

Melissa huffed then placed down the bag of rice she had. She rubbed her forehead for a bit then sighed deeply like what she was about to say would hurt her, and me for that matter.

"Wasn't no secret I liked Javon back then, Shanelle. Everybody knew it and could see it, but I guess you didn't care or whatever. I didn't think you two liked each other anyhow with the way y'all was always fighting and shit," she explained as she shrugged then turned to keep putting the food away. "Anyway, I wasn't surprised he would pick you. You weren't the neighborhood's white whore."

"Oh, Melissa," I said softly.

I could hear the hurt in her voice. "Don't do that, Shanelle, don't pity me."

"I'm not," I said quickly.

"You're lying. We both know the reason most of the black boys at school and in the neighborhood claimed to like me was because they knew I would fuck when you wouldn't. They knew I'd suck dick and you wouldn't. We both know Javon didn't see me the way I saw him."

"That's because you were his—"

"Don't give me that shit about being his little sister either. I'm not stupid. You were his little sister too, but he saw something in you he didn't see in me."

"Remember he beat the shit out of Oscar and his brothers for calling you a whore?"

"Wasn't because he liked me. It was because he's protective of all of his siblings and as my big brother he had to handle anybody causing harm to me. I was so angry with you, Nelle. Like why did you have to be so damn perfect? Like you're smart and black and beautiful and not a whore."

I walked over to Melissa and laid a hand on her shoulder. She had a lot of insecurities because of her addiction to sex. Not to mention, she was technically the minority in our family. She was the odd man out in a house of people of color.

She laid a hand on my mine and smiled. "I remember one time he and I were in my room. He had asked to talk to me so I chose my room so I could shut the door. He placed his lips on mine and I was elated because in my head, I just knew that meant he had always liked me, but that wasn't the case. He pulled back and asked me how I felt. I told him in no uncertain terms that I felt him stir something in my soul. He said that saddened him because what I felt when I kissed him is what he feels when he kisses you. He explained that, in his heart, I'd always be loved as his sister. That was the day I finally accepted you two as an item," she said after placing the last can of corn in the cabinet. She turned to me with tears rolling down her face. "Hey, if you kiss Javon and make him feel the way he made me feel that day, then there was no way I could compete with that."

I knew about that kiss because Javon had told me. That didn't mean I wanted to see Melissa hurt. "I'm sorry," I said to her.

"Don't be. I'm not mad, Shanelle. Inez was just saying shit to deflect attention off herself. It's what she does. You know that."

As Melissa and I hugged, I felt love in my heart for both my sisters. We may have been of all different races and ethnicities, but they were my sisters and I knew without doubt that we loved one another.

Still, the fact that Inez had effectively used manipulation to get the heat off her bothered me, not to mention all the other shit she had said. I couldn't wait to get her alone so we could talk again. She was going to tell me who the motherfucker was who had hit her and there would be no way around it. I wouldn't stand for one of my sisters allowing a man to beat her down. I just wouldn't.

I had to focus on that later though. As Lucky ushered us in, my eyes widened a bit. Brother man was fine. Black Italian leather dress shoes that looked fresh from the cobbler clacked against the marble flooring. He had a half-crested gold ring on his finger, which drew my attention. He was the color of raw honey that heat hadn't touched yet. His close-cropped silky black hair was tapered to perfection. His face was free of any hair and diamond studs were in his left and right earlobes.

He smiled and extended his big hand. "Nice to meet you, Javon."

Javon smiled and grasped Lucky's hand in a firm handshake. "Glad you could get out here on such short notice," Javon responded.

Lucky turned his eyes to me and I glanced away before looking back at him.

"This is my fiancée, Shanelle," Javon introduced me with a hand on the small of my back.

Lucky extended his hand, but for some reason I hesitated to shake it. I didn't know why. Just something in my gut clenched like a fist around my insides and wouldn't let go. But for the sake of decorum, I smiled and shook the man's hand. "Hello, Lucky. Nice to meet you," I greeted him.

The smile on Lucky's face was a lascivious one and he turned my hand and kissed the back of it. "The pleasure is all mine of course," he said.

My hand started to tingle. I cleared my throat then removed my hand from his. I glanced at the floor as I used my left hand to push my hair behind my ear. I felt when Javon's hand tensed a bit on my back. I would have chuckled and rolled my eyes if I didn't know any better. But I did know better. I also knew Javon's temper. So I kept it cute and stayed in my place for the time being.

We all made our way to the front room where staff had already placed out refreshments. Javon ushered me to the sofa to sit while he and Lucky took the two wingback Tudor-style chairs across from one another. After we had been served drinks of our choice, Javon got right down to business.

"I don't want to pussyfoot around or waste time," he said to Lucky. "I called you here because I want to offer you a seat at the table of the Syndicate. Lots of things are about to change around here and Mama spoke highly of you. You're already running a fine enterprise up North and you get your product through us already. Getting a seat in the Syndicate would mean you wouldn't have to deal with day-to-day details. You could turn that over to a general and deal with only the logistics, money, and distribution. Not to mention we each take our cut off the top when new product comes in. You could focus on other things like your overseas enterprises."

Lucky took a sip of his drink, crossed his ankle over his left leg, and studied Javon. "Lots of talk about you going on in the circuits. Is it true? Did you really off Cormac?" he asked.

"Whether I answer yes or no, the question will still remain if you want the seat at the table. But to answer honestly, yes, I did. He said he wanted my attention so I gave it to him. May not have been the attention he had in mind, but he got it nonetheless."

"You comfortable with cutting the Irish from the table like that?"

Javon nodded. "I have to be because I've done it now. They want to speak with me as well."

"And you plan to?"

Javon nodded once. "I'll give them time to speak their piece. We don't really need the Irish if you want me to be honest. We got the Mexicans, Africans, Jews, Italians, and once I make this change, I have Natives I can bring in as well. The reservations have potential to bring in a lot of money for us."

Lucky clicked his tongue a few times then chuckled. "That's some old-world shit you up against right now. Starting a war with them could potentially crumble the Syndicate."

"I'm aware. But they are not our only worries, especially since I plan to eliminate six chairs at the Syndicate anyway and replace the remaining six with new and younger people."

I looked at Javon. That was something new he hadn't told me. I mean I knew he didn't have to tell me everything, but I assumed with a move that calculating he would have run it by me. "Baby, how is that going to work?" I asked. "These are dangerous people."

He looked at me. I could tell he knew what I was thinking, which was why he nodded and answered, "I have the plans all laid out, but the first order of business is to see if Lucky is going to take the seat I'm offering. Bringing him on will start the process. The six chairs I eliminate altogether will have no dealings with Syndicate business. The six chairs I replace will form something like a council of elders. They will retire and I will allow them to have a hand in who they choose from their families to take their seats."

"Trying to ease the sting of being ousted," Lucky added with a nod and a smile. "Makes sense."

"Yes. So the question remains, are you in or are you out?"

"I'm in. Anybody crazy enough to carry through with a plan like this is crazy enough to head the Syndicate. The shit kind of reminds me of the story told about a great, great, great-grand of mine."

Javon smiled the first genuine smile he'd given Lucky all night. "Which is why I sought you out first to sit at the table."

Both men stood and shook hands like they were warriors readying for battle. I couldn't fight the sinking feeling in the pit of my stomach though. So many emotions had overtaken me in the last few hours. Maybe I just needed to sleep to shake off the feeling that when Javon made his announcement to the Syndicate bloodshed would be the end result.

Chapter 10

Cory

"Oh, shit," escaped my lips after I hung up with my brother telling him where I was, followed by a deep, satisfying smile.

This underworld shit had turned into something I hadn't expected of it, one that was reaping many specific benefits such as I was experiencing right now. Being Von's right-hand man, next to Uncle Snap, it was my responsibility to wine and dine our current supplier, Gemini, while keeping them entertained. I planned on being that dude for my brother. Planned on making sure these women stayed interested in what we got, which I did . . . well, was doing.

A quick glance down had me thinking about football and touch points as twin one, Aurelia, kneeled in nothing but her heels and a thong in front me as she swallowed my dick whole. *Gotdamn! Mami* was sublime with it. Tracing me from that sensitive spot between my nuts on up to the rim of my head, she didn't even blink when she swallowed my swelling dick whole. Never in my life had I had a female throat me without gagging like she was. The fact that I was still growing in her throat didn't seemed to bother her either. On my word, that move alone made me want to wife her.

Too bad that I wasn't the marrying type.

Sweet and musky scents mingled with the smoke of Mist in the air of the W hotel we chilled in. The sun was rising and I lay on my back, arm stretched out with my fingers curling to motion to the other twin, Arielle, who sat naked on her knees doing a line of molly she had finely chopped from several candy-looking tablets next to my bottle of Cîroc.

When she looked my way, I licked my lips and let my eyes drink up her sexy. Both twins had the same body type. Petite, thin but thick with the shape of a Coke bottle. Arielle's perky milk and tea–toned breasts made me want to suck the curved line of stars that ran against the contour of them. Gaze dropping farther, I dug how she had slight abs but only barely due to the softness of her stomach. However, what I liked even more was that sandy brown strip of hair that held a septum-like ring that hung on her clit. Damn, these two were bad.

Lifting a blunt to her lips, Arielle took a hit then walked my way in a sultry runway type of walk. Every word exchange between us was in French at this point. I commanded that Arielle give me a hit, as I combed my fingers through her sister's cotton soft fro. My eyes rolled in my head while mama worked my dick to perfection. When I drew in hit of that blunt, then took a hit of the Mist, I gave a slow grin while I reached for Arielle's hips and lifted her on my face.

Nothing but moist pussy was in my face and I enjoyed it all. Especially when mama worked that pussy in a circle against my stretched-out tongue. Sweet nectar coated my mouth and throat as I said, "Ahhhh!" then gave a throaty laugh with a, "Yeah," making her even more moist. A nigga was high. A nigga was in bliss, and I had to give my little brother props for creating a drug like he did. However, I never would. There was no way that I'd let him know that I took a hit of this shit. See, in all my constant work in being an activist lawyer then moving to into criminal law, I ended up developing several vices along the way.

Really, that shit started way before that when I was a teen. Drinking, weed, pussy, and the occasional light partaking of molly was my thing. Now Mist might become my next joy, but only in moderation. A nigga wasn't too stupid. Sure, I had a couple of females I used to get me what I needed on the low, fellow aspiring lawyers who gained a habit as a means of coping through the rigorous hours and work we all went through. I even used Inez's connection in the hospital as a means to get me a little something-something, once I found out she was a little junkie for her nigga. But, now everything was different.

I had a fresh prime source now through my big brother. My always protective brother, a nigga I hated to let down, but it was what it was. I mean, I could blame my habit on the shit we went through at kids. Yeah, a little of it was because of that, especially the drinking and weed, but I was a grown-ass man. I could accept and own up to my faults and embrace them at the same time. I did this to myself. As long as I could get high and keep this feel-good going, but also have a clear mind in order to handle business, then I was good at keeping my secret on lock.

"Ooooo," I heard both twins sigh at once as we made that bed rock.

It was time to flip and treat the other right, while allowing one to ride me. I was a creative nigga, so the night was still young for us, as I got my rocks off and dick wet with French twin juices.

By the time I was done with them both, it was sometime around twelve in the afternoon. Standing in front of my black and silver Benz, I adjusted my shades due to the glinting sun kicking me in the face. Rocking my cool stance, arms crossed over my chest, wide legged and feeling cocky, I watched a private jet lift in the air. Yeah, life was fucking raw right now. Just like the two pussies I left begging for more as they were escorted back to the airport by me.

For a moment, I thought Von would back out and pussy out of coming into such incredible power, but I knew him. My brother was the type to research his Ps and Qs. He'd find out all that he could just so he could weigh the pros and cons before settling on any business deal. That was only half of what made him a damn good businessman. For a second there, he did trip me up. But once he took that fork to that nigga Cormac's neck, I knew our time to rise to power had come..

Chilling in my ride, my mind went to Mama. No lie, her death seemed to kick my usage in overdrive. For the life of me, I didn't know what was up or what was down. I just understood that she was really gone. It was something that I was still trying to process.

"Hello?" I asked through the speakers of my ride while answering my ringing cell phone.

"Jojo and Naveen are fighting again. Can you get here?" It was Melissa. Her voice had a raw quality to it as if she was crying and it bothered me to my soul.

"I have something to handle, but I'll be there right away, I promise, Lissa. Can you keep them apart until then?" I asked, glancing right then left as I shifted lanes. Scuffling could be heard and it irritated me as I waited for her to answer me. "Melissa! Can you hold it down?" I shouted jarring her attention.

"Ah, yeah. I got it. Just come through please," she said hanging up in my ear as she shouted, "Oh my God! Stop!"

Fuck! ran through my head causing me to slam my fist against the steering wheel. I was done with those two beefing, I really was. However, there was something that I had to handle.

Whipping down the highway, I found my way near ATL's Old Fourth Ward district. Music blasted and I climbed out of my ride and stared up at an apartment complex. Keys jingled in my hand as I went up a set of stairways. Using my key, I stepped inside of a clean apartment that had the scent of fresh Clorox as the sound of a vacuum going off filled the room. Tossing the keys on the table, I paused to clear my cell of the various text messages I had received; then I walked through the place stopping in a large bedroom staring at Inez, who wore an oversized T-shirt and was reading from her medical book.

Closing the door of the room, I rolled my shoulders and sighed in annoyance and disappointment. I hated confronting her because she had a fucked-up temper; so did I. But, her messages I listened to this morning, and the texts I got from Naveen, needed to be addressed. We had to talk about her mouth with Shanelle. There was no way around it.

Yeah, I was her nigga.

Chapter 11

Javon

"Welcome. We finally get to meet the bloke who took over the Syndicate," was directed my way by a lone male sitting at a circular table surrounded by a team of Irish. "Who stole my father's chair."

Unbuttoning the sleeves of my black button-down shirt, I rolled them up and hooked my thumbs in the pockets of my dark jeans. With Lucky down with my plan, I immediately moved on the next phase with a group of niggas who reeked of disdain and homicidal desires. A quick flash of an amused smile appeared across my face as I stood in a tavern in Sandy Springs and stared the Irish down. At my sides behind me were Lamont, and Lucky who, funny enough, was watching in equal amusement clicking a lollipop back and forth in his mouth while his hands rested folded in front of him.

"Shit stain monkey," sounded in the room of Irish.

Around me but behind me, Lucky, and Lamont were my Forty Thieves acting as my additional protection. Each one stepped up only by an inch. The Irish side seemed to grow in that moment. Before coming in, each of us was patted down. I was assured that this meeting by their new boss would be private. But of course I smelled bullshit on that when I saw several undercover cars hiding around the block only a second away from the meet.

When we stepped inside and saw that, had I not brought my Forty Thieves, I would have been outnumbered by five extra Irish and an ambush was going down.

"Stole? No, I'd say abdicated or corrected a wrong that occurred before us." I had to thank my instincts and my mother's notes.

She explained that Cormac's crew were not to be trusted in any capacity. The Irish who sat at the table were ones who took out the old Atlanta crew of Irish by betraying the former leader, Branna O'Leary, also known as the Dublin Lass. Branna was one of the only people at the table Mama somewhat trusted and highly respected because of their shared views and being female. Also, because Branna didn't carry the weakness of racism in her.

Branna had come from Dublin in the sixties and used her pull and power to build up what she named O'Leary Tavern while transporting her father's crime syndicate to Atlanta. Even though her crew was majority Irish, Branna brought in other races who she thought would help seal her power in Atlanta, which it did. Through the growth of her power, her influence was noticeably impactful especially with her connections with the church. Cormac, who was in Ireland at the time with his own crew wanting to expand his own crew, staged a coup and took down Branna and the O'Leary clan, claiming their pipeline for his own.

Mama noted that he had his crew lynch and drag the black, Native American, and Latino members of her crew. Cormac used his resources to hunt her down. He broke into Branna's home and raped her. Then he cut her throat open, gutting her from her mouth to her pussy.

Being the type of extra-ass bastard that he was, because that wasn't enough Cormac then took her baby son Ennis. He later transported her marked and mutilated body, personally hanging it with an ultimatum in front of the Syndicate's unofficial headquarters. That ultimatum was, "Take him as Branna's chair replacement or war will come." It was foul how he came through the ranks and Mama voiced that. However, she was outvoted in her opinion and, suffice to say, they accepted him and then the rest was dust. Mama's distrust of Cormac's position and power that he used for the Syndicate continued even after her death.

For his type of evil, a fork for that motherfucker was a pleasantry in comparison to what he's done to others.

Fresh sunlight shined through stained glass. Dark wood paneling covered everything from the floor to the green walls. There were eight classic-style tables in the middle of the pub. The rest of the seating was booths. Behind us were Celtic tartans and Irish flags as well as pictures of various sports teams and plenty of flat-screen TVs. The Tarmac Carriage Pub was considered one of Atlanta's hipster spots. Funny enough you never saw many black folk, but that's beside the point. Various bar taps crafted to honor Ireland's history and mythology were lined up against a spotless bar top while glass pints sat in a stack.

"Do you mind if I have a bit of a pint? I heard this pub had the best Guinness around." Quietly watching the men in front of me, my attention stayed on a dark-haired young guy with a long ponytail wearing a leather jacket, sliced jeans, and black shit kickers.

Nigga's jade green eyes never left me while he played with a sharpened fork against his finger. From his appearance, I gathered he was Cormac's son and heir. From the lightly bearded jaw line to the asymmetrical shape of his face, he pretty much was Cormac's twin. When he snapped a finger and pointed, one of his crewmembers got up to grab me a pint.

This bulky bastard was bald and pasty pink with swastikas on his turkey neck. He also wore what I saw was the standard gang biker jacket. If I had a fat pit bull with a runny nose suffering heat stroke in front of me, I'd say that nigga was its twin. Anyway, dude took that glass behind the bar with him, pulled his dick out, ran it around the rim, pissed in it, reached up, and pulled the tap to finish filling it up, then topped it off with a thick blob of thick spit. After, that dude slid it my way over the bar.

I chuckled while I stared at the piss, spit, and beer concoction. "I'd thank you, but considering . . . Gentlemen, I'm before you at your request because your messages leaked through the pipeline to meet you at your insistence. Here I stand. I assume your loss has you questioning what is going to occur with your seat at the table. Correct?"

"Our loss?" Cormac's son repeated slowly as if in thought. "Rumor in the pipeline says you were the cause of that said loss. Would you lie to us about that?"

"I'm not sure, would I?" Keeping my place where I stood, everyone in the room bristled at my words, but I kept my cool. "I'm pretty damned sure that if one of the many units of the Syndicate went against their own law and attacked one of their own then, admittedly, went after family's younger family members, all retribution would have to go down right?"

Looking around, I noticed that the room became fuller with more Irish. This meant that I had a lot of room to work with and I liked the odds. Game on. With a roll of my shoulders, I picked up the pint, swirled it around then gave a low sigh. From how everything was situated in this joint, I knew off the bat that this "meeting" was a poorly crafted setup.

"Before we get down with the real business you all got me here for, let me introduce you to my man Lucky, representing New York. Why don't you all lift a pint up and tell him congrats on taking your father's seat; I mean, the nigga who killed your mother and kidnapped you to raise you as his own. Because you'll never get it now, Ennis," I said locking eyes on Cormac's son. "I mean, when your punk-ass father fell on his own fork, since he was so adamant about meeting me and all. That nigga looked just like a fresh sack of exploding haggis. That's that foul, vomit-looking shit y'all like to suck on right? Or is that the Scots?"

"What the fuck did you say, you darkie?" Ennis shouted turning beet red and glaring at me.

I knew I had his attention now. Chuckling, I gave a shrug. "Damn. You didn't know? Shieet," I said shaking my head and glaring at the pint in my hand. "I need to recruit Scots then. They have more loyalty and respect than your racist, sexist, pedophile, kidnapping, and morally repressed sacks of nigger shit y'all hate so much."

Flashing a hateful smile, I swiftly splashed the beer ahead of me. "Let's get this shit over with shall we, my friends?"

Swiftly with a sharp turn, I swung out to slam that pint against the head of a hulking redheaded beefy nigga with tattoos all over his hands. The force was so strong that the fleshy fat of that nigga's neck jiggled and rolled. Blood and spit flung out in a spew. Every Irish nigga in the pub either jumped up or flipped over tables to rushed at me.

"Damn, this is how I'm welcomed? I think I like it," Lucky said in laughter.

"Hell yes!" I shouted in excitement. Boastfully I laughed, adding, "I love a good stomping, don't you? Especially hateful motherfuckers. Lamont fought one of these fuckers. Racist naked mole rat spit in his eye and tried to cheat while calling him all type of racial bullshit."

Near the bar, Lamont was wrapping a tartan around the throat of one of the Irish's bikers. Unfazed, he twisted it with a grin. "No doubt! Told me to grab my tomahawk and go back to the rez. Motherfucker, you're on my land. Take your ass back to the side of Ireland that keeps being bombed and shit, then suck on my peace pipe," he said grabbing his crotch. "Now fuck off, son."

Finger squeezing his Glock, bullets rained out and Lamont beamed. "Today is a good day to get back at their asses."

Everyone on my side of the tavern flew into action. Lamont took a chair and swung it into the face of one of the Irish. The Forty Thieves began taking down whoever they could, all while Ennis sat watching me swing on his people. I already knew what he was waiting to do; it didn't take a rocket scientist. That's why I ducked and slammed my shoulder into a biker with sour breath, yoked him up by his throat then slammed his head down on the table.

With a quick glance around, I counted the tables again then grinned. *Bingo.* Quickly, I jumped on a table watching Ennis leap up with an evil scowl.

"You killed my father!" he screamed.

"My dude! He was never your father, and you piss on the true owner of this tavern: your mother. A true Syndicate queen right along with my mother," I said stepping backward. See, anger makes people do the dumbest things and I really appreciated that because I was using it to my advantage.

Now accepting, registering, or just plumb listening to everything I said, Ennis pushed his boys out of the way in the attempt to get me. Had this nigga had more sense and smarts, I might have attempted to extend an olive branch, but since Cormac brainwashed the nigga too deeply to be anything that Branna was, nigga was nothing but a lost cause for my plan. Mentally tossing that rock away, I grinned and readied myself to rumble with this fool.

He reached out attempting to snatch me up and roared, "I'm coming for you."

"My nigga behind me," I said pointing with my thumb to a big brotha from the Forty Thieves behind me, "Nuts, will be waiting as you try to get at me."

In my moment of tomfoolery, the room seemed to open for me, parting like the Red Sea. Kicking out, I slammed my boot in Ennis's face. In response, he snatched me by my ankle causing me to tumble off the table. Dude was quick with it. He slammed his fist in my face, scraping it with the fork he tried to slam into me.

With each punch from him, I used my forearms to block his blows while twisting side to side shifting backward. Having Ennis come for me was exactly what I wanted because it caused me to land near booth four. Earlier that day, before they shut the pub down and cleared it out, Tarmac Carriage Pub had a normal breakfast and brunch hour. Interesting enough, about that same time, Melissa, dressed in a wig, and with a group of some of her coworkers, headed to the pub, and had breakfast, seeking to taste their famous breakfast hour.

Lucky for me, during that chaotic dining hour, my sister was able to leave me a lovely present at booth four. Reaching under it, I felt around until I found what I was looking for pressed in a crack. Tugging, a large shopping bag worked its way in my hand. As I felt Ennis on me, I reached in that bag, pulled out what I needed, then swung it outward. The sound of metal meeting flesh, tendons, and then bone stopped everyone around me in their tracks as Ennis hollered.

Fresh blood spewed in interesting patterns everywhere. I used the rest of my force to slice that baby downward then up to point the tip of my machete at Ennis's neck. Sweat ran down my face causing me to blink. My rough breathing made my lungs inflame like twin fires while I pushed up from the floor.

"My arm!" Ennis screamed in horror. "My motherfucking arm!" he repeated as if in dismay.

With a casual bow forward, I picked up the mangled arm and surveyed it as if it were some strange object. Glancing back at Ennis, I tilted my head, flapped the arm around, then threw his hand on my shoulder while still holding the forearm part. "Yeah, that would be an arm, my man. Need a high five?"

That was when everyone in the room who was Irish tried to get at me. A deep, amused laugh erupted from me. I flipped his arm forward, tapped Ennis with it, then dropped it in front of him. Nigga was red with anger and it only egged me on. Smirking, I leaned forward and pressed the machete against his neck. I then slowly backed up not taking my eyes away from him.

"Now, see. All you had to do was give me respect and space. That's all you fuckers had to do, but naw, naw. You all needed to tug on each other nuts, like your so-called father did, and press me for my power. Y'all really think I'm stupid?"

"I think the Guinness has them drunk on stupid, my man," Lucky said while holding a gun to the head of one of the Irish.

"For real, man. I should scrape that shit up and make this cunt drink it now. I am really tired of the bullshit, but, whatever. See, what you all need to understand is this shit. Don't come for me like your father did," I said cutting a nice chuck of flesh from his neck. "He made that crucial mistake and didn't respect my request to leave me the fuck alone. Now, you all had to deal with what comes when you force my hand. Blame your kidnapping, fake father, Ennis. Don't blame me. Kill me if you think you can, but come for me again and the next thing I take will be your foot. Might give you some Kunta Kinte treatment; then I'll take your neck. A'ight?"

Tilting my head to the side, I stared intently at him, letting him know that through all this shit, I was not someone to fuck with. "We're all good with this meeting of ours now? Any questions?"

When Lamont's laughter broke the silence in the room, the Forty Thieves cleared a way out for me. Little brother hopped from where he was behind the bar, swinging a bat that he had taken from one of the Irish. That wild-eyed kid swung that bitch out and smashed their shit up before using it to barricade the rest of them who kept coming from the kitchens behind their swing door. At that same time, I took a final look around. Several of the Irish lay on their asses holding their heads, sides, or whatever parts of their body as I dropped Ennis to the floor. I focused my attention on Ennis where he lay bleeding out with a lopsided grin.

Today was a good day. I gave Lucky and Lamont a salute for holding it down, along with the Forty Thieves; then we then exited as quickly as possible. We all knew this battle wasn't over and I looked forward to our next "meeting" in the future.

After jetting by police and biking Irish, we finally made it back to Lucky's digs we had provided for him. Wiping my face, I casually glanced his way while he laughed and pulled at his shirt.

"Damn, again. This is how you do welcoming parties?" he said in his light accent. He rubbed his knuckles while wiping down his face and looking through the windows of our ride.

"You know it. Sometimes, to make changes, you have to kick up the sand. It's smart not to let the sand blow back in your eyes, but if you're prepared for it then you can make it through the storm, feel me?" I said chuckling and rubbing my jaw.

"Bro and his occasional philosophy," Lamont said climbing out of the car while rolling his shoulder and arm around. He closed the door behind him and looked around as was his job as my security.

Reaching my hand out to Lucky, brother took it in an amiable handshake. "You have my respect with how you knocked heads back in the pub, friend. Mama was right about seeking you out," I said watching him closely.

The nigga in me wanted to go deeper in my thanks to him with laying out an ultimatum in how he handled himself around Shanelle. But on some real shit with how the streets raised me, I'd have rather watched if shit went left, and let people hang themselves later. Shanelle and I had history and issues with cheating, so I was leery, but I wasn't a dumb nigga. She was attractive and so was he, so we'd see how far my trust could go.

Lifting our hands up and down in a familiar hand-shake I slid back as he moved to the door. "I've never been about Southern living but, my friend, you got my attention. Turning away your invitation was not going to happen, so I thank you and will make you and the Syndicate very happy with my seat. Contact me anytime. I'm down with your style of entertainment." Chucking the deuces, Lucky adjusted his shades then stepped out walking into the condo we set him up in while Lamont slid back in the driver seat taking me to our outpost home.

Once there, I showered then changed clothes. With Lamont behind me, I was on my way out to check into work when my cell went off. "Talk to me," I said recognizing the number.

"I called Cory but he hasn't come yet and Uncle Snap hasn't answered his cell," I heard Melissa say in rapid panic as she went into detail about Jojo and Naveen going at it again.

On edge from how rapidly she was speaking, I took a moment to calm her. "Hold up, sis, slow down. What is going on with Naveen and Jojo?"

"They are fighting again, tearing up Mama's living room! I tried to calm them but . . ." Tears made her speak slurred as she sniffled.

"Uncle Snap is in Lawrenceville. He should be coming back this way but, listen, I'm on my way with Lamont now," I said pissed off.

"What's going on?" Lamont asked as we locked up.

"Jojo and Naveen are at it again, pissing me off," I said as we stormed out of the loft.

Once in the car it didn't take us long to get to Mama's. We took a minute to make sure the area was clear before parking. Both of us rushed in the house. Immediately we heard nothing but, "Fuck you," and, "Nigga," and other bullshit. It took me two strides to cut between them. Yoking Naveen back by the chest, my lips formed a thin line in my anger.

"Chill!" I said low against Naveen's ear.

My body along with my hands were sore from fighting the Irish, so it was working my last nerve having to deal with my own brothers like this. Naveen struggled trying to get at Jojo again. Broken plates and pieces of the Mist e-cigarettes were everywhere with pictures of us all and Naveen's tools strewn in the mix of chaos. The house shook from Lamont struggling with Jojo and I just stared at them both in confusion. Not missing a beat, I locked Naveen's arms behind him holding him back.

"This shit about Mama again?" Lamont asked between gritted teeth.

"He's still can't do shit right, still slacking just like he did with Mama!" Naveen spat out trying to get to Jojo.

"I wasn't slacking! Why you hating, nigga? Why can't you just chill and let me do me!" Jojo pleaded in anger.

"Because that's how people get killed, just like Mama! What the fuck is wrong with you, Jojo! Where were you when you were supposed to pick up Mama?" Naveen said in angst.

Both teens had red-rimmed eyes. Watching them, I was reminded just how young they were. I hated how these two were so broken. They used to be close and now this shit. Moving Naveen behind me, I held him back and looked at Jojo.

"There's something about this whole thing with Mama that you're not telling us. We all used to try to be somewhat one hundred with each other and I need us back to that, Jojo," I said trying to keep my voice even.

Lamont gave a nod then muttered, "Yeah."

"Right, so, I need you to man up and be real with us because it looks like Naveen can't let this rest without hurting you and I don't want that for either of my little brothers. Especially with what's going on now, feel me? So, if you can't tell Lamont, or Naveen, tell me. I got you. I mean that because I love you," I said bending some so that I could look Jojo in the eyes.

Jojo bowed his head, relaxing and pulling away from Lamont to fix his glasses. He turned his back on us, and I motioned for Naveen and Lamont to leave.

"Let me handle this," I muttered. "Don't press me about this, Naveen. Just do as I'm asking. A'ight?"

Naveen, being stubborn like me, watched me with pain in his eyes, glanced at Jojo, then walked off outside, with Lamont following him. I listened to the screen slam shut, then I sighed.

"So, what went on, Jojo?" I calmly asked walking up on my baby brother.

Jojo was so rigged that it worried me. But as I listened, I could hear him crying. Reaching out I pulled him into a brotherly hug.

"What happened?" I muttered. "Did you see something you weren't supposed to? Did you do something you weren't so supposed to? What?"

"I didn't mean to leave her like that. I wasn't trying to . . . I was about to get her but—"

The sound of the door opening caused Jojo to cut off his words. When we both turned to see who had come in, Jojo's spine stiffened. His jaw clenched tight. His hands turned into fists and he pushed me off of him.

Puzzled, I looked down at dude. "Jo?"

"Everything good?" Cory asked as he walked through. "Got a call that y'all were being asses and fighting again." Cory slid his hands in his pockets. I watched him partially tilt his head to look at Jojo while raising an eyebrow.

An intense tension formed between the pair and I didn't understand it at all. I glanced between Jojo and Cory, noticing how Jo's eyes seemed to darken.

"It's all good. I just need y'all to leave me alone," was all Jojo said and he stormed out through the kitchen.

I realized that, for whatever reason, Jojo was avoiding Cory and it made me wonder what was really going on.

Chapter 12

Jojo

My world was coming undone. I was going to let Mom down. There was no doubt about it. I was sure I'd already done so. So much shit was going on and I had nobody to tell. I couldn't tell Javon. He would flip his shit. I knew he would. Von didn't put up with foolish shit and if he found out half the crap I had been doing, he would put his foot in my ass.

I plopped down on my bed and sighed. *Shit, man.* I knew secrets that were weighing on my heart. Secrets about Inez and Cory. Secrets about Melissa. Secrets about the day Mom got killed. My heart was so heavy it ached.

"God, help me," I said aloud. "What am I supposed to do with all this shit?"

Not everything was as perfect as Mom thought it was with her kids. The only perfect kids she had were probably Javon and Shanelle. They were actually what Mom had envisioned them to be. All the rest of us were faking it to make it. I was sick of Naveen cutting his eyes at me and looking at me like he always wanted to fight me, too. I didn't know what I did to him besides the fact he blamed me for Mom being killed.

I was lying; I knew why he was mad today. I started the fight this time and would start the next one if I caught him snitching to Cory about Inez again. Cory could do no wrong in Naveen's eyes. To Naveen, Cory was the fun guy while Javon was the one who got in our asses if we did something we knew wasn't right.

I stood and grabbed my backpack. I looked inside and shook my head. Little pills the color of Skittles peeked out at me. Before Mom got killed, I'd been mixing and making these "Poppers" in my lab. It was a mixture of ecstasy and hashish. Since hashish was in the cannabis family, being that hashish was the THC-rich resinous material of the cannabis plant, it was easy to dry it then compress it into cookie-like sheets. Once compressed into that cookie-like sheet, I let it harden; then I turned it into powder. Took me a minute to get the chemical compounds in the ecstasy and the hashish to work together like I wanted it, but once I got it down, the shit started selling like hotcakes at school and around colleges. Rich white kids loved that shit.

I ran a hand down my face. Mom had no idea that, before she died, I was already what she didn't want me to be before. I grabbed her picture from my nightstand then lay back on my full-sized bed.

"Sorry, Ma. I know you're mad disappointed in me, especially since I know you know everything I been doing since you can see me from heaven now. I'm sorry, and I promise I'ma chill on what I'm doing. See, Ma, you didn't tell us you were like this rich old lady so all this time I was selling them drugs trying to save up so when I went off to college you could go like on vacation or some shit you know? I ain't know you was on some Stephanie St. Clair, queen pin stuff or I wouldn't have done any of this," I confessed to her.

Water burned my lids as I glanced out the window. "Everything falling apart now, Ma. I know you see it—"

I stopped talking when the knob on my door turned. Once I saw who it was, I jumped off my bed and stood defensively. "What the fuck do you want, Cory?" I asked.

He walked in casually. His pupils were dilated so I knew he was angry or high or something. He walked around my room and pretended like he was interested in my science awards on the wall or my pictures and science books.

"Just checking to make sure you cool. You good right?" he asked as he turned to look at me.

"Stop making Naveen your fucking snitch. I know he told you about Inez and Shanelle fighting. I walked in on him doing it. You hit Inez again?" I asked him.

That was the secret between him and me. I'd walked in on it once and didn't try to hide that I'd seen it, but Inez begged me not to say anything so I didn't, but I tried to avoid Cory like the plague these days. Not to mention that he found out about my little secret. So between giving him half of my supply so he could sell it to Inez and her friends as well as to his colleagues, he and I ain't really have shit to talk about.

I loved my brother, I did. But he had some fucked-up ways about him, especially when he was high. I didn't like to piss him off either. I'd seen what he could do when he was angry and I didn't want no part of it. I wasn't a fighter. I'd rather talk myself out of tough situations. I'd been bullied at school about it a couple of times, but when I told Cory a group of white boys had robbed me of my money and my stash, he handled it and I didn't have a problem since, but none of the boys were able to play lacrosse again either.

"What me and Inez do ain't none of your business, li'l nigga, and nobody else's either. If I find out you opened your mouth and said anything, we're going to have a problem, Jojo, understand me?" he asked.

I knew he wasn't bullshitting, but I didn't care. "If you hit her again, I'm telling Von," I told him in all seriousness.

I expected Cory to threaten me with violence and bodily harm, but all he did was smirk and then chuckle. "He won't believe you and Nez will deny it. So there's that. You snitch me out and I tell the whole fam what you were really doing the day Mama got killed and why you couldn't pick her up."

That brought my bravado down a bit. My heart stopped a little, too. I didn't want my family to know why I was late picking Mama up. Didn't need to see the disappointment in their eyes or the accusatory glances. The guilt I already felt was threatening to kill me. My brother and I stared one another down like mortal enemies.

Cory ran a hand through his locs then pointed at my book bag. "You got that for me, though?" he asked like he and I were standing on the other side of enemy lines.

I tossed him the whole book bag, harder than I'd intended. Cory caught it then made a move toward me until the door opened again.

Javon stuck his head in the door. He looked from me to Cory then from Cory back to me. "Everything chill in here?" he asked.

"Yeah, we straight. I was just making sure Jojo was cool after everything," Cory said, tossing one strap of the book bag over his shoulder. "I'll be back later," he said to Von. "Unless you need me right now?"

Javon studied Cory closely for a moment. "Nah, just meet me back at the club tomorrow morning. We need to discuss family business."

Cory smiled like he had no problems. "I'll be there before you will," he said as he slapped Von on the shoulder and walked out.

I knew my oldest brother and I knew his mind was ticking a mile a minute. I always tried to watch my facial features around him. He could always pick up on stuff that way. So I removed the scowl I'd set for Cory when Von brought his attention back to me.

"You know you can talk to me about anything, right?" he said to me as he stood to his full height and crossed his arms over his chest.

I nodded. "Yeah, I know, bro."

"Anything. And if anyone is fucking with you or making you do shit you don't want to, you know can come to me right?"

"Yeah."

"You better not get yourself into any shit, Jojo. Understand me? I'm letting you into the business by allowing your cigarettes into the club, but don't make me regret this shit, a'ight?"

I chuckled trying to hide my mood and my nervousness. "I won't. I swear."

Von didn't say anything for a while, still studying me. I prayed like hell he didn't ask me anything else because I knew if he kept on asking, he was going to break me down sooner or later. There was only so much of his interrogating I could take before I folded.

I was happy when he nodded once then walked out of my room, closing the door behind him. I sighed hard then plopped back on my bed. I was way too young for all the shit that had been placed on me and if I wasn't careful the walls were going to cave in soon.

Chapter 13

Shanelle

I knew I was being followed from the moment I left the office. Javon hadn't come in that morning as he was with Lucky doing something with the Syndicate. He was supposed to be flying back to New York soon and wanted to talk to Javon about the new pipeline that would be coming though. I let the men be men and I came into the office to keep up appearances.

Three young men were following me. I could tell the shortest one was the leader as he was quiet as the other two laughed and talked loudly as if they wanted to be spotted. I glanced around as I walked. I was happy to see that no camera was aimed at my truck from any angle. Being on the top deck meant no security would come running if I screamed.

My heels clacked against the pavement as I made my way to my truck. I thought all three of them were stupid. Obviously someone had put them up to it because they were in a parking garage dressed like they belonged in the latest hood video. I had my Bluetooth in my ear, talking to one of my assistants.

"I'll be back in the office by six in the morning. Keep my schedule clear for the rest of the week," I told him then hung up as I opened the trunk to my truck and tossed in my purse and leather carrying case.

As soon as I went to slam the trunk down, I felt something hard pressed against my back. "So, why don't you open the purse and hand us that wallet. We like the ring and the watch you got on, too. So hand that shit over, too," a raspy voice demanded.

I took a deep breath and wondered if I was going to have to be the reason another black mother had to bury her sons. There was no doubt in my mind that I would kill if pushed. The game had changed. Mama was gone. Javon was a crime lord—and he wasn't answering his phone, which pissed me off more—and I, for one, wanted to kill somebody. She was on my mind heavily. I'd had a dream about her this morning.

"Ain't shit what it seems, baby," she had said to me. *"I don't even think you can trust the people I told you to trust."*

Her words stuck with me. Her face was pained. I dreamt I was there when she was shot. I tried to save her but I wasn't quick enough. No matter how hard I tried, my body wouldn't propel forward. It felt as if I was running in slow motion.

I hadn't laid eyes on Javon since he left. He sent me home so he, Monty, and Lucky could go see the Irish. Lucky was anxious, eager to go. Javon told me with Lucky representing the Italians, it would let the Irish know where the Italians stood.

I said nothing as I reached into my purse and grabbed my wallet. I hurriedly took off my watch and my ring.

"May as well give me those diamonds in ya ear, too, bitch," another one said.

The one thing I hated was to be called a bitch. The bitch who donated an egg to me loved to let her nigga call me bitches. All kinds of bitches he liked to call me. Nigger bitch. Black bitch. Virgin pussy bitch. I showed him who the real bitch was in the end though.

I snatched the earrings out of my ears. Today, I wasn't in the fucking mood. My period was on. I hadn't had dick in days. Some rancid dick pussy of a nigga was beating on my sister. My two little brothers couldn't stop fighting. My sister, Melissa, was still somewhat in love with my fiancé, Mama was dead, and now niggas wanted to rob me. I was not having a good day.

I turned around with tears in my eyes. Judging by the way they laughed, I was sure they thought it was because I was scared. To be honest, I was. I was afraid of what I was going to have to do to them.

"You got what you want. Now, please, let me leave," I said, trying to give them a warning.

"Shut up, bitch," the one with the gun said.

My eye twitched. That word "bitch" rang bells in my head; or were those bells because he swung the butt of the gun and cracked me in the temple with it? I fell to my knees, one of my heels flying from my foot. I shook my head then kicked the other shoe off before I stood.

"Who sent you?" I asked.

The three males chuckled. "How do you know someone sent us?"

"You're in an office building's parking garage, which means this isn't random. You were waiting for your target, which I'm assuming is me," I said. I stood to my full height and got my bearings. "So again, who sent you and what do they want?"

The shortest one stepped forward with a toothpick in his mouth. "Some people wanted to send yo' nigga a message."

I shrugged. "Why didn't you just go to him?"

"Niggas like him seem to react better when you send messages through people they have a connection with, feel me?"

"What would you like me to tell him?" I asked calmly.

"Yo, this bitch is crazy," the one with the bad acne quipped.

I closed my eyes, took a deep breath, and then said a few Hail Mary's.

The short one chuckled along with the one who had the gun to my head. "We don't need you to tell him shit, but you'll give him the message all the same," Shorty cracked.

I shrugged. "You would have been safer just giving him the message," I said.

The elbow strike was so swift to the face of the one who had the gun that the bumpy-face one was too stunned to run from the bullet I put between his eyes. I used the heel of my foot to stomp the knee of the one who'd hit me with the gun. The sound of it cracking was like music to my ears. Shorty went for his heater but I mule kicked him in the nuts before he could. My skirt was a little tight so it didn't have the impact I wanted, but it gave me distance. Shorty fell and his gun slid underneath the van parked behind him. He tried to run for me like a raging bull, but the bullet to the top of his dome dropped him midflight. I didn't have time to fuck around. I was sure someone had heard the shots and the cops would be coming soon.

I stood over the one who had hit me. "Who's a bitch again?" I asked him.

"Don . . . don't shoot, please! I know, I got some information," he pleaded through tears.

"About what? Who sent you?" I demanded.

"This white nigga with a funny accent sent me, all right? Nigga sounded Irish or some shit. He ain't have no arm. Nigga looked like he had been in a fight or some shit. Wanted us to hurt you bad."

"For what?"

"To send some nigga you fucking a message! Bitch, I don't know," he yelled belligerently. Slobber and spit rained from his mouth.

See, I was going to let him live, but the word "bitch" set off my kill button. I put two in his chest without remorse. I heard the sirens already. I knew I had no clear way out as there was only one way to get out of the garage. I quickly wiped my prints from the gun and then tossed it near one of the bodies. I ripped my clothes and my tights. I'd already been assaulted with the gun, but it wasn't enough to tell the story I wanted to tell. I slammed my trunk closed, and rushed around to the driver side door. I took a deep breath and balled my fist then threw my head through the glass.

I screamed out so loud that I was sure the devil heard me in hell. Blood rained down my head and chest. The cuts hurt. My face and neck burned like hell. I took a deep breath then rammed my head into the door. What happened next, I didn't know. The blackout was instant.

I woke up two hours later, in a hospital bed with two dog-faced detectives looking down at me.

"Good. You're awake," the first man said.

I started laughing. The nigga was the exact replica of Andy Griffith. The joke was on me though. My head was pounding and the laughing made it worse. I closed my eyes and moaned.

"Who are you people?" I asked, feigning ignorance.

"I'm Detective Monroe and this is my partner, Detective Stillwaters."

I couldn't help it. I laughed again. "You can't be serious. Stillwaters? Really?"

Stillwaters looked as if he had eaten too many donuts and had something stuck in his throat as he breathed with his mouth open.

Detective Monroe actually bit back a smile. "Ah, we're here to ask you about the men who attacked you in the parking garage."

I moaned again as I tried to sit up.

"No, no, no, now. I think you should lie still," Detective Monroe said, pushing me back down in the bed.

"I . . . I . . . I don't remember much. Three guys came out of nowhere. Attacked me from behind. And I woke up here," I lied with ease.

The two detectives glanced at one another. "So you didn't see who killed those three men, Ms. McPhearson?" Monroe asked.

"They're dead?" I asked with wide eyes.

"They are."

"Oh God," I whispered. I knew I was putting on and any other time I probably would have been ashamed of myself.

"Now we know what happened to your mother a few weeks ago and this is a shame that something like this would happen to you so soon, but if you can remember anything, anything at all, it would be a great help."

"She's lying you know," Stillwaters cut in. "No way in hell she doesn't remember something."

"Dick head, I said I remembered the three men attacking me. That is the something I remember," I snapped.

"They didn't say anything?" Monroe asked, ignoring his partner.

"Yeah, they said, 'Give me the wallet, bitch, and your jewelry.'"

Stillwater cut in to sarcastically ask, "Your wallet, huh? Not your purse, but your wallet."

"You know what, fuck you, okay? I just woke up in a fucking hospital after being assaulted and you're worried about particulars?" I spat.

"Ah, yeah. We're detectives investigating a crime. In case you're too stupid to know, particulars are important."

"Hey, look, Still, cool it with all that, okay?" Monroe asked of his partner.

"I sure as hell hope y'all have some information on who killed my mother while you're hounding me, a gotdamned victim of assault and robbery," I snapped.

"Thought you said she was a college graduate. With a vocabulary like that, I beg to differ," Stillwaters said.

I eyed his gun. I could take it before he could blink, shoot him and his partner. Only I'd kill him and just give Andy Griffith a flesh wound. But that would open up a can of worms I didn't want.

"I'm angry and I'm in pain," I said then pretended to calm down a bit. "I was robbed and assaulted. Forgive me if my college vernacular flew out the window."

"We . . . I'm sorry, Shanelle. We don't have any more leads on who was involved in the drive-by shooting that killed Ms. Claudette. She was a nice woman and the juvie center will miss her greatly."

"It's all the same to me, Monroe. If the gangs didn't kill her, one of them kids she took in would have. Tell me, Shanelle, who's watching that boy in high school while all of you are off working or doing God knows what?" Stillwaters asked.

His line of questioning and off-hand comments made me suspicious and, I could tell by the way he was looking at me, he was just as distrustful of me.

"You're talking about Jojo?" I asked, just to be sure. *What the hell has Jojo gotten into now?*

"Yes, that little motherfucker."

Monroe laid a hand on his partner's shoulder then whispered in his ear. Stillwaters grunted then went back to writing on his notepad.

"Hey, is Jojo in some kind of trouble? If so I need to know," I said.

Monroe smiled. Clearly he was the proverbial good cop. "He's in no trouble, I can assure you. You and your brothers may want to keep an eye on him though. Just to be on the safe side."

I couldn't wait to get out of that hospital bed so I could get home. Just what the fuck was Jojo into that the cops would tell me to keep an eye on him? I didn't want any police anywhere near me as it was. I was mad and annoyed. I needed to get to my phone. Needed to contact Javon so he could know what was going on. Although I'd lied to the detectives, the pain I felt was no fabrication. I could feel the bandages around my head and neck. I was happy when the detectives decided I was of no use to them. They left me with their business cards and I left the hospital whether the doctor had released me or not.

Chapter 14

Javon

A little birdie had hit me up with a nice little morsel of news. I was on my rounds with Uncle Snap, Lucky, and Lamont, educating myself about who to fuck with in Atlanta and who not to. It was during our drive through ATL and various meetings with our contracted underlings, that I lucked up on being told, by Uncle Snap, to visit a part of Atlanta that housed a group who was causing problems on my payroll. The Caribbean Lions. My intent was to visit with this crew and invite myself to a meeting they were having with the same hopeful connect I wanted to meet, the California connect.

Again this wasn't by accident, as I was going to make it appear.

Now, as I said, this little situation that I was prepping to step into had nothing to do with beef or issues on my payroll. Awhile back, I had actually been invited by the Caribbean Lions leaders, a sibling unit going by the criminal name Rize, to meet with them once I stepped into my new roll in the Syndicate. According to Mama's notes, the Lions had a longstanding pipeline from the Caribbean, London, some parts of South America, and Canada. Like me, only in the last several years, the younger leaders had been working to secure a pipeline to Japan and gain a seat with the Syndicate.

Because of my research, I began playing with the idea of meeting with the Lions after looking into how professional they were with their hustle. Let me break it down though: Rize consisted of Khalil Brixton and his sister, Trinity, the current leaders of the Caribbean Lions. They were a small growing force, one that I was very interested in. Especially with Rize's suggestion to meet them after they had heard about the Irish. Unfortunately for them, the streets talked about some trouble going on within the crew and I now had ears that regularly blew sweet information my way on whoever I wanted to keep an eye on and they became my focus.

When later information fell in my lap about Rize meeting with their connect, I found myself at an advantage, which had me moving our meeting up. I also had done research into networking with the California connect, who Mama was close to before her death. This was my chance. I'd learned that this connect was Sato Ayame. She and her partner had additional pull in several Asian areas such as Taiwan and Korea. Watching the outside of a two-level, brick-front shop—a shop rental once owned by Mama, as Uncle Snap had explained to me, but was now my inheritance—a huge smile spread across my face in thought.

"For years, Claudette had been watching and micro-managing the growth of the Caribbean Lions by fostering their business transactions and supplying them with a little money here and there. The idea was to create a new pipeline as a means to bring versatile growth with the Syndicate. But when Mama introduced them to the table, they wanted nothing do to with young, new blood. So she let them sit back and grow on their own," Uncle Snap detailed by my side.

We sat in a blacked-out XL Escalade in the alleyway opposite the restaurant. Monty had picked up Lucky and brought him our way so that he could learn a little of what he'd be dealing with as a chair. Both he and Monty sat in his low-rider waiting for Uncle Snap's signal. I had him on speaker so that he could hear via his Bluetooth while he and Lucky spoke about bullshit.

"So if we follow through with her notes and they prove themselves resourceful we can bring them in." Uncle Snap stretched his legs out and checked his Glock.

I wasn't sure about all of that just yet. Just because Mama had notes that specified to trust certain people didn't mean I shouldn't act in my own way and size people up. Not everyone can be trusted. However, I liked the idea of bringing in fresh blood, so the crew already had my attention.

"Who's their enemy?" I asked while in thought.

Rubbing his bearded jaw, Uncle Snap grunted then shifted in thought. "Let's see. Around here, they have some beef with the six-nines over in Bankhead. Niggas always hating on the Lions grew out of nothing. There some beef with the Kango's, an Australian crew. We got some beef with them too because the niggas hate not having control of how we do shipments."

I reclined against my seat, tapping my thigh while listening. Everything Uncle said I put to memory including every name he spat out verbatim as he rattled the enemies off like a list. After a while, I sighed, and shook my head. "Damn, sounds like half of the A has issue with these cats."

"You think that's something, nephew? Shit, that's just a fart in the wind. Let's see there's also X-clusive. A black and white crew in the suburbs. We have beef with them too because their preppy fuckers never do business right. They always undercut and manipulate to take more product than they should. Then the Irish. Cormac made it his mission to wipe out the Lions, which is why their leaders are your age."

"If they managed to hold it down through that, and find a way to be interesting enough to gain the attention of the west side, then I need to meet them. Let's start this meeting," I said hopping out of the car.

"Go in through the back. I have the keys," Uncle said motioning with his head. "One thing?"

"Yes, sir?" I said out of old habit and respect.

"What are you going to do about Naveen and Jojo?" he asked in sincere concern. "Those two used to be close but now they are fucking up Mama's and mine's house."

An inward chuckle resonated through me then came out. I knew something deep was going on with Jojo and I could tell that he was being stubborn with it. I just had to wait on him, which I intended to. Now with Naveen, little dude was like me with having a perceptive mind sometimes. Except, he never could hold his thoughts in like I could and let people hang themselves. That part of him wasn't a strong suit, so I knew that I was going to have to talk to him soon about how he was feeling about Jojo.

"I plan on speaking to Naveen when I carve out some free time," I explained.

"Good. The family needs you as a whole, but individually they need you, too," Uncle Snap said with a clap of his hand against my shoulder.

After that, we all headed inside with no issue. Cooks had the stoves lit up with savory foods that made my stomach growl. I watched Uncle give hugs to people I didn't know. It was he who had a beautiful older woman with salt-and-pepper locs hand me, Monty, and Lucky plates of the fucking best jerk chicken and rice I had ever had.

"Damn, don't tell anyone, but I think this is better than some shit I had up in Harlem, gotdamn. *Che buono!*" Lucky said with a huge grin. He stood next to a woman with an ass he was leaning back to admire while asking for more food on his plate.

Me, I went on my way through the doors, fork in my mouth, plate in my hand, and that's when I introduced myself.

"Can I tell you that your family in the back have a gift with food? I mean my friend is locked in a state of ecstasy while my baby brother has his nose stuffed in the rice, not saying a thing."

Looking behind me, I saw Lamont give a thumbs-up and continue to take huge scoops of food.

"What type of roots is this huh?" I said chuckling with a grin stopping near a table to look at everyone in front of me. As I looked around at the group of people over my plate, the brother-and-sister team Rize both abruptly stood and stared at me in bewilderment.

"My brotha," Khalil said in a slight accent with his locs braided on his skull like a crown, giving me an equally confused look. "I'm confused. Did we schedule for our meeting today?"

I allowed myself a moment to take a forkful of chicken and roti. I took my time to savor it before responding, "I gathered that since the streets are heated about you all meeting with a very important connect, I'd allow myself a chance to peek in on how you all operate. Is that good with you, brotha?" Going back to eating, I waited for his reply.

From my peripheral vision, I could see Khalil arguing with his sister in hushed tones. Baby girl was a creamy milk chocolate connection of beauty. She appeared to be around Lamont's age. She wore her microbraided hair in two ponytails. Around her bare waist was a tartan plaid shirt tied in a knot over her black baggy yoga pants with waist beads as she sported a cropped short-sleeve top. As she spoke, her bangles shook and she pointed her red-tipped nails our way as if making a gun shape. She looked me up and down. She shifted on her feet to do the same to my family, pausing to stare at Monty the longest with a curl of her lip before speaking with her brother again.

"Damn she fine," I heard Lamont say near me and it caused me to chuckle.

"I'm not here to bring trouble," I said holding up a hand. "I am here to do business though."

Both siblings studied me, scrutinizing me briefly before giving me a reassured nod.

"Have a seat. We've been wanting to meet the brotha who took over for Mama awhile now, especially after hearing how you took down those rassholes," Khalil said taking his seat.

Trinity flipped her chair in front of her to straddle it and rest her chin on the back of it.

I was amused. That's why a smile spread across my face and I smirked. "Oh, yeah. They were a problem that needed to be handled. Unfortunately for them, they are proving to be a bigger problem that I'm enjoying handling."

"Exactly. I was just having that conversation with my people. See, the lot of them believe we should extend a hand and I'm like nah. Now why would we work with people like that when they've been nothing but grief?" Khalil said while leaning to the side and running a hand over his locs.

From how he was leaning, it had me checking out that he was looking at a specific person in his crew. A light, bright-looking nigga in baggy clothes and a close crop fade. My eyes narrowed and I stabbed my fork in the chicken, took a bite, and chuckled.

"Yes, I can dig how you might feel about that. Suggestions are like assholes, ya know? Only when explaining to people that debased remarks such as that can get you killed will the person understand. Get me?"

Khalil sat in silence. His sister Trinity burned holes into their crew's faces with her heated gaze.

"I mean, take the Irish. They will do all they can to come into your world and fuck it up. Like, I don't know, insert a plant who might make ridiculous suggestions that have only caused you to lose out on deals and almost get you killed. You ever have a situation like that?" I asked steady picking at my plate and eating.

Khalil slowly stood to reached out in front of him and splay his hands on the surface of the table before him. "Actually, my brotha, I have, which is why I called this meeting so early. Niggas been talking. My own people been talking."

Everyone in the room started to bristle. A few of his people began to speak up. "We're loyal to this fam," one said. "Yeah, we'd never break loyalty," another said.

I smirked with a low-key chuckle. "They're right, Khalil, but I mean I don't want to get in your family business like that."

"No, get in it," Trinity said standing with a sudden accent. "What do yuh know?"

Shrugging, I made a show of things and took my time before answering. Moving casually around I glanced at everything then pointed to the one Khalil stared at. "Him."

My man Khalil gave me a chin up with a curled upper lip while looking down his nose at me when I stopped in front of him. He then said, "Nuh ramp wid mi."

"No need for me to," was all I said after he said, "Don't fuck with me."

Like that, Khalil went bat shit crazy. He furiously pushed his chair over, snatched that dude up, and yanked him in front of me. "Who yuh working fah, nigga? Mi knew yuh were off." He snarled in heated fury. "Mi knew yuh were actin' shady fah months now, D'Andre."

Glaring at me, D'Andre held his hands up and shook his head. "No, no. I'd never play you, boss. I mean that on my daughter, fam."

"Shoot him in his right pinky toe and see how true that is," I suggested egging dude on. For some reason, I dug his style. If done right, he might make a great general in training up new soldiers for the Syndicate.

Behind me Lucky chuckled then whispered, "He works for the Irish."

I nodded watching the entertainment before me in silence. "Yeah. Saw him exit out the back of the pub when we left," I eventually said.

"But a wah di rass? Oooo, mi hate liars. Put that on yuh daughter? Fah real, D'Andre? That's so foul," Trinity said through clenched teeth, her accent thickening.

It was Trinity who walked to D'Andre and slapped him so hard that he flew face first on the table. Baby girl slammed his face against it multiple times. She twisted him by his head, smashed her kicks against his face then lit him up with her Glock hitting his legs. D'Andre's body shook then fell back near me. Damn, I was kind of impressed.

Interesting enough, there was blood on my boots and a neck under it. Was I the cause of it? Maybe. Was I the one who pulled the trigger that had my boot covered in another nigga's fluids? No. Not this time. What was I doing through all the fun? Shieet, holding a plate of chopped jerk chicken with roti and standing in front of a table full of Jamaicans and others representing the Caribbean.

Thanks to Trinity dropping that nigga in front of me, I figured that I'd play as well by stepping on his neck and watching him struggle to breath, all while eating. That's how I got blood on my boot.

"How long have you been with the Irish? Saw you exit their pub, my friend," I asked licking my fingers then setting my plate down on a table beside me. "My bad, Khalil, go on and handle this homie."

Both Khalil and Trinity stood over D'Andre. Trinity motioned to one of their people and I watched someone disappear to the back coming forward with a woman and a little girl. It was then that Trinity punt kicked D'Andre in the head then walked over to the girl.

"Yuh hear his lying ass?" she asked the crying girl.

The girl shifted her baby on her hip and covered the infant's face nodding. "Yeah. I knew he wasn't shit. Knew he'd throw us to the wolves."

"A wah di bloodclaat dew yuh? Das why mi tell all dem females dat come 'round dat yuh have ta protect yuh pussy. No matter who it is. Trust no shifty dutty dick nigga like him or yuh end up in fuckery like yuh are now." Trinity flipped her hair out of her face and kissed the girl's cheek. "Thank yuh for coming to me, Peachy."

"You ratted on me, Peachy?" D'Andre gurgled blood coming from his mouth.

"Hell yeah, I did! When I saw you with those niggas who shot up my last man, I was too done. I hate your ass for this. I knew you weren't getting all that money from the family. Knew it!" she spat out.

"Bitch, so? You were still living off that shit like I was. I'm going to kill your trifling ass," D'Andre said trying to get to her.

Too bad he didn't make it far.

Plucking the sleeping baby from the girl's hand Trinity cradled the infant against her heart then let a bullet pop off against the mother's temple. Eyes frozen in pure shock, Peachy fell to her knees backward gone to the world as Trinity then turned her Glock on D'Andre with a wink.

Gotdamn, rang in my mind. That girl was sick with it.

"Mi dun trust no thieving sketz rats," she said with a smug smile. "As for yuh, wah yuh story, oh yuh. Yuh half Irish, eh? Thought yuh could get in on some *Sons of Anarchy* bullshit and run out on us? Damn that's shady. Yuh baby girl is going to hate yuh grave."

"Don't touch my—" was the last thing D'Andre ever said.

By that time Khalil allowed his switch blade to run against his neck and left him there to bleed out from ear to ear.

I wasn't sure why they killed the mother, but I gathered she was on some bullshit too. Scratching my jaw, I just shrugged it off. It wasn't my business on that end of things. I watched Rize give both people a salute then go to sit down. I also noticed how Trinity would glance past me toward Lamont every so often. If anything sparked between them, then I knew shit would be interesting. Once the pair sat like a king and queen at their table, the bodies were quickly moved out by the rest of their crew. Immediately after, several old ladies came out with cleaning solution washing the floors clean as if nothing had gone down. My boot even was given respectful treatment, which I appreciated greatly.

Waving a hand for us to sit, Khalil reclined and sighed. "I hate doing that type of shit, but it has to be done. Clean house or bugs will flourish."

"No judgment on my end. I find that a smart business move. Right, Uncle?" I said toward Snap.

Uncle Snap rocked back in his chair. He folded his hands and gave a slight chuckle as if he was privy to some secret only he knew. "That's correct, nephew. If I may speak on his behalf. In a couple of minutes here, you'll be meeting with the California connects."

"Explain to us how we should interpret a move like that, considering your history with my mama." I said finishing it for him and nodding at him in respect.

Khalil cleared his throat. He stared me in the eye with a mature expression on his face and slowly he leaned forward. "It's simple: we wish to expand and grow. We're hoping to get the attention of the Syndicate in hopes that they'll see that we mean business. Yeah, we all are some kids from the street, but we've made old-world moves worthy of respect; and this branch of the California pipeline we hoped we could lay at their feet."

Digesting what he said, I leaned back to tent my fingers against my lips before speaking. "As of now, the Syndicate is in the process of changing as you all know," I said.

"Yes, Ms. Claudette taught us so much," Trinity said in earnest. "We'd never try to break our ties with her,"

"I'm counting on that. Allow me to introduce you to our newest chair, Lucky Acardi representing the NYC circuit and pipeline. With him now in the fold, I'm planning to bring something fresh to the Syndicate. If you all continue to prove to be on the same mind level as me, nothing but good will come toward this family. I promise you that. You all held Mama down, and I intend to do the same," I explained.

It was then that the front door of the restaurant opened. Everyone stood as two of the Lion's main bodyguards walked in with large men behind them. Anxiousness had me readying for whatever as I saw to the right of me. Monty and Lucky also shifted their weight waiting this out while Uncle kept my back protected. As the group moved in, one of the Lions locked the front door then nodded our way.

The group parted like the Red Sea, and then before us was a woman I was familiar with from my research, Sato Ayame; but what had my mouth dropping in surprise was the male at her side, my assistant, Danny Ito. Apparently my research wasn't shit, because there was no way that I knew he was part of the California connect. Shit, from the confused look in his eyes, I could tell that he was thinking the same about me.

Dressed in a clean black-and-white suit, I watched Danny step up, then bow before speaking. "Khalil and Trinity of the Caribbean Lions, we are thankful for your gracious invitation."

Sato Ayame stayed where she was. She watched all of us with knowing eyes. Dressed in a clinging caramel-toned dress with matching shoes, she held a clutch in front of her as she stood in regal authority. Hair pulled into a long ponytail, it hung over her shoulder, showcasing her diamond-studded ear.

"Ito Daisuke," Khalil said bowing, then turning toward the woman next to Danny. "Sato Ayame. Welcome to our home. Allow me to introduce my personal guests, Javon McPhearson, current head of the Syndicate, along with his newest chair, Lucky Acardi, representing New York City."

Danny turned my way then bowed. I wondered if he would betray our connection, but he didn't as he said, "It is a pleasure."

Returning the gesture, I gave him a look that let him know that we would be having our own meeting later to discuss this. "Indeed. Welcome to Atlanta," I said turning to give my respects to Sato Ayame as well.

"Everyone, please have a seat," Trinity said, all sassy tones in her voice turning very professional.

Once everyone took a chair, business commenced with Sato Ayame saying, "I am very familiar with the Syndicate and the recent changes within. I find this meeting very accommodating in us all gathering in such a manner. So, please, let us all speak to each other as friends. I am Ayame and, Javon, I look forward to signing a contract with you. Isn't that right, brother?"

Danny looked my way then gave me a smile. "I believe working with Javon would be for the best of us. Let's get to business shall we?"

Glancing at my uncle feeling cocky, I grinned.

"What just happened there, nephew?" Uncle Snap said in my ear with his hand curled near his mouth.

"Money, that's what happened. I'll explain later," I told him.

Once everything was over, he and I did have our talk, where I explained that I knew Danny. As we spoke on it, Lamont went to his ride to drop Lucky off. Exhausted from the day, I was chilling in the back of the truck with my arm partially over my face glancing at my cell when it rang while Uncle Snap drove.

"Talk to me," I said glancing at my cell. Because I had been so busy, I realized that I had various missed calls.

"Von, it's me, Naveen. Shanelle was in the hospital," I heard him say in worry.

Angst hit me hard as I cursed. "What the hell happened? Fuck that. I'm picking you up."

It didn't take nothing to get to Mama's house. Uncle Snap drove us there like a madman in order to get Naveen. Once he hopped in the car, he told me everything.

"You weren't answering your phone, so the hospital called the house because Mama was still down as her emergency contact," he explained hurriedly putting his seat belt on.

"I know, I know. What happened?" I asked repeating myself.

Naveen had this panicked look on his face that only made everything worse for me. I swear I almost snatched that little dude by his neck but I kept my cool. I needed to know about Shanelle.

"She's not there! I don't know where she's at though," he explained causing me to dig my phone out.

"What do you mean . . . Never mind, I got this," I said calling the missed call number on my cell.

Reaching the hospital, after being put on hold, I finally got through and learned that she had discharged herself. Pissed, I went off livid.

"Mr. McPhearson, I'm sorry but we can't stop her from leaving if she is adamant about it," the woman said in my ear.

Livid and not thinking straight, I went off, "If she's adamant about it? Have you all lost your goddamn mind? She was attacked and you all let her go?"

The nurse on the end began stumbling. Had it not been for Uncle Snap taking the cell from me, I would have gotten in her damn ass. I was fuming, furious that they had lost Shanelle. Rubbing my face, I felt my world tilt with all types of crazy thoughts, until Uncle Snap's voice drew my attention. I heard him explain to the nurse that Shanelle had a phobia about hospitals and that he appreciated the nurse's patience to be helpful. He then became silent before calling my name.

"Von, she called you, nephew, multiple times. She's at your place," he said. "We're on our way," he adding making a U-turn.

Glancing at me, Naveen reached out and squeezed my shoulder. Little dude had tears in his eyes and that made everything harder for me. "If she left on her own, then she's not that hurt, I hope. I mean that," he said with worry in his eyes. "Nelle never gets sick and always acting like she's not hurt even if she has an accident. This is the same thing," Naveen explained. "I know she's okay, Von.

I feel it," he continued. His voice held a tone of admiration and care that he tried to hide due to machismo.

I didn't know what to say. All I could do was nod, because it was true. When we were kids, if she ever got hurt, Shanelle would never let Mama know. She'd just show up with a Band-Aid or something, while acting as if she could take on the world. That's how she always was, but I couldn't stop myself from being worried about her.

Once we made it to my place, I rushed up the stairs opting not to take the elevator then quickly unlocked the door to my place. When I opened the door, Shanelle stood there bruised with anger in her eyes.

"Where the hell were you!" she shouted rushing me and hitting me with her fist. "I've been calling all day, Von, all day! Fucking pigs were questioning me as if I were a criminal. I mean I am but fuck! I needed you."

"I know, I know. Bay, I know." Stumbling back, I reached out, picked her up then held her to me. My thoughts were racing and all I could do was hold her. "What happened?" I whispered against her, forgetting everyone behind me.

"I called you, Von," she said struggling to hit me again. "The Irish. I think the Irish came after me."

Tension had me pulling slowly back as I made her explain to me what happened. Bastards had, yet again, fucked with the wrong one. Retaliation was going to be a motherfucker once I was done.

Chapter 15

Jojo

"Damn, Jojo, what took you so long to get here, nigga?"

I cut my eyes at the white boy who called me that. I'd told that son of a cracker over and over not to call me the N word. He didn't have the right to, but he never listened. Next to him stood his blond sister who was every black man's worst nightmare. She was a beautiful white girl who was irresistible to most niggas, even me. We fucked a couple times, but I had to leave her alone. Pussy was too wet. Too good and too distracting. She was twenty-one and shouldn't have even been fucking with me when she had been; but she wasn't too happy when I cut her off. She had nothing besides sex to offer me as she was using me so she could keep tabs on me for her brother.

We'd agreed to meet by some abandoned railroad tracks near downtown ATL. No one would be around at that time of night; at least, no one who would care what we were doing there. Cars drove over the bypass above us, clueless to the drug deal going down just a few hundred feet below them. About twenty or so men and women flanked Crum and Calista, all dressed in their usual preppy attire.

"You call me that again, Crum, and I'ma break my lacrosse stick across your pug face. You don't get to call me the N word," I told him. No, I didn't like to fight, but I didn't say I wouldn't.

The tall, all-American-looking white boy stopped smiling then frowned at me. "It's just a word, son. Stop being so sensitive. If you say it to one another, why can't I?"

"Fuck you, Crum. You bring the money?" I asked. I didn't have time school him on why his dumb ass didn't have the right to call me a nigga even if my black brothers and sisters did.

Crum chuckled and signaled to one of the boys from his clique. X-clusive had been one of my top buyers since junior year. The money I made from them kept me afloat when I needed to order shit like chemicals and tools for my lab. It was supply and demand with X-clusive. The more they demanded, the more I supplied. Crum tossed the bag at my feet. I normally always made these drops alone, but for some reason tonight I wished I hadn't. I didn't know what it was, but the hair on the back of my neck was standing up.

I checked the money quickly before tossing the bag of product to him. I watched him look in the bag eagerly. He pulled out a Ziploc bag full of the Skittle-like drugs. He grabbed a handful, tossed a few in his mouth, and then shared with his twin sister.

"This my last delivery. I'm out," I told Crum. "And you shouldn't eat those like candy. It's easy to OD that way."

Crum frowned as he chewed. "I don't understand. How is this your last shipment? We're supposed to have homecoming next week. We're going to be out of this by the end of the week. You can't leave us hanging like this. What the fuck is that?"

I shrugged and threw the book bag strap over my shoulder. "You have to find something somewhere else."

"What the fuck, nigga? We can't find this shit nowhere else. We're X-clusive. Your shit is organic and exclusive, which is why we fuck wit'chu. But you can't just roll up here and leave us ass out without a proper change of channels," Crum barked.

His face had turned red. No doubt from the drugs enhancing his anger. Poppers worked quickly. Once mixed with human saliva, it traveled to through the tongue to the bloodline quicker.

"Jojo," Calista said. "This isn't right. You know you can't do us like this. One more shipment for homecoming—"

I cut her off. "No, I'm out. I'm done. I can't do this no more. Got too much shit going on right now." I didn't need to tell them that now since Mama was dead, I didn't have no use for doing what I was no more. It was better I got out while my hands were still clean.

Calista turned to her brother. "I told you Rize was going to get to him. I knew that shit. You should have killed this motherfucker when I told you to, Crum. You never fucking listen to me."

My defenses shot up. *Killed me? What the fuck for?* "Yo, wait a minute. Ain't nobody doing business with Rize. I don't fuck with them like that," I said quickly. My Spidey senses were telling me to get the fuck on.

"He's lying, Crum. I saw some people from Rize's crew pushing this shit over at Georgia Perimeter. He's the only little motherfucker making this shit. How else they get it?" Calista yelled, pointing at me while she looked at Crum.

The Poppers had kicked in. Her face was red, eyes watery and glossy. My mind went to Cory. *Motherfucker! Is he selling my shit to Rize?* It was well-known around the way that those two groups beefed heavily. *Shit. I thought he was only supplying to his friends.* I had no idea he was pushing my shit on the other side of town.

When I looked back at Crum, his face was masked in a scowl that told me shit was about to go left.

"So you take my money and then go sell to my ene-mies?" he asked low and deadly.

I started backing up. I felt stupid for parking my car a block over now. "I just told you, I ain't selling to Rize!"

"Get him," Crum yelled to a couple dudes from his crew.

"Shit," I said as I took off running.

Trying to keep the bag on my back and run as fast as I could was proving to be a challenge. I was glad I wore sweats, a T-shirt, and Jordans instead of my usual preppy attire. Tiny stones and pebbles flew from beneath my feet as I ran full speed ahead. The only thing I could think about was getting away until bullets started chasing me.

"Fuck!" I yelped out once a bullet grazed my ear.

Fear had never been as strong as it was in me at that moment. Tears clouded my eyes.

I'm sorry, Mama.

How fucked up would it be if I died the same way my mother did? What would happen to my family? We were already barely hanging on by a thread as was. My insides heated up then cooled down when another bullet barely missed me. My stomach started churning, a bout of dizziness threatened to take me down. I knew at that moment, I was so close to death the only that could save me was a miracle. My breathing accelerated as buildings and trees blew past me in a breeze. I took off across the street, barely missed being hit by a car. The wind on my face slipped into my throat and made my chest tighten. All I could think about was getting to my car. If I could make it to my car, I'd be safe.

Chapter 16

Shanelle

I was in a blissful state. After Naveen and Uncle Snap made sure I was okay, Javon asked them to leave so he could be alone with me.

"Damn, baby, you really fucked yourself up," he said after removing the bandages from my head and neck.

I had stitches in a few places and my head had been feeling like someone was trying to pry it open. I stood before him naked, body still aching. The water beating down on my body felt good as we stood in the shower.

"I had to," I said.

"I know, but damn. You're crazy as fuck you know that?"

I'd told him everything from start to finish. I was a little annoyed that he hadn't told me what went down with the Irish. Maybe I would have taken care how I handled myself. I would have been more careful.

"So I've been told. Many times. You need to tell the rest of them to be careful, Von. And add more security detail. Put the Thieves on the family since you have Uncle Snap and Monty watching over you."

I noticed he hadn't mentioned Cory as his right hand in a while. I wondered what was up with that. Javon nodded as he continued to look me over. His hands were tracing all over my body, massaging, touching, caressing. When he moved my hair to the side and kissed my neck, I moaned lightly. It felt good to be this way with him. The past few weeks had been crazy.

"I got it covered, baby," was all he said as he laid a hand on my stomach. "So when are you going to let me plant my seed in here?"

"Javon, no," I said.

I wasn't turning him down because I didn't want kids. I was turning him down out of fear. We had way too much going on and me being pregnant would add unneeded distraction. Not to mention, if I lost another child to violence or otherwise, it would send me to the madhouse. I never wanted to know what it was to feel your child move then know the exact moment it stopped. To have to push a dead baby out was the most cruel shit nature had thought to do to a woman. I couldn't bear going through that again.

"It'll be different this time," he said wrapping his arms around me. "There are no other women and we don't have to worry about how we will take care of him or her now. We have money."

"And we also have problems, people problems. Our siblings are fighting. Inez is getting beat on by some nigga she's dating."

Javon pulled back then turned me around to face him. I didn't even have to look into his eyes to know Mr. Lover Man was gone and had been replaced by the protector. "Say what?" he asked.

"Inez, she and I got into a fight because I saw the bruise on the left side of her face."

"So she's back with another motherfucker who can't keep his hands to himself?"

I nodded then sighed. "Looks like it."

Javon didn't say anything. He was quiet for a long while as he picked up my sponge, added peppermint soap to it, and began to wash me.

"I'm clearing my schedule for a day or so. We need to have some family time. I've been focusing too much on other shit and not enough on my family." He grunted then said, "Some shit is going on with Jojo and Cory, too. They've been acting real strange around one another."

I told him what the detectives had said about keeping an eye on Jojo.

"What the fuck, baby? Why would they say some shit like that? They watching Jojo? He in some kind of shit?" Javon blurted out.

Although Cory was blood, Jojo had a special place in Javon's heart. He found Jojo hiding in some bushes when Jojo was seven. He was covered in bruises, blood, and his own feces. I'll never forget the day Javon came running in the house to get Mama. He told her he found a kid who was hurt.

Mama tore out of that house like her ass was on fire. For thirty days while Jojo was in the hospital, Mama was there for her him and so was Javon. Javon read to him. He fed him. Once Jojo was released and Mama was able to foster him, Javon kept the boy around him so much people who didn't know them always asked if it was his son or little brother.

They never told us why Jojo had to stay in the hospital so long, but Jojo had been a part of our hearts from the moment they brought him home. Was he spoiled? Yes. We'd all spoiled him. I knew Javon would lose his mind if anything happened to him.

"I don't know, Von, but we need to find out. I don't like the fact that the cops know something about Jojo we don't," I said.

"I'm going to fuck him up. Swear to God, I'm breaking my foot off in his ass. I told him, Shanelle. I told him to keep his hands clean and focus on school," Javon fussed. "Little sneaky motherfucker," he mumbled.

When Javon was angry was when he was the sexiest. His eyes would darken, brows would furrow, and his face would set in stone it seemed. His chest would expand with each deep inhale and exhale. The muscles in his chest and arms became more defined. I missed this Javon. I missed the man who only had to worry about what time he had to be at work the next morning. I missed the man who worried about how much his next check would be and if he would have enough to take me out for the weekend after bills.

There was nothing wrong with the new Javon besides the fact that he was a changed man. I knew shit would never be the same and I was okay with that in a sense. But I also knew the old Javon was moving further and further to the back of the line. I could see it in his walk. Feel it when he talked. He was the king of streets and it was starting to show in ways we hadn't thought of before. With more of his time being dedicated to the Syndicate, the less time he had to be worried about what was going on at home.

I brought my hands up to caress both sides of his cheeks, stood on my toes then kissed him. The tension in his body slowly ebbed away. Jojo was put on the back burner as Von lifted me around his waist. The kissing had my nipples hard and my breasts swollen. My pussy was throbbing. It needed to be filled beyond capacity, which I knew Javon was more than capable of doing. His big hands gripped my ass cheeks and pulled them apart. That shit turned me on more. His kisses traveled from my lips to my neck. When he bit down then sucked on that place between my neck and shoulders.

I threw my head back and purred low. "Javon, baby, stop," I pleaded. "My . . . my period's on."

He lifted his head then looked at me. "Shit ain't ever stopped me before. Water stops it, right?"

"Something like that," I said, but forgot about it when his lips found my left nipple. "Oh, my God."

Gotdamn, Javon was a master with his mouth. He never denied my breasts the attention they deserved. He moved from one to other, aggressively suckling like a greedy infant. I hissed as my period always made my nipples sore, but that shit felt so good, I didn't even care. He adjusted the shower head so that it rained down between us. Water got in my eyes and mouth, but when his placed my back against the wall and his fingers found his way to my clit, I knew I was in trouble.

My clit was so hard and sensitive that as soon as he touched it, I damn near climaxed.

"Damn, baby. This pussy wet," he said.

"All for you," I replied.

He smirked. "Better be."

He lifted me enough so he could rubbed the mushroom head of his dick up and down my slit.

"Ughhhh," I growled low.

I hated when he did that shit. Every time he rubbed it up and down and his head got close to my opening, I caught my breath in anticipation of him breaking skin. He never did.

"Javon, please fuck me and stop playing," I demanded.

He chuckled. "As you wish, but tell me something," he said still rubbing his stick against my pussy.

"What?" I spat out. My eyes were closed, head thrown back about ready to explode.

"You plan on fucking Lucky?" he asked.

My head shot forward and my eyes flew open. My pussy damn near dried up, and I was about to curse him to hell. That was until Javon pushed inside of me so deep whatever I was about to say got caught in my throat. One of his hands was beside my head on the tiled wall while the other one palmed my ass while he moved deeper inside of me.

"Oh shit," I whispered.

"Thought I didn't catch that, huh?" he taunted while fucking me slow.

All I could do was whimper and try to catch my breath. "I . . . I . . ." That was all I could get out.

Javon's dick was so hard it felt like I'd impaled myself with steel. Steel that had the power to touch every inch of my walls and make me come so hard I feared I was going blind.

"You what?" he growled low in my ear. "Huh? You what, Shanelle? I saw the hesitation to touch him and I know you," he said, hips still pumping into me like he aimed to engrave his DNA with mine.

The more he talked, the harder and deeper he went. By now I was on the verge of going crazy. I yanked at my own hair with one hand while digging into his shoulder with the other. Javon grunted then groaned low. My pussy muscles were quaking. I knew he could feel it. I was doing it to make him come quicker. This nigga was trying to kill me with his dick. I had to make him come or he was going to fuck me senseless.

Then, on the other hand, I didn't want him to stop. The shit felt so good I wanted it to last forever. He was right. There was hesitation to take Lucky's hand, only because he reminded me of who I used to be. The old me would have fucked Lucky by now and Javon knew that. However, I had no intention.

"Oh gotdamn," I cried as I felt Javon's dick grow harder.

He grabbed a handful of my hair and snatched my head back so I could look at him. The harder he pumped into me, the darker his eyes turned. I knew he was on the verge of coming, but he was trying to convey a message before he did.

"You fuck him and I'll kill him," he warned. "And for you, you'll wish you were dead."

As soon as the last words left his mouth, he fucked me harder and faster until he released all his pent-up aggression inside of me.

Chapter 17

Inez

It didn't used to be like this. We used to be good to one another. There was a time when he didn't hit me, but then the drugs happened. I'd do anything for him, anything at all. I even stole drugs from the hospital for him. I lied for him. Covered up the truth for him. Took a fist to the face for him. And it still wasn't good enough for him.

So now as I lay in the middle of the floor with him standing over me, fist balled because I'd fucked around and said the wrong thing again, I wondered when we would get back to the way we used to be.

"I'm sorry," I cried then cringed when he drew back again.

He wasn't himself. Both of us were high out of our minds. Mama wouldn't be so proud to see us now, I bet. The beatings were worse since she was gone. His drug use was getting worse. I was going to have to tell soon or we were going to kill one another.

"You gon' do what?" he barked down at me before backhanding me again. "You gon' tell who?"

I screamed out then tried to back away from him, but I couldn't. Normally I'd fight back, but the new drugs wouldn't allow it. Drug use made me weaker while giving him super human strength. We'd been fighting again. I found text messages in his phone from other bitches. I was never gon' be good enough for him. There would always be others. I hated him for that. It angered me. So I threatened to tell Javon that he had been hitting me.

"Nobody, baby. Nobody, I promise. I'm not . . . I won't say anything. *Por favor, lo siento. No voy a decir a nadie, nena. Es tú y yo contra el mundo.*" I spoke the last part in Spanish in hopes he would calm down.

I got no such luck. It seemed to enrage him more. His locs swung like wild worms as he grabbed me by my hair and dragged me across the floor. The carpet burned my thighs as I tried futilely to get away. I knew if he got to the bedroom, the beating would be worse. I screamed and yelled his name to no avail. I couldn't fight back. I shouldn't have smoked the Mist and then popped the Poppers. I was out of balance, in a state of delirium.

Mama help us. We're crumbling. We're falling apart without you. We kept it all together for you. Why you leave us, Mama? We can't do it without you.

I missed out on my internship at Grady so I lied and told Javon I'd gotten on at Emory. That had been Cory's idea. As he tossed me in the room then kicked the door closed behind him, I tried to back away, but for the life of me I couldn't get away. It felt like the weight of the world was holding me down. He stalked me like a madman. He wasn't the man I'd fallen in love with. Neither was I the woman he had fallen in love with. I didn't know the people we were.

I crawled over the nightstand. I grabbed the lamp then hit him in the head with it. He fell back. I found strength I didn't know I had. I made a mad dash to the bathroom and locked myself in him. He sounded like a wounded animal in the room. He was roaring and throwing shit around. My wrist was against my lips as I backed away from the door. I jumped when a loud thump landed against the door. I caught a glimpse of myself in the mirror and jerked away from my reflection.

Both of my eyes were blackened now accompanied by a red bruise on my cheek. His handprints were around my neck. A patch of my hair had been snatched out by the root. He needed help. We needed help. The ghosts of who we were destined to be before Mama found us reared their ugly heads. I hated it. I hated the way we were, what we had become.

"Open the door, baby," Cory said. I could tell his face was against the door.

"No," I whispered. "You have to calm down, baby."

"I am calm," he yelled then pounded on the door. "Open the fucking door!"

A cold shiver shook me to my bones. "No," I screamed. "Sick of you hitting me, Cory. I'm telling Javon. I swear to God," I cried.

A barrage of hits, bumps, and thuds hit the bathroom door. "Inez, don't fucking play with me! *Abre la maldita puerta!*"

"No! Go away, Cory. Go calm down and come back. Then we can talk."

He kept kicking the door anyway. I knew he was going to kick it down sooner or later. I looked around the bathroom for something to defend myself with. When the door came flying off the hinges, I realized there was nothing there. He stepped through, a scowl on his face that put the fear of God in me. I had nowhere to run. Cory grabbed me by my hair and tossed me out of the bathroom.

I screamed as I rolled over my head. I may have been high, but I was tired of him hitting me. So if he wanted a fight, then he had one. I kicked him in his dick as soon as he came for me. He went down hard, holding his dick while doing so. As I hopped up, I remembered the bat I kept behind the door. His phone started to ring. I rushed for it and the bat, but stopped when I saw Jojo's face pop up. I grabbed the phone then headed for the front door.

I could tell Jojo to come get me. He knew about Cory and me. He would come get me if I needed him to.

"Hello," I answered while looking for shoes so I could get out.

"Help me," Jojo said before I could tell him what was going on.

"Wha . . . What? What's wrong, Jojo?"

"Help me, sis. I'm trapped. Where Cory? I need help, please!"

Cory came storming from the bedroom and I threw the phone at him. "It's Jojo," I said frantically. "Something's wrong. He needs our help."

Cory stopped stalking me. He stared me down. I could see the devil in his eyes, but I also saw that flicker of something turning off. He kneeled to pick up the phone.

"Where you at, Jojo?" he asked into the phone, all the while keeping his eyes on me. "Stay there. We're coming."

Cory hung up the phone. I was happy he didn't come for me. He went to the closet and grabbed down two guns.

"Get your shoes on," he said to me.

I didn't ask any questions. Jojo needed us. That was all that mattered.

Chapter 18

Cory

Shit, I was fucked up. I mean I was on that level of fucked up where even I knew I needed to step back and chill. Of course, that clarity didn't come forth until Inez threw that fucking phone at me and told me Jojo was in trouble. Thinking about that though was pissing me the fuck off and I wanted to slam my fist against the side of Inez's face. *Fuck.* I was on another plane, the type that had the sane part of me looking from a locked chamber in my mind, telling the fucked up half of me to chill. The fucked-up part of me that was wrapped in anger about my childhood and Mama's murder. The part that was using everyone around me to get my high and get whatever fucking shit I wanted. Money, pussy, promotions at work.

Damn, I was fucked up and, sadly, I liked it too much.

Quiet and in my thoughts, I glanced in the rearview mirror at Inez. She had been smart not to sit near me. Part of me was pissed at her ingenuity to not even broach the waters of sitting by me as if we were good about how she hit me. See, I knew her mind. In her mind, it was all me in this. I was the lone abuser, the lone monster, but how I'd tell it, I'd bring up the time she wilded out on me and sliced me across the chest with a kitchen knife because she was pissed about me not coming home at night. Or the other time she sliced my arm, because I hadn't brought her a pair of shoes she wanted. Or when she cut my abs, because she thought I was talking to some young bitches in her complex, which I really wasn't. That was one day I wasn't thinking about pussy actually.

But fuck it, let's act like it's all me.

Glaring at her, I rubbed my nose. These drugs were fucking me up majorly and fucking her up royally. Whenever I got pissed it was because she threatened to speak with my brother about what was going on between us. It always angered me. It felt like a fucking copout on half the shit she did to me, like blow out the tires of my cars and bash the windows in because she was pissed about me ignoring her when I was watching the game or writing a deposition. Most times I could hide what was going on between us, but the time she busted out my windows I had to borrow money from Javon to get that shit fixed. I told him it was some chick I was fucking who got mad about some shit I'd done. It was partially the truth. Granted, she was fucking high as hell when it happened. Yet, she did that shit. In this battle with each other, we provoked each other, equally. Even-steven. So, I'd be damned if she'd put it all on me and have my brother find out about it.

That nigga Javon was faultless. Even in his anger, nigga always could emote that shit just right. I never could and wouldn't it be my luck to end up with a female with the same type of anger issues as myself. I don't even know how it came to be, when the switch turned from me seeing Inez as family to seeing her as being my own family, my own makings of a Shanelle. I really don't know, but it went that way.

We were good before I allowed my drinking to turn into being addicted to using different types of drugs I could find. I thought I was micromanaging it, being a functional addict but that truth slipped further and further away from me, then disappeared when Mama was killed.

I was now a monster-ass nigga and I kinda liked it, but only when I got perks and only if I could make Inez do whatever I wanted and needed. See, it was crazy. Inez's background was simple and to the point. She came from a house of drugs just like a few of us did, so she knew firsthand what living with an addict could be like. However, when she got into med school, I guess the stress of it all made it easy for her to fall into using the very same drugs she thought she hated at one time, just to make it through her education.

When she couldn't easily get what she needed at the hospitals, she took from my stash that she found. When I learned of that, shit pissed me off until I saw how pliable she became. So, in our addiction we became addicted to each other, feeding off each other, vibing off each other, until we fell into the void. We were once good to each other. Once, uplifting to each other, and now, all we were to each other was damaged goods.

"Where is Jojo now?" I said with an edge in my voice.

Inez stayed pressed against the door of my ride, as if trying to make herself invisible as she held her cell phone to her ear. "He . . . He said that he's near Princeton Street. Behind the old dean's house of the high school," she directed with a tremble in her voice.

Jerking forward, Inez gripped the seat of the car in a rush. "Wait. He said he's running past some houses. Stewart Street. He passed a big white mansion."

"Tell that little nigga to find a safe spot to hide and wait on me. We're in the area and if he keeps moving, I won't be able to get him," I said speeding down Princeton. "I'm pretty sure the cops are on the way since his black ass is running through money village."

I was annoyed yet again. I was pretty damn sure that Jojo had gotten himself mixed up with X-clusive over his distribution. I told him to be smarter about it and to spread his business wide, but nah. He never listened. Now he was in some shit, and I had to clean it up.

Gunshots rang to the right of me. It was close to the point that I whipped my ride around, headed toward where it came from, and ran up to a bunch of preppy white and black kids sprinting down the block. Shaking off my high, I pressed the gas, and sped up in my Benz. I knew that shit was loud and was drawing attention, but I didn't give a fuck. Niggas were gunning for my baby brother and that wasn't fucking acceptable.

"Oh my God! Cory, go left, there he is! He hopped a fence," she said all loud and shit in my ear.

"Calm the fuck down, Inez!" I barked at her looking over my shoulder at her and snarling.

Inez slunk back in my car and then proceeded to tell Jojo to stay where he was, which was a smart move.

My attention was on getting my brother at that point, and once I made it to where he was, I parked, and jumped out of my ride. A lot of the crew who followed my brother ran off when they saw me, but a few kept going not noticing me. Sprinting as if I were playing football again, I tackled a blond nigga who had a gun. Forcing my forearm in his throat, my lips pierced and I tilted my head in annoyance.

"Crum? So, you thought that you could kill my brother," I said in annoyance. "Nigga, his black life matters, and I guess all that terror your people got about us is right in this moment, because your life don't mean shit to me right now. Say night-night."

Flipping his gun from his hand, I used his own finger to pull the trigger. I watched in satisfaction as I blasted a bullet into his skull. The shock on his face was humorous to me and annoying at the same time.

"Damn shame, another white suicide due to doing white thangs." Pushing up, I looked around. The softness of grass pressed in my palms and I pushed my locs out of my face as I squatted in place.

"Jojo!" I shouted.

It was then that I was ambushed and felt myself partially lifted up when someone rushed me. Falling backward, I struggled with whoever was on me until I got a clear hold of the kid's neck and snapped it. My lips curled to flash my teeth, and I rolled away dropping the random kid on top of Crum. Gotdamn, this base mix of drugs had me feeling like Hulk.

Laughing, I stood up. It was crazy, because I had no emotion about what had just happened. I just blew it off, brushed myself off, and rolled my shoulders. "Who's next?" I nonchalantly asked.

Tensions were thick and, again, I enjoyed it. I was about to say something smart-mouth again, when a sudden rustling came from the left of me. Like a deer frozen in fear, I looked to the left of me and got ready to body block another nigga until I saw that it was Jojo. Little nigga appeared out of the foliage of some bushes and held his hands up staring at me.

"It's me. It's me," he said in fright.

Two strides had me slamming my fist in his face. The force was hard enough to knock him back on the soft ground where I stood over his stupid ass. My body was like a furnace in my rage.

"What the fuck type shit got you being chased by these pussy-ass bitches huh? You fuck up another deal, nigga?" I barked at him still high off my kills and the drugs coursing through my system. Liquid ran down my nose and I wiped it away noticing that it was blood while I hunkered over him.

"Cory, leave him alone please! He almost lost his life, you see he's hurt," Inez screamed at me rushing over Jojo, pulling him into her arms. "Oh, Jojo! They shot you." Tears fell down Inez as she rocked him against him.

Realizing what she said was true, I stepped up, but fell back when Jojo pushed out of Inez's hold. "Fuck you, nigga," Jojo yelled at me.

His eyes were bloodshot behind his crooked glasses. Behind him was his book bag and he held his bloody arm as he glared at me. To me, he looked crazed and I liked the look.

"I asked for help, not for you to beat my ass. I'm tired you putting hands on me, on Inez!" he said in fury and pain.

Fists clenched I stepped forward and snarled, "Nigga, fuck your tears. Grow the hell up and get your life, dude. Sometimes you have to be roughened up to get the bigger picture. You think Mama was able to do what she did if she didn't have it in her to fuck people up like me, huh?"

"I'm not trying to be like Mama or you. I just—"

"You just what huh?" I interrupted. "You out here slinging. You've been slinging when she was alive, so what the fuck do you think you been doing, huh? Being just like me and Mama."

Tears ran down Jojo's face. He stared at me as if he hated the very air I breathed and, funny enough, I didn't give two shits. His thoughts meant nothing to me in my high. He wasn't blood, so he could kiss my ass with the emotional bullshit.

"I'm not trying to be like you. Not trying to be kingpin and shit. You're selling to Rize and their Lions? X-clusive came after me because I told them I was done. Mama is gone, so there was no point in me selling anymore," he said fisting his hands. "When I said that, they thought I was selling with Rize because they had my Poppers. I know I wasn't selling to them so that leaves you. Only had the bulk of it, so you almost got me killed!"

Confusion had me tilting my head at my baby brother. I blinked several times, trying to process. *Like what the fuck?*

I laughed. "Nigga, who are you to question how I handled your product huh? Second, I don't know a motherfucking thing about Rize or some Lions. I don't sell in bulk to the streets. My bulk supplies only go to the rich fuckers I get through my work as a lawyer. I sell up to make ducats, and sell down to fuck around." I laughed. I liked that rhyme, might remember it for later.

"They said Rize and the Lions have Poppers. Only you had them, nigga. Only you! And now they're trying to kill me," Jojo repeated in exasperation.

His shoulders rose up and down. Sweat beaded his temples. His hair was disheveled and nappy. His clothes were fucked up. His new kicks were all kinds of dirty, which annoyed me. Then, on top of that, he purposely kept himself in front of Inez in fear that I might go for her, I figured. As if I was going to beat her ass in front of him. Shit. I wasn't going to put my hands on the girl. Or him. Not yet. I wasn't in the mindset of it. Give me some damn credit here. Either way, what he was telling me had me thinking. Until I figured out what was up.

"I sold a bulk of the Poppers to the nigga whose club we took for Melissa as a way to keep him in my pocket. I'm thinking that in order to gain some ducats back, he sold to whoever Rize is," I said in thought starting to feel beyond pissed off. "It wasn't me and if X-clusive is coming for you like this, then I'll handle it."

"How?" Jojo asked staring at me with a stern look.

"Nigga, I'm the right hand to a killer, that's how. I'll take care of it. I'm dropping you off at Inez and mine's crib. She'll patch you up, won't you?" I said looking at Inez.

"You know I will, *papi*," she said with slight tone.

"Chill with ya nuts finally dropping, nigga. I'm not in the mood." I thumbed my nose then stared at both Jojo and Inez's scary fucking asses. Man, fuck them.

I was incredulous about Jojo asking me how I was going to handle this situation. I was a handler. This was my job. Yeah, I hadn't been by my brother's side as he learned the way of the crime syndicate. Shit, the fault was really all mine. I think. Come to think of it, I hadn't been getting calls from Javon since he came in on me and Jojo talking. Scratching the side of my face in thought, my eyes were wide with my high and I rubbed my ears hearing everything in the night and nothing. *Damn. Von might be suspicious about me being MIA a lot. I guess I could flip that to my favor and say it was me working. Hmm, maybe.*

Inez grabbed Jojo's book bag. She frantically rushed around to clean up the surrounding area, while looking around for anything or anyone who might be watching us. After clearing the area, she made sure not to look my way, while helping Jojo to the car. Remembering that Inez had responded in a rude-ass tone, I jumped out of my thoughts and focused back on her. My hands itched to do harm to her, but I kept it cool. Considering how Jojo was watching me, hauling off and punching her ass and yoking his little ass up wasn't going to happen right now, so I decided to be chill.

"Right." I turned to look at him over my shoulder while driving off then stopping around a corner. "Tell me everything you know about X-clusive. How they operate, their base, and where they sell. I'll handle the rest."

Shifting in the back seat of the car, Jojo reached out to grip the back of my driver's seat in rage then turn to extend his finger toward the window. "First off, you killed one of the main leaders, Crum, and his sister."

My eyes followed as he pointed outside the car. Sprawled in lush grass lay the bodies of the kid I killed and the girl whose neck I snapped. They looked like rag dolls and I had no remorse. Shrugging, I dropped my foot on the gas then sped away.

"Shit happens," was all I said as I went into my pocket, pulled out a blunt, lit it, and drove off with everyone in tow.

Chapter 19

Javon

Yeah, my family was coming apart at the seams. I sat in Mama's house, staring at her portrait with my fingers over my mouth, my pointer and middle finger over my nose. I was in thought. Deep thoughts. Lucky was back in NYC. The Syndicate was quiet for now and the streets were abuzz about the death of two rich white kids in the same neighborhood as Jojo's school. When I received the word of that, I had been at home, enjoying breakfast with Shanelle. She had made me a big breakfast. Grits, scrambled eggs, toast with grape jelly, thick-cut bacon, sausage links, and sweet potato pancakes with maple pecan syrup.

She had gone all out and was flexing the fact that she had taken cooking classes just to get better at it for me. I was feeling some small type of normalcy because of it. After putting in an extension of my PTO at work, having the Forty Thieves beef up their security on us and sending word to the Syndicate that I was going to need some time to myself, I realized just how little time I had been spending with the fam. Coming into the fold had taken out a lot of my energy and it took Shanelle's loving to get me right on track.

As I sat eating, and feeding Shanelle as she sat on my lap in nothing but my open button-down shirt, the news drew our attention. After that, my cell went off with word from the Forty Thieves about the buzz the killings were causing. Now, I sat with Shanelle behind me staring at my mother in thought. The family needed to talk. I needed to know if Jojo had heard anything at his school about those killings. I needed to talk to Melissa to see what was good on her end with the club. Lamont and I needed to have a discussion about what Shanelle said to me about Inez. In the midst of all of this Uncle Snap, Cory, and I were currently gearing up to speak with Naveen and see where his head was at as well. We all were going through so damn much that it was important that we all checked in with each other; otherwise, the reality of everything could do more damage to us, and not good.

"Do you think we'll be okay, baby?" Shanelle whispered against my ear as she stood behind my chair with her arms around my neck.

"All I have is hope with that, baby. Mama's death and her plan have been opening a lot of wounds and weaknesses in us that I never noticed before," I said while thinking. My fingers shifted into an L against the side of my face as I tapped my finger against my temple. "I'm not liking the feeling that I'm getting in my stomach about this."

"I know," Shanelle said moving so that I could stand. "Me too. I had a dream that Mama said that she wasn't sure if the people she told us to trust should be trusted after all. That she might have been wrong."

"Damn. Really now." I shifted in my chair to study Shanelle's beautiful face and I started thinking back to last night between us.

She was right in her actions of persuading me to slow down in my desires to make up for what we lost. This wasn't the time for her to carry my seed so that we could try to create life again. We had too much going on right now to even think about starting a family. I just hoped that my seed didn't take root during our shower session;

otherwise, we'd have a lot of adjusting to deal with in the middle of a dangerous time for the family.

The sound of Shanelle's heels on the wooden floor let me know from the rhythm that she was pacing and now stood near the big bay window of the room. When I turned to look her way, I smiled. I was right in my assessment. While studying the tension in her back, her voice traveled to me in subtle sadness. "Yes, really. I'm worried for our family."

If there were any way to take away her pain and worry I would. "I'm going to work this out, I promise, starting today." Taking my time to stand up from my chair, I turned to look at Mama's picture again, and I whispered my promise. "I need you to do something though."

"Anything," I heard Shanelle say behind me.

"Hit up Uncle Snap." I suggested. "Right now, I have him speaking to the streets to get some more intel. Just call him and tell him to come home so that you and he can make us some dinner." Pulling her hand to me, I kissed her palm and continued, "That way, he can fill you in with what I've been doing as well. Think you can do that?"

"Yeah, I can. Sounds good to me," she said with a soft smile on her face.

"With the Irish pissed, I need you up to date with everything. That was my fault for not having the time to give you the knowledge. I should have had you by my side anyway, but that's another thing for another time." I watched Shanelle give me a cute smile and nod, as her way of saying, "No shit," without actually saying it.

"Shut up, woman," I teased with a lopsided grin as I touched the mantel of the fireplace and stepped down the stairway. "I'll be with Naveen." Pausing, I looked toward her again, "And if Jojo shows up, send him down my way. Talk and take care of the family for me while I'm talking with Naveen."

Cutely biting her lower lip, Shanelle understood what I was asking without me saying it. Basically, I needed her to be me while I tried to heal the family one by one.

"I will, Von," she said tucking her hair behind her ear, showing the stitches, scratches, and bruises there.

"A'ight," was all I said as I went below.

Finding Naveen was simple. He was in the craft shop he had moved down there, working in a zone. Quiet, I looked around noticing the huge monitor behind him. I saw Shanelle going through the house on her cell. I saw everything else on the monitors then I paused and quirked an eyebrow because there was a new section on the monitor: Jojo's room. What the hell was going on?

Walking in, I stared at the blueprints and various pictures of objects he had up. "What are you crafting now?"

I also saw a picture of his girlfriend and him directly in front of him. They were hugged up, in that typical IG pose: him kissing her forehead, as she held him and stood on the tip of her toes. Navy's girl was a pretty nutmeg brown East Indian girl who grew up with a hood mentality. That was the only way he'd date an Indian girl; otherwise, he stayed with black girls, I learned by watching him. Studying their picture, I realized, again, just how young he was and how much his life had been turned upside down. It hurt to see that his world now was focused on the next thing project he could build in tandem for the Syndicate and in maintaining Mama's properties.

Sparks lit up over whatever he was fiddling with, along with the smell of smoke. Bobbing to whatever music that he was listening to on his headphones that rested around his neck, I watched him reaching around his space for things. Young Naveen stood over his workbench doing his thing being a master of his world.

Like usual, his hair was knotted on top of his head. He wore a white wife beater with dark jeans and boots. The difference in me watching him now was that I noticed the Glock that he had against the small of his back and the one I knew he had strapped to his right ankle.

Damn, our family had changed. Shanelle had taken to teaching all of them how to shoot and it was showing.

"Soldering a new version of the Mist cigarettes and something else, I don't know what it'll be used for. Maybe for my car. Just getting out of my head," he said as if it were an afterthought.

"Sounds good. So check it, me and you need to talk." I walked up to him and leaned against his worktable crossing my arms over my chest.

Not looking my way, Navy continued his work. "About?"

"For one thing, why are you watching Jojo's room?" There was no point in bullshitting around.

"I don't trust him anymore is why. He killed Mama," Navy said matter-of-factly.

Thumbing my nose, I felt a flicker of irritation. "So, there's nothing he can do to make you drop this huh? Jojo didn't pull that trigger."

I knew when Navy began clanging objects around on his station that he was getting pissed off. "He might as well have. Shit, he did in my opinion. There's no excuse for him not getting her, and I'm not letting him off the hook for it either. I'm tired of everyone kissing his ass because he's the baby." Navy stopped his clanging then looked my way, taking off his protective glasses. "There's only a year difference between us, and I got more maturity than him, and he's lying about where the fuck he's been? Naw, I'm not letting this go. That's why I'm watching him. He's sneaky."

"What you doing isn't chill, little brother, and you know it. This isn't you. You and Jojo used to be tight, close at the hip, and now you're calling him sneaky. That shit isn't adding up. Something is going on with Jojo, we all see it. We need to see behind what we want and the blaming and go deep at this shit. Navy, you of all people should know that," I tried to reason.

Pushing back from the table, Navy walked to where he kept his tools and pulled his gloves off. "Why? Because we went through the same shit? Because my birth father got a kick outta making me sit in the back of the kitchens of his restaurant to play with the rats and be eaten? Because my criminal-ass father would let my uncles fuck me? Because my aunts used to burn me with cigarettes calling me a demon and living shit. Because of all of that I should know when someone is hiding shit?"

"Navy, we all grew up in pain. I share that with you. We all had to do shit to survive. Step back from your anger and look at this from all sides is all I'm saying," I explained.

There was boiling pain behind Navy's eyes. He loved Mama as much as us all if not more. I remembered when Navy came to us. Mama just showed up with him one day and made me promise to protect him at all costs. I never understood why. I just remembered that day, she had a wild look in her eyes and, I swore, speckles of red on her dress. Like I said, I never understood what it was back then, but being where I was now, I thought I was slowly coming to an awareness of just what Mama did to protect Naveen.

"I don't want to," was all he said.

Stepping to him, I rested a hand on his shoulder and I squeezed. "You have to, for Mama. If you don't we'll continue to fall apart, Navy."

"And if I do, I won't have Mama anymore. Jojo is doing something. I feel it and he's lying about where he was when Mama was killed. I won't let that go!" Tears rimmed Naveen's eyes.

I pulled him into an embrace understanding finally that this anger, this blaming Jojo for Mama's death, was the last thing he had that could keep the feeling of Mama alive for Navy. That understanding was deep to me. Fucked up, but deep and reasonable. Shit. My way to keep her alive was taking on the Syndicate and I knew that it was eating me alive. So, I got where Navy was coming from, which was why I held him as he cried.

"I understand," I said low. "And I got you. I can't let this tear us apart, but I got you. I'll stand by you as best I can in this, baby brother, I mean that. We'll figure this out but you need to get that camera out of his room."

Navy said nothing; he just stepped back and went back to fiddling with shit.

Something in me kept staring at the camera as my mind started clicking in thought. "I mean that shit, Navy. Do me that solid," I urged then looked his way. "How long has that been up anyway?"

"For almost two weeks now," he said with no emotion in his voice.

"And you've been going over the footage?" I asked curious.

"Nah, not really. Jojo hasn't really been doing anything for me to go over it. It's the same thing. Go in his room, sit on his bed, maybe work on some schoolwork, or bring up his chem kit and do some shit with that. Fuck with something under his bed. Scratch his nuts and do whatever. I ain't been watching him that hard," Navy explained.

Stepping back from the monitor, I crossed my arms feeling the weight of the world on my shoulders. "Put it on a couple of days ago. Last time I was here and you two blew up."

Without a thought, Navy pulled up the last time we were here. "What are you thinking?" he asked eying me.

"Just watching," I quietly said.

At first everything was like Navy said. A large chunk of it had Jojo's room empty until it came up with the fight. I watched him bang around his room in distress. He flipped things around until he grabbed a book bag. Digging in it, he seemed too satisfied with what he saw. That's when Cory busted in. I watched my brother go at it with Jojo. I surveyed him walking up on Jojo to intimidate him with his size, then take that backpack from him. Heated, constrained words were exchanged. My eyes narrowed while I carefully observed. I was so deep into it that I didn't realize that I was digging my fingers in my arms. Nor did I realize just how quiet Navy had gotten, too. We both stood there just watching in silence, mentally recording everything until Shanelle's voice on an intercom pulled us back to reality.

"There's been an accident with Jojo, Cory, and Inez," she screamed on the intercom.

Glancing at Navy, I moved his way quickly. "Say nothing, and don't react. If there was a time when I needed you to be me, today is that. If you react in any fucking way, I'll harm you, get me?"

Surprise had Navy backing up. He gave me a slow nod and licked his lips. "I'll watch my temper and won't slip up."

"Thank you, baby brother. Go ahead." Sidestepping out of his way, I let Navy jet out.

When Navy was the first one out of the bunker, I knew that even though he was angry with Jojo, the video was fucking with him. As well as the idea of losing Jojo would be the straw that broke the camel's back in their relationship and I felt the same way too. But the three of them, hurt? In an accident? This was a pain deeper than losing one's mind. Besides, my mind was processing what I just saw. I wasn't 100 percent about some things there, but that quiet voice in my head knew I was reading the body language and lips right in that footage. Uploading the video to my cell, I glanced back at the monitor.

"We're on our way up," I said shutting the bunker down.

As soon as I made it up top in the house, all I heard was yelling.

"What the hell do you mean it was nothing?" I heard Shanelle shout. "He was shot at! You almost wrecked the car and you look high, Cory."

"Look, get out my face, Shanelle. You're not listening to me. We also got into a wreck because some Irish motherfuckers started chasing us outta nowhere." Cory started to explain.

While I walked into the main living room, I glanced around to see two of the Forty Thieves standing by the front door. In front of them, I saw Jojo sitting on the steps with a bandage on his arm. His glasses were cracked and he appeared to have been in a fight. Naveen was at his side with a scowl on his face trying to help Jojo and Inez. My little sister looked to have been in battle herself. She too had some bandages on her, on her neck, wrists, and arms, as she stood in the middle against the stairwell trying to disappear, it seemed to me. Then, taking a look at my brother, I noticed that he also had some scratches on him though he looked better than Jojo and Inez combined.

I felt my jaw twitching in response to the madness.

"If the Thieves didn't call me, you wasn't going to say shit, nigga! What the hell is wrong with you, Cory?" Shanelle shouted pointing with her fingers.

Everything felt surreal.

I felt a hand on my shoulder that made me feel the
presence of Mama in the room. I waited for her to say
something, but realized that it was all falling to me.
Turning, I stared in the face of my uncle as he pulled me
back.

"Tell me what happened clearly," I asked of him, keeping my temper at bay.

My uncle also seemed weary. He ran a hand through
his salt-and-pepper hair, then looked my way. "First,
some Thieves are bringing Melissa around the back with
Lamont, so there's no issue there."

Crossing my arms over my chest, I kept finding myself
watching my brother's erratic movements while he and
Shanelle argued. "Good, that's a blessing, Unc. So what
went down exactly, I ask again?"

"Damn, I'm too old for this." Taking a seat, Uncle Snap
grabbed his clear Mason glass again and looked up at me.
"You know why I hold on to this piece of shit glass huh?"

Shaking my head no, I moved closer to him listening.

"It's the last thing your mama ever touched to her lips.
Back in the day as she aged and couldn't fight niggas
as easily as she could in her youth, she'd mix a type of
acid in different-colored Mason jars and pack 'em in her
purse. She used to throw that shit on anyone who got in
her way. The unused ones she'd give to me with my favorite lickah or moonshine." Uncle Snap gave a sullen laugh
before glancing up at me. "Anyway, nephew. The Thieves
reported yesterday in their watching of the family that
Cory left some apartment complex in midtown with Inez."

Quirking an eyebrow, I frowned. "What complex? He
doesn't have a spot down there and neither does Inez.
Why was she with him?"

"Hold up off that just now and listen, nephew, because
we need this handled now and quickly," my uncle said

taking a deep drink of some amber liquid from the glass. It was probably sweet tea and Crown Royal.

"I told you to beef up the security, forgetting we all still had at least a few of them watching us. But anyway, watching Cory, they followed up to Jojo's school," he explained as a feeling in the pit of my stomach became heavy.

"They watched as Cory whipped through and ended up picking up Jojo who was being chased."

"By who?" I quickly interrupted.

"From their intel, some preppy-ass kids," he explained.

"Do they know why? Did they question them?"

Uncle said, while shaking his head with a deflated look on his face, "No. By the time they caught up with Cory, the kids had bolted off."

I dropped down in a seat next to Uncle with a heavy heart. All this time, Mama had been sending Jojo to that prep school to give him a better chance at life. From what Uncle was saying, it didn't mean shit if Jojo was being attacked and harassed at the school. Everything that was going on wasn't making any damn sense for me. None. There was a thread that was off, a couple of them, and it was bothering me to my soul.

Disappointed at myself, I shook my head. "So, then what?"

"From how it sounds, Cory picked up Jojo and left two bodies behind him," he explained swinging his glass around. "Inez patched Jojo up and they all stayed the night at that apartment in midtown. Then, today, on their way to the house, they were sideswiped by the Irish."

"Back up though." Scratching my head, I leaned forward with a tilt of my head and with an eyebrow rising in agitation. "Why the fuck was Inez there and why the hell were two bodies dropped?"

Raising his shoulders Uncle Snap dropped his hand splashing his drink with it. "Shanelle's been trying to figure that out. All Jojo will say is that he was being chased because they were pissed at him about some school shit. Won't say what. I gathered he's being bullied. Then, all Cory will say is he found them trying to kill Jojo and he handled it."

"Wait, you don't kill people who are bullying. What the fuck shit is this?" I stood up, but Uncle grabbed my arm.

Stepping up to me, we stood face to face. Almost brow to brow. We hadn't had a moment like this in years, since I was a kid acting up. It's what had me dropping my resolve out of respect. That old man gave me a look of concern that put me in my place and had me shutting up to listen. "You're not hearing me. They were shooting at him, nephew. Since that's the case, he handled it. Must have gotten in a scuffle with them. Besides, he's not himself right now."

"This shit is insane. Are you hearing yourself, Unc? Everyone is lying, then the Irish pop up and attack? I'm not chill with that," I said pissed all the way off.

"I know, but one thing at time. We need to handle Cory," Uncle Snap said.

"Why?" I snapped at him.

"You don't see it do you? The nigga is high," my uncle said letting me go.

Turning, I watched my brother use the back of his hand to rub at his nose. He then flashed a curious grin, flipped Shanelle off, then stumbled back. Shanelle followed right after him, not giving a damn about his rude actions. Her pretty face was contorted in rage and she blasted out something he didn't like. I observed Cory's face flip into a mask I was very familiar with as kids. It was the same one he wore when he had to cope with attacking one of Toya's boyfriends. It was a look that, if I hadn't been watching everyone so closely, I would have missed. Especially when Inez became tense, tucking her body in as if someone was about to hit her and something akin to paralyzing trauma flashed across her face when my brother flipped his switch. Thinking back to the video. I recalled seeing Jojo mouth her name in anger.

As my mind worked its thing, my feet followed. Two strides forward, and I found myself snatching Cory up, and slamming him backward over a table. I followed with my forearm to his throat as I slung his heavy body up against a wall.

"The Irish really attack you, or you caused the car to flip because you were high?" I said in Tagalog so that only he and I could hear it.

Something in my brother's eyes softened to the man I knew him to be, but it quickly disappeared with his pride, flipping to anger. "Man, get off me with that bullshit. The Irish chased us down. I don't know what you're talking about with the rest of that shit, man." Half of what he said was slurred and half was in Tagalog.

"Boss, the Irish is a factual thing," one of the Forty Thieves said speaking up. "We took them from the wreckage and took care of the wounds, then brought them here."

"Yet, this motherfucker is floating around, talking any kind of way to my fiancée and the rest of the family," I said low turning my attention back on my brother. Taking a sniff, my lip curled in anger. "I smell liquor."

"I'm in pain, Von! Chill, get off me," Cory said struggling.

Checking him out, shit wasn't adding up. I noticed marks on him that looked old, shit that wasn't aligning with the wreck.

"Von, get off of him please. Please, we were in a wreck," Inez pleaded, pulling on my arm.

It was then that Jojo stood up going off, "Why you always defending him? I'm tired of this bullshit, tell the truth . . ." he said then stopped, freezing his words.

Jojo then spun around and took two stairs at a time disappearing.

"Naveen," was all I said for Navy to jet off and follow.

Placing my attention back on my brother, I felt him laughing under me as he tapped my arm. In his struggling the nigga made a vital mistake. His movements caused a bag of something that looked like Skittles along with Mist tablets for the e-cigarette to fall from his pocket. Motherfucker was basing!

I looked down at that shit then looked slowly back up at my brother, then back at the drugs. Back and forth I went until I felt my brother tense under me. This wasn't my little brother. Flashes of us as kids played around in my mind. In it, as we grew, I saw the small things that I used to ignore, like the weed he'd steal from our mother's boyfriends, or the little sips of beer or liquor missing from their cups while his breath smelled like a distillery.

I also saw his anger at not being able to protect himself or me for that matter from the whippings our mother would give us or the ass kicking her boyfriends with put on us until we could find safety at his old-ass father's home. Yeah, against the wall under my hold wasn't my brother at all. Nope, this was shadow of his anger, alive and in full color. Mama's death broke him.

"Stop playing. We're in some real shit with the Irish man. That . . . that's not mine." He lied to my face. "Look, had I not gotten that message from you about the Irish, I would have been fucked up. We all would have been, right, Inez?"

"Y . . . yeah," she said stumbling, looking down at her feet and not at me. "He found that with those kids."

Something was off with her and it wasn't just the bruises that lined her pretty face. Keeping my hold on my brother, I used my free hand to gently grab Inez's chin then raise her face up at me. I didn't know why, but as soon as she started crying, I realized the truth of the matter, as the video replayed in my mind and pieces about my brother's own temper aligned. I learned as a child through Mama the valor of a man isn't always about his fist. Men who are uneducated, weak of mind, mentally incapable, or just plain dumb were the type of men who always resorted to using their fists instead of fighting with their mind. Since my brother, *my goddamned blood,* was on some dumb shit, I figured that I'd fall right in line with him. You know? To wake his stupid ass up since he wanted to act 'sleep.

Everything happened in slow motion. Blood or not, that I was about to kill my brother ran in my mind as my fist connected with his jaw followed with my foot against his chest. Yeah, the Irish were out of control, and I had every plan to deal with them. But, for right now, I had a junkie problem that needed handling.

Chapter 20

Uncle Snap

I didn't know what to make of what I was looking at. I just didn't. These weren't the people Mama spoke so fondly of. These weren't the children who had it all together. The children Mama had raised wouldn't behave in such a manner. I didn't want to accept that the shit had hit the hand we fanned with, but what was playing before me was the downfall of all Mama had spent years putting together.

As soon as Javon dropped Cory, I knew for sure shit had changed. When Javon's foot connected to Cory's chest, I knew it was time to move in, but I didn't. I watched as Javon and Cory fought like two niggas on the street. Cory was like the Incredible Hulk. Seemed like the nigga bulked in size each time he inhaled and exhaled. I guess whatever he was high on made him a super nigga or some shit.

He threw a punch at Javon that made him stumble back, but he didn't fall. Javon righted himself then threw a combo of punches that bloodied his brother. Cory may've had unnatural strength in the moment, but the devil in Javon was bigger than the one in Cory. Javon rushed Cory, scooped that nigga up, and then took him down. It was like watching the best of the best in the WWE or MMA.

"Nigga, you must be out your mind to be putting your hands on her like you don't know what it is to be a man," Javon growled after he had put Cory in a chokehold. "So you a junkie now, nigga?" Javon asked as he yanked him off his back and pretty much kicked him across the room again.

"Stop, Javon," Inez screamed. "Leave him alone!"

She made a move toward Javon, but Shanelle stepped in front of her. Her hands were already fisted and she had placed herself in a defensive fighter's pose.

"Don't do it, Inez," she warned her sister.

Inez nibbled on her bottom lip and eyed Shanelle down. Her fists were already balled by her side too. Her eyes were dilated and she held a look that said she was on the edge and threatening to fall over. And I knew neither one of them was scared to get down. Lord knew I didn't want to see those two go at it. Wasn't no need. But Cory needed what Javon was dishing out to him. That li'l nigga needed some tough love, and if I were ten years younger I would have taken that stupid nigga to task myself.

I watched Shanelle. She was watching Inez. She hadn't said a word or made a move to break the brothers apart. The look on her face said she was waiting for Inez to make a move or the wrong move. I knew Shanelle would fight for Javon. Had no gotdamn idea Inez and Cory were even fucking. They had kept that shit under wraps.

Dishes went crashing to the floor. Chairs fell over and Cory finally found his footing. The mask of anger and pain on Javon's face showed him in father mode instead of being a brother. Blood poured from Cory's nose as he snatched his shirt off and threw it. He was so damn high I didn't think he realized just what was happening.

"What the fuck you hit me for, Von?" he asked. "So you want to be that nigga now? Think since you running shit, think 'cause you're a kingpin or some shit you got the right to put hands on me now?"

"Shut the hell up, nigga. You out here being stupid so I'ma treat you like you stupid. You wanna be a junkie so I'll treat you like one," Javon told him. "Put your hands on her again and next time I'm chopping those motherfuckers off."

Cory's face twisted as he slapped his chest. "You see this shit, huh? You see what the fuck she be doing to me? All these gotdamn marks on my chest and back from her ass cutting me, coming after me for stupid shit. Why ain't nobody going after her? What? A nigga ain't got a right to defend himself from a crazy bitch?"

Just then Monty and Melissa walked in. "Holy shit." Melissa gasped. "What the fuck is happening?"

Monty ran a hand through his hair, but said nothing.

"Do you hear yourself?" Javon asked Cory with a frown. "What the hell you and Inez got going on that you two trying to kill one another?"

"Everybody can't be perfect like you, nigga," Cory shouted then threw his arms open wide. "I'm fucked up and I own it. It's me," he said while slapping his chest. "Live with it or get the fuck from around me and mine."

Javon's head jerked and he snarled. Cory picked up a glass and threw it at him. But Javon was quicker than he was. He closed in on Cory. Somebody had been washing dishes in the sink before all hell broke loose. The water was murky and I could still smell the faint hints of bleach in the air. Javon grabbed Cory by the back of his hair, spun him around, and then forced his face into the sink full of dishwater.

Inez screamed and ran for Javon. Before she could swing at him, Shanelle had tripped her up. Inez did a tumble over her head. Once she realized what Shanelle had done, she jumped up and ran for her, but Monty stopped her midflight. He bear hugged her and kept her in place.

"Ahhhhh, you stupid bitch. I'ma fuck you up," she screamed at Shanelle, who only shook her head.

"I'll kill you, nigga," Javon spat at Cory. "You understand me? Before I let you become this thing you're trying to become, I'll dead you myself," he said then snatched Cory's head up.

Cory tried to catch his breath but, before he could, Javon shoved his head back into the water.

"Think you want to die, li'l bro? You wanna go visit that cunt we called a mother? Say hello to her in hell when you get there. Tell her she ruined her sons so badly that one of them has decided to become an abusive junkie so the other one killed him."

I'd never seen that boy flip the way he was doing. I was half scared to touch him and too drunk to test my strength in the moment to pull him off Cory.

Shanelle rushed over to Javon. "Baby, stop. You're really going to kill him," she said as Cory's flailing arms started to go limp.

Javon wasn't himself.

"Ay, nephew, you gotta pull back. Mama wouldn't want this. She wouldn't," I told him.

"Javon, please," Shanelle pleaded while touching his arm.

It was a gentle touch, one that seemed to quell the beast inside. I was sure that if I would have touched him, he probably would have swung on me. Javon snatched Cory's head from the water then slung him backward on the floor. Cory coughed and spit up water. Inez started kicking in Monty's arm. She twisted her body until she got one arm loose and swung on Monty. She hit the boy so hard he bristled but then caught himself. She rushed over to Cory, tripping over her own feet. Tears were in her eyes.

The worst kind of love was a junkie kind of love. I knew from experience, not my own, that when two addicts fell in love they not only shared love for one another but also shared their love for drugs. They were enablers for one another. I shook my head, disappointed and sadder than a motherfucker at this point.

"Why . . . why you do that, Javon?" she screamed as she cradled Cory's head in her lap. "I hate you," she yelled. "I hate all of you. Baby, you okay," she whispered to Cory who had started shivering.

He didn't say a word, just stared at his brother with a hatred I couldn't fathom.

"Get out," Javon said coldly. "Both of you, get the hell out of Mama's house. You're done. I don't know either one of you. He's not my brother and you're not my sister. Get out."

Shanelle's eyes widened. "Javon, baby—" she started but then stopped when he shot a look over at her.

That look silenced every other brother and sister in the room, including Naveen and Jojo who were on the stairs looking on. I had to respect Javon for doing what he was. He needed to apply this kind of tough love. I'd seen Mama do the same to many a nigga who had gotten beside themselves.

"Mama was out here every day putting her damn life on the line only for you two ignorant drug addicts to tarnish her damn legacy. Out here on drugs and selling that shit. I'm out here trying to keep all this mess together."

Inez was wailing at this point. "He needs help, Javon, please," she begged.

"I don't give a fu . . . Get out," Javon spat, this time deadlier than before. "Get out before I drag both of you motherfuckers out of here."

Inez gently laid Cory's head on the floor then stood. She moved toward Javon and Shanelle stepped in front of him.

"Stop, Inez, please. I don't want to fight you, sis, but I will," she said.

"Fuck you," Inez yelled at Shanelle then looked at Javon. "You so busy sniffing up that bitch's ass you ain't have time for him. When he was receiving awards and shit from school, you chose to go support Shanelle instead of him. Ain't shit he ever did been good enough for you. And you," she said to Shanelle, "you don't care about nobody but him." She pointed at Javon.

"That's not true and you know it," Shanelle said.

"Inez." Cory mumbled it. "Fuck 'em," he said running a hand across his nose. "Help me up and get me out of here, baby."

I felt like I was in a movie or some shit. Cory was Eddie Kang and Inez was crackhead Felicia. Shit woulda been funny except it wasn't. Inez did exactly what Cory asked of her. She helped him up. He stumbled then looked at Javon.

"You're dead to me," he told him.

Javon's upper lip twitched and in a matter of seconds it felt like all hell broke loose again. I watched as Javon moved Shanelle and rushed at his younger brother again. The back door to the kitchen was already open since Monty and Melissa came through the back. I didn't know what to think when Javon tossed Cory outside and then shoved Inez out with him when she tried to swing at him. It was the most heartbreaking shit I'd ever seen.

Chapter 21

Shanelle

Javon slammed the door then looked at all of us as Inez and Cory sped away in one of the Forty Thieves' trucks.

"I'm not playing with any of you. Go the route they took and you're out of here," he said with finality.

Most people would have thought he was angry behind the snarl and furrowed eyebrows. I knew better. There was hurt and pain there. There was regret. That was the straw that broke the camel's back.

"Jojo, you knew about this? You knew they were in this jacked-up junkie love relationship?" Javon asked our youngest brother.

Jojo cast a glance down at his feet then back up at Javon. "I ain't want to tell because I promised Inez I wouldn't," he said.

"Let me tell me you something . . ." Javon started then stopped. "Did any of the rest of you know?"

"I didn't," I offered up quickly.

"Neither did I," Uncle Snapped added.

Monty shrugged. "I suspected they had some kind of thing going on but I didn't know nothing 'bout no drugs, bro."

Melissa's face was red. "We got high together a few times. But . . . but it was just weed. I swear," she clarified when Javon tilted his head and stared pointedly at her.

"I saw her hit him before, Von. She went crazy on him. Tried to stab him and he shoved her off him, but I never saw him hit her," Naveen said. "She like was mad because some chick from work called his phone so she went off. I saw her fight him, but I never saw him hit her."

I shook my head. Obviously Cory and Inez were abusing one another and on drugs. They were able to hide that shit so well that neither Javon nor I knew and that bothered me. Javon had no words, which was obvious in the way he punched several holes in the wall then kicked over the small round dinette table Mama kept in the corner of the kitchen.

Just as I was about to say something else, we heard a loud crash in the distance. Uncle Snap set the Mason jar down quickly and headed out the door. As soon as he did, we heard a few of the Thieves yelling for us to get down. Seconds later, bullets riddled the house. Pictures fell over, dishes rattled, flower vases screamed as they cracked open, cotton from the furniture flew through the air as Javon grabbed me and hit the floor. Uncle Snap fell back into the house.

"Get down," Javon screamed, eyes on Jojo and Naveen.

It was too late for Naveen. Bullets knocked him backward and he went flying over the staircase.

"Noooooooooooooo!" I screamed. "Ahhhhhh, Navy!"

Jojo dived over the stairs and hit the floor while covering his brother. Monty had grabbed Melissa. They clumsily fell down the stairs in the basement behind them. Uncle Snap had taken a bullet to the shoulder. Thieves had us surrounded as they returned gunfire.

"Baby, let me go," I whispered to Javon. My eyes were wide as I looked at him.

He nodded, knowing what I needed to do and I army crawled to the sofa. Naveen had shown me what he was able to do the other day. I pushed a small brown button and watched the couch come undone and reveal a secret compartment.

"Always cheat. Always win. The only unfair fight is the one you lose," Mama always told me when she was with me at the gun range.

I pulled out a full-auto mini Uzi then tossed it to Javon. I grabbed the full-auto Uzi then rushed to the window facing the street but it was cattycorner so I had the protection of a brick wall and the three Thieves flanking me. I put it on semi versus auto so I could have more control of the gun. I put my right leg back, leaned on the seal, and put all my weight forward on my hip before unleashing a hail of bullets that sent the men on one motorcycle head first into a parked car. The sound of the gun rocked my eardrums and made bells ring. I leaned forward a bit more, and spotted another motorcycle with two riders coming up the rear. Before they realized what was coming, I released rounds that sent the bike skidding across the road. One of the gunmen got up to run and I let the rounds from the gun light into him. He did a "Thriller" kind of thing with his body as the bullets rocked his body then hit the ground.

"Damn, shorty, handling a full auto like it's light-weight," one of the Thieves commented.

I couldn't be bothered by sexism at the moment. I glanced to my left and saw Javon had rushed through the back door around the side of the house.

"Shit," I said as I focused back on the Escalade that had turned around and come back down the street.

I heard a fight going on in the backyard and knew Javon had spotted gunmen trying to sneak around the back. I heard the rat-a-tat-tat of the Uzi Javon had and felt my heart rate speed up. I unleashed a barrage of bullets on the Escalade and watched it crash into the old lady's house across from ours. I heard Javon yell out.

Tossing the Uzi, I grabbed a Glock .30 with a .45 caliber and rushed out back. Just as I did so, I saw Javon take down a masked man with a riddle of bullets to his chest.

"You okay?" I asked when I saw the five bodies lying around.

"Yeah," he said.

I watched as Javon ripped the masks off several of the men. The four-leaf clover tats on their necks told who they were.

"Fucking Irish," he spat. "These niggas won't quit."

Just as quickly as it began, it stopped. The streets were quiet. Sirens were in the distance.

"What are we going to do?" I asked him.

"Deal with it," was his response.

"Yo, boss, you better get down here and look at this," one of the Thieves said as his chest heaved up and down. "It's your brother and Inez, fam. This ain't good."

My heart dropped to the ground as Javon and I took off running. Out of all the shit the family had just gone through, to have Cory and Inez snatched away from us was sobering. I was right behind Javon as he ran full sprint to Willowbrook Street where we saw the truck Inez and Cory had driven off in.

"We found the truck like this," the guard said.

There was blood everywhere, but there were no signs of Cory or Inez.

"The Irish had to take them, fam. All this blood and no sign of them?" the guard said.

Javon brought both his hands to his head and let out a roar that would have intimidated even the alpha in a pride of lions.

"Fuck, fuck fuck," he yelled.

I knew there was regret mixed with his frustrations. He'd been so angry after fighting with Cory that he hadn't been thinking clearly. He'd forgotten that he had stepped into a whole other lifestyle. He'd had tunnel vision when he should have been seeing the bigger picture. I could see it in his eyes when he gave me a wild look that he was blaming himself.

"Boss, you need to get back to the house. Cops near. Get back to the house and let us handle this," the guard said then looked at me when he realized Javon wasn't listening. "Get him to the house."

"Javon, come on, baby. We gotta go," I said pulling on his arm.

"Give me your gun," the guard said to me.

I'd forgotten I even had the thing. I tossed him my weapon and Javon's. Javon grabbed my hand and we hightailed it back to the house. We rushed in to find Jojo, Melissa, and Monty surrounding Navy, who was laid out on the floor. Uncle Snap was at the table holding a bloody white towel to the wound in his shoulder. My eyes watered. Just that fast, I'd forgotten Navy had been shot. I rushed in and kneeled beside him. If we had lost three siblings in one day, I'd need Jesus to help me keep it together.

"He ain't bleeding," Jojo said. "I saw him get hit, but he ain't bleeding."

Javon walked over and kneeled down.

"That's because I got on a bullet blocker, you stupid piece of shit," Naveen croaked out then strained to sit up.

A sigh of relief swept through all of us.

"A what?" Melissa asked.

"It's a bulletproof fleece," he said. "Got it when Mama was killed. Ordered it online. Was scared to get gunned down in a drive-by shooting like she did."

Only Navy would have been paranoid enough to do such a thing and, in that moment, I was glad he did. Sirens outside the house silenced us all. I rushed over to the couch to push the button so it would go back to being an unassuming sofa. We knew the cops would be inside of the house soon. I looked at Javon wondering how and when we were going to break the news to the rest of them that Cory and Inez were gone and, most likely, dead.

The next few days were hectic. Between police interviews, the media camped out in our neighborhood, and no news of Inez and Cory, the family was a wreck.

"I'm sorry, Javon, but with that much blood loss, it's safe to say they're dead," Detective Monroe had said one day after the shooting. "Who would do this? What enemies, if any, do you have?"

"I . . . I don't know who or why. I don't know anything other than someone came into our neighborhood and shot it up. I don't know why," Javon lied.

"Yeah, but why would they target you and your siblings?"

"Why you think they targeted us? Couldn't we just happened to be caught in the crossfire?"

Stillwaters scoffed then said, "Yeah fucking right."

Detective Monroe smiled. "I'd like to believe that. I want to believe that, but your mother was killed in a drive-by. Your sister, fiancée, or whatever y'all are, got assaulted in the parking deck coming from work. Cory's and Inez's bodies are gone and, I can't say for certain, but I'm sure I saw Jojo over there hanging out with those two members of X-clusive we found dead some days back. So, now see, Javon, I can't believe your family just got caught up in anything."

Javon and the detective stared one another down. "Tell you what," Javon said, "if you want us to keep talking, do so through our lawyer. We got nothing else to say otherwise."

"You sure that's the route you want to go, son?"

"I ain't your son. You want us to talk, call my lawyer."

"Told you, Monroe, you can't be nice to the likes of him," Stillwaters said.

Javon shot daggers through Stillwaters with his eyes.

"We'll be in touch," Monroe said then walked out calmly.

The day after that Javon left Mama's house at six in the morning and didn't come back until two the next morning. He didn't say much. Ate even less. The stress that was on him could be seen with the naked eye. I had no idea what he was doing while he was out until he told me.

"Can't find them nowhere, baby. Nowhere. I've looked high and low," he said.

We were in Mama's room sitting on her bed. I hadn't left the house since the shooting. It was safe to say, with so much police presence, the Irish wouldn't be back anytime soon.

"I been to that apartment they got in midtown. Praying and hoping they were alive and would show up. Pooled in all my resources and nothing. Can't find them."

"I'm sure the Irish have them . . . their bodies. They want you to come to them on some 'falling on your sword' type shit," Uncle Snap said.

We hadn't even realized he was in the doorway. His arm was in a sling and he had that Mason jar close to his chest. Uncle Snap had been trying to get Javon to reach out to the Irish for days now.

"It's okay to lose one battle, nephew. But they, Cory and Inez, deserve a decent burial. Mama deserves to hold them again," Uncle Snap told Javon.

I wouldn't let on I agreed with Uncle because, with all the stress Javon was under, he needed me on his side no matter what decision he made. The house had been quiet. There had been no fighting between Navy and Jojo. Everything had been hush-hush.

"Send word to them that I'd like to meet and get my brother's and sister's bodies back," Javon said. "I'll lay the guns down if they just let me have their bodies back."

Uncle Snap nodded and set out to do what Javon had ordered. Two days later, the Irish responded. Two dead raccoons were sent to Mama's address with pictures of Cory's and Inez's faces taped to them. The raccoons had been shot then sliced down the middle with the guts flayed open. Javon's eyes didn't leave that box for a long time. Melissa started crying loudly. Jojo dropped his head then locked himself in his lab in the basement. Navy sat stunned on the couch. Monty had been hiding somewhere only Javon knew and Uncle Snap couldn't be read. I swallowed back bile at the disrespect shown. My stomach twisted in knots knowing Cory and Inez were dead and that we would never see them again.

Javon disappeared for two days after that. It had been five days since the shooting. He didn't call. He didn't text. Uncle Snap had no idea where he was. I had to step in the role Javon normally filled. Monty came home and told me he had been chilling with the female leader of Rize. I didn't even question him. Just told him he wasn't to leave the house, not until Javon got back. I'd never too much believed in God or prayed much, but for two days and two nights, I prayed harder than I ever had. I prayed for my surviving brothers and sisters. I prayed for Uncle Snap but, most of all, I prayed that God brought Javon back home to me.

God must have been on stand-by for me. He must have just been waiting on me to reach out because Javon walked in soon after my prayers that last day. As soon as I woke up and realized he was in the room, I jumped from Mama's bed to his waist. He was dressed in black from head to toe.

"Oh shit, baby. Don't do me like that ever again," I whispered in his ear.

He held me just as tightly as I held him. "I won't. I'm sorry," he said.

We stood that way for the longest.

"Where have you been?" I asked.

His only answer was to put me down. He walked over to the chair by the bay window in Mama's room and undressed in silence. "How is everyone?" he asked me.

The hardwood floor was cool underneath my feet as I watched him. "Hanging on," I said.

"We have to plan a memorial for Cory and Inez. We can't find their bodies, but we'll still send them off in style," he said.

He was confusing me. He was way too calm. Something wasn't right. Once he was only in his boxer briefs, I walked up behind him and laid a gentle hand on his back. "Baby?"

"I was wrong for how I treated them. If I had to do it all over again, I wouldn't be so angry," he said.

"Javon, where did you go? What did you do?"

He turned to look at me. "Both of them loved to dance so make sure we get a good DJ who knows how to blend different styles of music. Also, make sure nobody wears black. We'll celebrate them instead of mourn them. Can't do another drab funeral so we'll celebrate."

At that point, I knew he wasn't going to tell me where he had been or what he'd done so I left it alone. When he pulled me into his embrace, I knew I had to trust him. Whatever he did when he was away, it was for the good of the family.

Later that night, the phone woke me up. Javon had been watching it all night. The TV was on in Mama's room. BREAKING NEWS flashed across the bottom of the screen on Fox News channel. Something or some group called the IRA had been ambushed outside a popular pub in Belfast, Northern Ireland. Several members had been gunned down. That was after a building known to be the IRA headquarters had been bombed. Javon flipped the channel to the local news station. Fox 5 was reporting another bombing at an Irish pub in Sandy Springs.

"Hello," Javon answered.

I didn't realize he had the phone on speaker until an old, deadly, and stern voice came through. "It's done," was all the voice said on the other end before the line went dead.

I sat in stunned silence. I didn't know what Javon had done and how he had enough pull and power to do it, but I had no words. There was an aggressive knock at Mama's bedroom door.

"Who is it?" Javon asked.

"It's your uncle, li'l nigga," Uncle Snap answered.

"Get the door for me," Javon asked of me.

I complied, my feet slapping against the cool floor as I made my way to the door. As soon as I opened it, Uncle Snap nodded at me then made a beeline to Javon.

"Nephew, the phone call I just got . . . You had something to do with this?" he asked Javon.

Javon stood to his full height and walked over the window to look out. "I tried to be nice, Unc. Tried to do shit with decorum, but they wouldn't let me be. So I pulled out my ace in the hole. I know people, you and those in the Syndicate, thought I was flying by the seat of my pants on a lot of shit I'd been doing. Granted killing Cormac was a random act of violence; yet, the rules stated I had the right to do that. Still, the Irish gunned for me. And they kept coming."

"Rules of the game, nephew," Uncle Snap said.

"Rules?" Javon asked then turned around. "Ain't no damn rules. Always cheat. Always win. The only unfair fight is the one you lose."

Mama's words rang loudly in the silence of the room as Uncle studied Javon. Clearly he was a changed man. He was hurting. So was I. So was Uncle. We all were.

"The Irish ain't shit without the IRA and you went for the jugular? You just started a war that the Syndicate didn't approve," Uncle Snap said. There was something in his voice akin to nervousness and apprehension.

"I don't need their approval."

"Nephew, you do. That's the way shit works around here."

"You're still operating on old rules and the old system. The Syndicate as you know it will be no more, Unc."

"But, Javon, listen—"

"No, you listen. Ain't nobody gon' come in and take my members of my family and I not do shit. They couldn't even give me their bodies back so I could give them a proper burial."

"They don't ha . . ." Uncle Snap started then caught himself.

I tilted my head and frowned a bit. Uncle Snap glanced at me. I tried to read him, but he quickly averted his eyes. What the fuck was that about? Was he about to say that the Irish didn't have Cory and Inez? Or was I tripping? I had to be tripping. Maybe he was about to say something else. Had to have been.

But before I could say anything, Javon continued. "I asked nicely. Lay down my own sword and those mother-fuckers laughed at me. Sent me two dead coons to show the level of disrespect they had for me. I did what I had to do," he said.

"Yeah, but how, nephew? How the fuck did you do this?" Uncle Snap asked, pointing at the TV.

I knew he was referring to the bombings and shoot-
ings. Javon was quiet for a few seconds, but it seemed
like forever.

"Some secrets . . . If you reveal your secrets to the wind,
you shouldn't blame the wind for revealing them to the
trees."

Another famous quote from Mama. I could tell Uncle
was offended that, as his right hand, Javon refused to
tell him what he had done. Uncle's face reddened and he
sucked his bottom lip in. He backed away from Javon.
The look on his face was flat as his eyes narrowed.

"A'ight, nephew. If that's how you wanna run the ship,"
he said, shaking his head disapprovingly before exiting
the room.

Once we were alone, Javon turned to me. I had my
mouth fixed to ask all kinds of questions, but he stopped
me with two words: "Trust me."

I opened then closed my mouth before nodding. Javon
had done something that he couldn't even reveal to Uncle
Snap. That was so telling that it chilled me to the bone.

Chapter 22

Javon

A Week Ago

"*My baby, almost every well-laid plan starts with good intentions. Sometimes, it just goes south if you are weak of mind and if the universe just deems it not meant to be. You might mean well and end up doing wrong. It happens, and you can't be mad about it or hurt about it for long. That never solves the wrongs that were done. One day you'll understand that and you'll see that you can't be everything for everyone, baby boy. I just pray if that day comes it doesn't break ya,*" I heard in my dreams.

A light tap on my shoulder woke me from my dream of me and Mama sitting on her back porch shucking peas. I was about twelve then and had gotten in trouble for fighting some kid for Cory. My baby brother was being bullied for a bike and the kid tried to beat his ass and take it. When I found that out, I went after the kid and almost cracked his head in. I later learned that my sticking up for Cory was in the wrong.

Cory had taken the kid's bike and he just wanted it back. Funny thing with that though, the other, flip side to it was that Cory had taken the bike because the kid he stole it from had taken it from his little sister and

Cory was just protecting and defending the girl. So, long story short, I learned that day that in Cory's actions, he had good intentions, he just went about them the wrong way and dragged me into it. That was always how it was between Cory and me. It seemed that that never was going to change. Well, it had now.

Thanking the stewardess for waking me, I shifted in my seat, and opened the bottle of water given to me to take a deep swig from it; then I glanced out the window of my plane to see the cityscape of New York City. I had the weight of the world, namely my family, on my shoulders and the pain in my knuckles was proof of that. Rubbing them I listened to the words of the woman who adopted me as a means of saving me from my fate, only to damn me in it later in life. I shouldn't have gone at my brother like I did.

Never should have laid hands on him and treated him like the stranger I thought him to be, but I did. I had regret over that the moment I kicked him and Inez out. I had remorse now that I had lost him and my little sister. In that moment, at that time, I felt like there was nothing for me to do with them both. They were killing each other just to succumb to drugs. The shit was baffling to me. What hurt worse was that they felt ignored and unsupported by me as well. I thought I had given my all to every single one of my siblings, while trying to grow in my relationship with Shanelle.

I never thought the day I chose to shift my love for her from a sibling to one of romantic investment that it would flip my whole family upside down. Had I really been that selfish in that regard, to ignore them and stunt my siblings' connections with one another? I really didn't know. All I knew now was, after searching through Atlanta and having connects searching around every nook and cranny, I came up empty in finding

Cory's and Inez's bodies. That reality broke me to the core. It had me extending my PTO into vacation time at work and had me on a plane to New York City.

The shooting had jeopardized the family and I needed to rectify it by any way possible. Tucking Mama's journal in the front of my jacket, I sullenly walked through the airport with my lone Forty Thief as my security behind me until I saw a familiar face.

"Welcome to NYC friend. I'm here with whatever you need," Lucky said in his Bronx accent. "I'm deeply sorry for your family's loss."

Gripping him in a quick warrior handshake, he led me to a waiting chauffeured car. "I appreciate it," was all I said as we drove away.

"Is everything set up as I asked?" I said watching the city rise up before.

Lucky sat back relaxed, studying me. "Of course. The Old Italian is currently waiting for your arrival. Can I ask, though, the fact that he was willing to meet with you one on one like this is crazy. How'd you pull this off, new blood?"

New blood? I had to inwardly laugh at that jab because it was true. I was new to the game; however, I felt like I was playing at the table since birth. Never reveal your hand, I learned at five. Be careful who you trust, I learned at eight. Don't turn your back on an enemy, I learned right after that. So, I sat in the back of a car I had asked Lucky to pick me up in, staring at a brotha who I personally picked to be a part of the Syndicate due to Mama's notes, and I smiled.

"Simply. You all owe me and, beyond that, you all owe Mama. I feel like cashing in tonight and discussing business before I head back out and home. So don't be sorry for my loss. I plan on fixing that tonight," I explained taking the cigar that Lucky offered me.

Lucky's light eyes widened. He ran a hand over his pant leg then he chuckled. "Our debt to your family runs deep, and goes back decades."

"I know it does," I calmly said.

"Hell, many in my circle hoped you didn't," Lucky amusingly stated. "I'm just being honest."

Enjoying the taste of my cigar I rolled it between my fingers appraising it. "Then you all have been taking me for granted." I took another a deep puff and allowed the smoke to snake from my lips. "What I have planned will use up a good number of IOUs and bring us right back around once we're done."

"Damn, are you so sure about that, my friend?" Lucky asked raising an eyebrow studying me. Brotha sat back in a gray tailored suite. I stared at the herringbone pattern of gray and green socks that peeked out from under his pants and the brown spotless leather Italian shoes he wore.

Noticing that I wore something similar in all black, I gave an arrogant nod. "You're sitting at my table as a Syndicate member, aren't you?"

"Touché," Lucky said with a smirk. "I enjoy learning from your new blood ass, friend. Please enjoy my hospitality as your host and I'll make sure you stay comfortable with your short visit."

"I appreciate it," was all I said.

Lucky drove us through Manhattan, giving me a history lesson on how it was once an enclave full of Italians and other ethnic groups. As he spoke about how all of New York City had changed and was still changing thanks to gentrification and other shit, in my mind I kept replaying my fight with Cory. I knew that if I could right it, I would. I'd give half my soul for my brother. I wished he had remembered that when we were fighting.

Nodding as if I were listening, though I partially was, I watched as we pulled up through an alley that connected to a major hotel.

Once we got out and walked into the side door of the hotel, Lucky led me to a private conference room. Inside at the center of the room sat three men, including the Old Italian, as Lucky called him, who sat at the head. Next to him were several familiar faces that I had done my homework on. One was a Jewish mobster, and the other a Catholic mobster. I felt as if I was on the cusp of history and I embraced it for my family.

I walked into the room to see the men Mama had spoken about in her notes. I would have laughed at the fact that they indeed looked the part of old-time mobsters had I not been in a business-only state of mind.

The blend of sweet and spicy smoke from cigars accosted my nostrils. I stood with no fear, shoulders back, eyes on every killer in the room, showing them that I could hold my own if they ever sneezed wrong to test me. Several of the men swiveled crystal tumblers of skillfully shaped iced and amber liquid.

When Lucky pulled out a chair for me, I took my time to sit, before I was finally addressed.

"Lucky explains that you've come to collect on a debt we owed to Claudette." The Old Italian asked of me in a measuring tone, "Do you understand exactly what you are pulling here?"

Offering nothing but brief curl of my lip, I folded my hands together and pressed my fingers against my lips before speaking. "I wouldn't be here if I didn't."

I guess that I pissed someone off with what I said because one of the men in the room gave a grunt, and other shifted in a creaking chair right after. I couldn't care less. Every last one of these old geezers owed not only the Syndicate, but my family personally. Starting with the man who was Lucky's uncle.

"Humph. Interesting—" he said before I interrupted him.

"Long ago, my mother came to New York and ended up saving your life, sir. I think that story is not only interesting, but also telling of her character. It reflects on how she raised her children."

The Old Italian shifted in his chair, lifted his drink to his lips, and took a sip. He hovered it just above the table and watched me. "Your mother saved my life, yes. She stood in the line of fire and took multiple bullets for me, risking everything. Do you understand what that is, young man? Because I'm not convinced, as of yet, that you carry that same fire and leadership. And as you know, what you ask of us does not come free even with what we owe you."

I opened my mouth to counter the insult he had spit out and the bald-faced lie he just told me but, before I could, the old man held a hand up. Motherfucker must have known that I had something else up my sleeve to counter that lie. Yes, the three men in this room had enough power to collectively start a war that none of us would come through alive if they didn't want us to, but in their elder years they took more to running things behind the scenes. That was all well and good, but they still owed Mama and I intended to collect by any means necessary.

Straight up, I was pissed at that. The insult stung deep considering everything I had been doing to keep the family safe and secure in the Syndicate. But, I was taught to be a businessman, so anything I had to say in grievance would be said to the Old Italian privately.

However, I couldn't stop myself in saying, "My leadership and fire has brought the rise of the Syndicate to a new era. One that many of you just cannot reach. But, yes, our problem is with the Irish."

The Old Italian nodded.

The Jewish mobster said, "Tell me how you came to be in the crosshairs of the Irish again."

I told him what he wanted to know. Told them how Cormac had sent men after me while I was in public with my fiancée. Told them how when I wouldn't comply with Cormac's demands, he kidnapped my little sister and my little brother.

"By then, I was no longer in a talking mood. He had already shown he had no respect for me by removing my mother's chair, sitting at the head of the table, and taking what didn't belong to him. I had to put up or shut up. So I put up. Cormac's dead and now his family comes after me and mine? They wouldn't even give me the fucking bodies back. They sent dead raccoons to me with pictures of my brother's and sister's faces attached," I snapped. My eyes watered and I had to catch myself so I wouldn't let my emotions get the better of me. "I tried to do shit diplomatically. Even went as far as to tell them if they just gave me my siblings' bodies back, I would back down. They spit on me. Spit in my fucking face!"

"So now you're here and want to call in your mother's debt to repay them." The Catholic priest's croaky voice made me turn his way.

"Yes," I answered with no qualms.

"Calling in this favor means you want us to start a war with the Irish, a war that may come back to bite us in the ass one day," the Italian said.

I sat up, back straight, eyes never leaving the Italian's eyes. "Frankly, I don't give a damn. The Syndicate is mine and I won't stand for any level of disrespect. Not when I tried to back out of the fight peacefully. I was willing to concede this fight if only for their dead bodies to be given back to me and my family. Cory and Inez deserved a proper burial."

I stopped talking then. I could feel my anger rising. So much so my fisted hand started to shake. Part of me wished Shanelle were here with me. She could help level out my anger and emotions, but I had to do this shit on my own. Had to prove to myself and others why Mama chose me as the leader over everyone else.

The Old Italian looked at the other two men in the room then back at me. "We do this for you and what do we get in return?"

"Not a damn thing," I snapped. "This is a debt owed to Mama and since she is gone, you owe it to her kids, me specifically as the leader of the Syndicate. Don't try to play me like I'm some remedial dimwit. I came to you with respect. I passed through all the proper channels by reaching out to Lucky first and having him bring me here. I respected the chain of command and I expect the same in return," I said sternly. So much so that each of the old men glanced at one another and nodded one by one. I knew what was owed to my mother. They wouldn't fleece me out of anything more.

The Old Italian looked at Lucky and said, "Get the others in here. Father Seamus to be exact."

Lucky nodded and went to do as he was told. I watched as about fifteen to twenty other men walked into the room. Some were in suits. A few others in clerics clothing. All of them dangerous.

The Old Italian stoically stared at me then chuckled. "Father Seamus, hand our young man the file of information about our little Irish family in Atlanta."

A fat, old, leather-faced man with muddled brown hair quirked a glossy eyeball my way. He sat as if he were king, dressed in an all-black suit with a cleric collar around his neck. The disdain in his eyes let me know that he didn't trust me. Which I really didn't give a fuck about. I was just here for business. I watched him shift in his groaning chair, handing a stack of folders to a female attendee. I observed the exchange is patience.

Curious enough, she looked like Lucky, like she could be his sister. That was all that I noted about her, besides the Glock tucked against the small of her back.

"As you see," Father Seamus started, "the Irish MC became problematic for us, even back in Ireland, once they start mixing with unsavory rednecks. They forgot how not to draw attention to themselves and we in Ireland had to limit our partnership. Alas, that is corrected now and their dealings with the heartland pipeline will become yours, once we switch hands."

"With the people I pick, of course," I added while reading through the pages of papers before me and noting the images.

"Indeed. As of now, the Irish MC is responsible of transport of meth, heroin, guided transportation and protection of firearms and other weapons of mass destruction as you Americans seem to believe only come from the Arabs, to the heartland and South circuits from Ireland. It is from there that it passes to the hands of the MC leaders on the West Coast."

"Seamus." The Old Italian clucked his tongue in a tsk and shook his head. "Do not insult the nation that lines our pocket and harbors our families."

Inwardly, a frown spread across my face. I wasn't jigging on how the father spit out that insult as well, but I let it ride.

"But of course. It was just a light critical assessment of course." The father crossed his heart with his rosary tapping against the table, then continued. "When you eradicated Cormac, you effectively isolated and ended their ties to Ireland," the father explained.

"Father Seamus, Cormac was a problem for even this table. You know this," the Old Italian stated. "Mr.

McPhearson did us a favor by ending that pissant. I
never knew why Claudette kept him at the table. She
could have rid herself of him and brought in another.
But she did things her way and I won't question it now.
My concern is our property in Atlanta that they weren't
managing well. That must be prioritized in being handled as well."

Everyone at the tabled grumbled in agreement and I
sat back feeling vindicated in killing Cormac, although I
would have felt that way regardless.

Clearing his throat, Father Seamus looked my way
then flippantly swept a hand out. I knew his type. All
he saw was a black kid in front of him. No, a dangerous
black man. An insect for him to crush and probably try
to turn into his bitch if I had been a young child. Dude
made my skin crawl. I was nothing to him. Just a monkey
and it pissed me off, but amused me, only because I was
that monkey he'd have to work for, or die for, once I was
done.

"Within the files, you have all the information you
need," he drily stated then added, "as requested via our
debt owed to you."

I tilted my head to the side at the figures, real estate,
pipeline boundary lines, and more, as Father Seamus
spoke up with his slight Irish brogue. "I'd say this is a
good change for Ireland to revive the stalled pipeline. 'Tis
my suggestion that you introduce yourself to the Irish
MC, before they make a play first. For they will stop at
nothing to end you in the name of Cormac."

"As for the rest, it is agreed that we will supply you with
your additional needs," the Old Italian announced.

"I want them hit so hard it will take them years to
rebuild what it is lost. I want them hit in Ireland and I
want the rest in Atlanta to feel it," I said coolly.

A collective murmur went around the room. Father Seamus looked as if all the blood drained from his already pale face.

He looked at the Old Italian. "You can't very well be thinking about hitting me home base in Ireland," he said, almost incredulously.

"If that is what Javon demands, we must comply," the Old Italian replied.

"That is me home. That is where the main supply for the pipeline comes from. My son—"

"Don't not beg in front of company, Seamus. What must be done, must be done." He cast a gaze at everyone then stood. "This meeting is adjourned. Mr. McPhearson, walk with me. Unless you have questions?"

I could tell Father Seamus was about to blow a gasket. Something about that made me smile on the inside. I didn't come to fuck around. I meant business and it showed.

"Yeah, I have a question," I said in response to the Old Italian. "If you all knew Cormac was an issue then he should have been handled by . . ." Slamming my finger down on the table before me, I glared. "Every. Single. One. Of. You. I shouldn't have had to handle him."

"Cormac was in the Syndicate. We have no dealings with the Syndicate other than when Claudette pulled us in for business. That was her turf and she handled it how she saw fit," the Jewish mobster stated.

"He is right," the Old Italian said. "We had no power in the Syndicate. That's something you should think about."

The grumbles started again; then I pushed back from the table, grabbed the thick stack of folders, then walked out. I didn't give a shit what they said, whether they had a say-so in what happened at the Syndicate's table. They knew Cormac was a problem and if he had something to do with Mama's death like I suspected, then I would hold it against the Old Italian and his comrades. They knew the man was a ticking time bomb.

"Hey!"

It wasn't until I heard Lucky behind me that I stopped.

"You pissed them off, fam."

"Yeah, then we all even with it then," I grumbled. "Look, where does your old-ass uncle want me to meet him at, or walk with him at?"

Lucky gave a chuckle then stepped around me with his hands in his pockets, the ends of his shirt bunching up. Dude walked ahead of me with a cocky swagger and said, "Follow me."

We walked a bit, took a glass elevator up to another level then ended up in a private penthouse suit. The room was immaculate. Yes, we were in a hotel, but the feel of this place was straight luxury home living. Glass was everywhere. I'm meaning the windows. If you wanted, you could see all of Manhattan in one clean swoop. The skyline was impeccable leaving those who were swayed by such displays of wealth feeling like a living God. Plush white drapery accented silver Art Deco–designed framing along the large windows. Beyond those windows was a large patio space with lush green grass and a few trees.

Inside, it was as you would imagine a mob boss of today would live. A huge bar was separate in its own parlor where Lucky relaxed talking to an older black woman. I couldn't see her, but I could clearly hear the age and culture of my race in the tone of her articulate vernacular. *Interesting.*

Where I stood was a sunken sitting area with two large dark leather couches with those dimple marks throughout them. I call them therapist couches. In between them was a floating glass table with a decanter of liquor, two glasses, and two cigars with a cigar cutter and lighter next to it on a tray.

Behind me on several white or gray walls were old-world paintings, mixed with several current artworks. A glass fireplace was in the center of the penthouse next to where I sat waiting. It wasn't long after that the Old Italian made his appearance. By that time, I was sitting studying the files. I didn't even stand when I heard the sound of his shoes clip-clopping against the dark wooden floors as he walked into the room. By that time, I was still very much annoyed as fuck.

"Javon Williams-McPhearson," the Old Italian said with excitement in his voice.

My head snapped up at him using my government name. In doing so, I saw the old man walk around undoing his blazer. He made a graceful motion in taking a seat opposite me; then he took off the simple white brimmed hat that he wore, setting it on the table between us. The old man had a still youthful quality to him. All white hair from the tip of his wavy low-cropped hair to the white beard around his face. The man had a slight golden coloring to him marking him clearly as being pure Italian. He had a Robert De Niro quality to him.

Rumor had it, true Italians had black African in them due to the Moors and, at that time, Persians, anyway. So, to see it in the old man didn't trip me out at all. I just wondered if he was the type of Italian who embraced that ancestry. Glancing at Lucky, whose back was to me as he spoke to the same elder woman I could not see in the partially closed-off parlor, I gathered that the old man did embrace that truth. Again, that was interesting to me.

"I know that you know my full name too." He reached forward and grabbed the crystal decanter of amber liquid in front of us. Liberally pouring a stream of liquid into the two glasses that sat next to the decanter, he pushed a glass toward me then said, "I'd be disappointed if a son of Claudette's didn't."

Rebuffing the glass, I shifted the folders away and stretched out an arm over the back of the chair. "No, thank you. I don't indulge while I'm doing business."

"Smart young man," he leisurely stated. "Then you are more like Claudette than I assumed."

"Of course I am, sir. Which is why it amuses me that you lie in front of your council of mobsters about just how interwoven the debt is." Leaning forward, I pushed the glass away then reclined, keeping my gaze on the old man and folding my hands over the files on my lap. "Each and every one of you owes my family a debt. Many. That will not erase itself just for me being here."

A quick glint of anger flashed across the old man's face. "What do you know of debts owed! Debts paid off with Claudette's murder!" he barked out, ice clinking in his glass.

"Nothing was paid off with my mother's death! Nothing!" I found myself shouting fist clenching at my side. A simmering passion blazed through me as I stared at a man Mama had mentioned countless times in her journals. A man who allowed her to die, in my eyes, if Cormac had anything to do with her death.

"If anything . . ." I paused and toned down my anger before continuing. "If anything, it's double bound due to your neglect in not protecting her and not protecting the one thing she loved. Us."

Silence blazed between us. An unspoken challenge of wills had been kicked off because of what I now clearly could see: our love for Mama and our grief.

"She chose him over me," the old man grumbled low.

The tone was so harsh that I noticed Lucky looking our way from the parlor and taking a few steps toward the room before a hand stopped him. It was then that I could see the elder woman. Immediately, I pushed up from the couch and almost fell backward in fear. I was staring at Mama. She was alive, looking over Lucky's shoulder. I blinked rapidly, trying to comprehend who I was looking at because I was there when we buried Mama, so I had to be losing my gotdamned mind as I stared at her mirror image.

When Mama's twin moved around Lucky, she turned her back to me. African-print fabric swirled against the floor where she moved. She wore what I could tell was a couture-style dress, with dripping diamond necklaces around her neck. On her fingers were various rings and around her wrists were diamond bangles. Coiled gray hair swung against her back, and because she was closer, I could see she was slightly younger. This wasn't Mama, but it was almost a twin in a sense, with varying differences, such as the jewelry and her state of dress.

"I loved your mother dearly," I heard by my side. "Even in our . . . complicated friendship. I loved her, and tried to move heaven and earth for her. So when whispers in the crime world started that some heat might have possibly been coming for the Syndicate, your mother was the last one I ever thought would be the one to be eliminated. She knew something was brewing. Told me as much, but she told me it was what came with the territory. Said not to worry about her. I was too late, son. There is much that you can't even begin to know. So tell me clearly, what of the debt specifically are you pulling here?"

With a glance, I stared at the side of the face of a man who was in just as much pain as I was over Mama's death. My shoulders almost dropped at what was told to me, but I kept my cool, then turned my attention back to the woman in the room.

"She stopped a bullet from going into your heart," I said.

I couldn't believe how much that woman looked like Mama. I turned to back to the old man.

"Yes. That's the first debt I owe her." A gentle smile spread across his face as he lit up a cigar. "Let me share with you why because what I want to share wasn't appropriate for our meeting with the others."

He made sure that I understood that in the life of a leader, not all parts of you are meant to be shared, just the overview; and I respected that. "It was the late eighties. Your mother came to New York at my request to work for me and as a means to secure her own rise in the South as a queen pin. After King had died, word on the street was that his woman was taking his place. I knew this to be true as King and I done business before. Good business. I'd met Claudette before then, got the scars to prove it. I felt something for her the moment I first laid eyes on her. With King gone, I figured she was fair game on the other side of business if you know what I mean."

I nodded.

Plumes of smoke rose between us. It was then that I turned to grab that offering of amber liquid. Yeah, just moments before I said I didn't drink and do business, but I needed something to be able to handle all I was hearing. I listened to him tell me things about Mama I had no clue about. I was sure that there were more journals that I needed to read about Mama's early days.

"She glowed in her intelligence and ability to command a room. At her side was her trusted right hand and protection. A young kid named Snap. At the time, I was intent on having my own time with her, because her beauty and the way her mind could summarize business deals and plans aroused something in me."

I glanced at the Old Italian, then chuckled. It didn't take anything to fill in the cracks of what wasn't being said. Shit, I was experiencing a taste of that same game through Lucky. So, I chuckled low realizing that this was the additional piece of Mama's life not written in the journals I did read.

Sliding one hand in my pocket just to relax, I said, "You made sure to keep him busy?"

"Of course, I tried, but Claudette wasn't about to allow him to be treated like the help. He was her right hand after all. Besides, whenever Claudette visited, my coffers runneth over with coins. So she kept all of us busy anyway. She was good like that. Could make me work when I said I wouldn't."

I listened to a rich, deep rumble of laughter come from the old dude as he spoke on. "It wasn't easy to get along with Snap. I tell you that. A man knows when another man is after something that he had laid claim to; but beautiful Claudette insisted that he'd learn everything, so he complied. She asked me not to do and say certain things around him because it angered him. I respected her so I kept my mouth closed. I was rewarded behind closed doors."

The old man moved away from my side and walked to the large panel windows overlooking the city. "We took over the city. I wined and dined her. In our prior years of friendship, it was a simple thing to do. We spoke of when we first met, which was in Vegas where it was her smart thinking that got King to the top of the food chain of the Syndicate and me in line to run the Commission."

As he spoke, I sat back amazed at the brilliance of Mama and ingenuity she had to make a business deal no matter the cost. Which led back to the debt business, as the day turned into night and we both sat back full off of seafood, Italian pastas, and wine.

"There was a property in Queens that I was showing your mother the ins and out off, when I was ambushed by several of my rivals. Before that, in my limo, your mother and I . . . engaged ourselves in the act of coitus. It was during that when I learned that she was with child. Had I known prior that that day would have been the day of all days that I was to be tested and challenged for my life, I wouldn't have ever brought her to Queens. On my word."

A pained expression appeared on his face. It made the old man furrow his brow and close his eyes at the memories as he spoke.

"There was blood everywhere, too much to be normal." The old man's voice softened and he shook his head. "She ran right out in front of me like a gazelle. Pushing me back into the limo, using her body to shield me, as bullets peppered the limo and our bodies."

From the way he cleared his throat, I could sense that he was holding back tears. "It was a simple acquisition of property. I was go to in, collect my money from the family who was running the butcher shop. Only, the Ajello family was adamant about ending me and everyone associated with me that day. Alas." He flipped his hand then pressed it against his eyes. "She lay in my arms bleeding everywhere. Do you understand what I'm saying?"

"She lost the child?" I quietly asked, feeling a sharp pain in my heart.

The old man was eerily quiet before he finally answered me, which had me thinking. Especially when I heard Lucky's laughter nearby.

"Indeed," he finally said. "She was in shock. Calling out to the father of that child, Raphael. I listened to her telling him that she was sorry for failing him and their bambino. I didn't realize until we escorted her to the hospital and put her in protection just how much she loved the man. Rightfully so, he hates me for her being shot and I hate him for the loyalty and love he was able to win from her. However, I owe him as well, which is why I never told him that she was carrying his child. Your mother bound me by my word to not tell the truth of the situation. She never told him either. By the time he got to the hospital, they had her stable and all she told him was that she had been shot."

When the old man looked at me, it was if he was being shot at again. The pain was exceedingly raw and it hurt to my soul to know that I knew what it was to lose a child too.

"I killed every last member of that family, Javon. Personally washed in their blood. Made them experience pain and loss that I did, the day they decided to overthrow me. This is what you must do as you rise in power, Javon. Never let your enemies know your fear!"

Again, a subtle silence fell between us. I sat in shock at everything that was shared with me. When a man loses all he loves, if you don't kill him, then he will rise like a demon and take all that you cherish, so I learned. Never leave your enemy breathing.

The old man cleared throat again, then shifted back in his chair. "So, this debt is lifelong, generational, because it was almost your mother's death, then it was death of the unborn child. It also includes the thievery of her ability to have any more children after."

Folding his hands in front of him, the Old Italian stared at me in assessment. "In totality, that has put the responsibly on my shoulders to answer any call that Claudette or her children may have. Which is why I allowed you to speak so disrespectfully and why I omitted some information with my council. They didn't need the details; you did. So, now we continue this negotiation and I will use my power to help you in any way, son."

After handling business in New York, I came back home. Everything during my trip fell how it was supposed to. I guess that was Mama guiding me in her lessons again. I ended up having everything negotiated it to a T. What I did in meeting the Old Italian had been a major gamble. But, in the end, I learned a lot and knew that if I didn't have Mama's notes, and her explicit messages that if I ever needed to pull an ace these were the people who you start with, then I would had been signing my own death certificate. Mama had been clear in making a big note about that in her journal.

So, in addition to being aware of all of that, I personally needed to recognize that my rash plan could end me. I had to have that understanding that if my attempt to personally kill every Irish that I could get my hands on would ever go south, then I needed to be aware that the family would be left to their own devices, and Mama's plans and dreams would be nowhere. So that was why I made sure to add one more clause to the debt I'd collected from the old man. Mama's plans were birthed with ill intent. I had to be the living embodiment of Mama's contingency plan. I now had to man up and follow through with everything.

Chapter 23

Javon

This was the quiet before the storm. The moment when old secrets could either shake up our foundation, or help educate us. Checking out the woman of my life, my "before all else," who had held me down through everything, I studied how Shanelle sat in the middle of the bed after debriefing her. She was beautiful how she was positioned in the middle of the bed surrounded by pillows, and turned-down bed linens.

I was fresh out of the shower, skin still slightly moist even after oiling my skin. I had on drawstring pants and a towel around my neck. Shanelle was baffled. That was apparent in how her head was tilted to the side, and how she stared up at me and blinked slowly in disbelief.

Honestly, I was the same way when the Old Italian told me about Mama's secrets. It was wild to even think of Mama having such an experience, but she did. So, I wasn't sure where to go with expressing that to Shanelle. So, I walked her way in concern, my bare feet feeling the familiar knots and dents in the wooden floor under me.

"So, why can't you tell Uncle Snap?" she asked speaking low just in case we were being listened to.

When I dropped down beside Shanelle in Mama's bed, the bed creaked and the comforting softness pressed in my hands. I couldn't help but remember the times I used to come in here as a child to wake Mama up or help her clean. Now, her room was ours, along with her secrets; and I missed her deeply.

"Because, it would break Uncle Snap's heart," I heard myself explain while still in my thoughts.

I shared the rest of my trip with Shanelle. Explaining where I went and who I met and why. When it came to Mama's secrets, I did my best in relaying everything.

"I don't understand," Shanelle said taking my hand and shifting in the bed to lay her head against my shoulder.

Honestly, I wasn't sure how I could explain it, but I chose my words to the best of my ability. "With seeking out those old heads, I had to pull up a lot of old history. Old things between Mama and the Old Italian up North." I worded it like that because, as I spoke, I was rehashing everything again. "Mama always told Uncle Snap that she wouldn't give him a kid, but she did; at least, she was carrying when she went to NYC to do work for the old man up North."

Taking my time, I tossed my towel away from me. I then locked eyes with Shanelle while we spoke. "While she was working with the old man, she saved his life by taking a bullet for the dude. It wasn't on purpose, she had said in her journal. She wrote that it just fell that way. But, according to the old man, it was on purpose because they had been ambushed by a rival family. He said there was a lot of blood. Too much blood, baby."

Frowning, I knew what I was sharing about Mama would bring up my similar history with Shanelle. Emotion shimmered behind her eyes. I knew that she was putting the pieces together. My hands wrapped around Shanelle's legs; then I pulled her to me, so that I could lay a kiss on her temple, wrap her legs around me, and hold her close as I knew she enjoyed.

"She lost that baby in the middle of the battle. Blood everywhere. The Old Italian witnessed it and it broke his heart. His life was spared by her risking her own life, and sacrificing her child, and her ability to create life again. That started the life debt. I didn't know the full story of it all when I presented to him that I was cashing in on that debt but, in the end, it worked out for us, baby. We talked for hours and he understood why I chose that deep of a debt in my request for help in taking down the Irish."

Pausing, I brushed my knuckles against Shanelle's neck to check if she was still listening and make sure she was okay before continuing. "The old man gave me a pass because Mama's kids were being attacked in a ruthless, dishonorable way. Besides, I learned that he and Mama had a small sexual thing in the past as well and that he was still in love with her."

Eyes bugged out, Shanelle covered her mouth. I knew what I shared was bringing up our own pain and losses. There was no way around it, but I knew that I could bring her comfort, so I did. I leaned in to kiss her moist, fluttering eyelashes.

"Get out of here. Really?" she softly muttered, her voice coated in unshed tears.

"Yeah, baby." I nodded with a lighthearted sigh. "It was hard to read all of that in the journals and hear it from the old man's mouth. Before going to NYC Mama and Snap fought over that."

"Wait, is Lucky—" Shanelle started.

"No. I actually was able to meet his mother. Funny enough, but not really because it broke my heart. She resembles Mama," I explained then scratched my head. "If he was, I'm not too sure how I'd feel about that. I mean what's the point of all of what she had us do, you know?"

Resting her head against my chest, Shanelle closed her eyes and slid her hand against my stomach feeling my abs. "Maybe to give you both seats as a means to show her love and atone for her mistakes? I get why she was in tears when we lost our baby."

What she said hit me heavy. If Lucky had been Mama's child from the affair with the Old Italian . . . damn. I couldn't call it though. The game would change and the idea that Mama set this all up for us both to rule would make for some interesting camaraderie within the Syndicate. Shaking that thought off, I moved on trying my best to not break down about Cory and Inez. I needed to check on the rest of the family before I did that, so I got up, and helped Shanelle up while thinking about Jojo and Naveen.

"I need to check on Jojo and Naveen, on all of them," I said tilting Shanelle's chin up. "You good? Don't think I didn't see how you went commando on the Irish. That was the sexist shit I ever saw."

She blushed when I said that. That brief flash of a blush wrapped me in a brief moment of light in the darkness that surrounded us.

"I had to hold it down, you know that. I had to for the family. I'd do it again if it would bring Cory and Inez back," she said.

My silence was painful at the mention of them. It was one thing to think about them but hearing their names out loud brought back that fresh pain. I clenched my fists and looked away before standing up from the bed. In my mind I could imagine how pissed and scared they were when their truck flipped.

"Von?"

Their screams echoed in my mind. I felt hot suddenly. Felt burns over my flesh, smelling the scent of smoke, hearing the deep laugher of a male voice hurting me, then the memory of large hands snatching up Cory.

"Von!" Shanelle shouted at me.

I was losing it. I lost my brother because I wasn't strong enough for him. Lost him because I wasn't devoted enough for him. Then, Inez, I failed her the most. It's sad but I should have protected her from Cory. He wasn't who I thought he was. Wasn't able to separate himself from the demons. Fuck, I hadn't either. Everyone saw Shanelle and me as perfect but we weren't. I fucked up all the time, every day with her. I just learned from it and she forgave me. I wished my brother were here, not to tell him all of that but to show him that I accepted him and not the addict he became.

"Von!" I heard again.

Turning and shifting against the sheets, my name being shouted again had me drowsily opening my eyes. Face pressed against my pillow while I lay on my side, I realized that I was staring into the teary-eyed gaze of Shanelle. She sat on her knees in bed with her hands against my arm hovering over me. The panic and worry in her voice had me waking up further.

"Your hands are bleeding, baby," she softly said coming to me to gently take my hands. "Von, you dug your fingers in your palms."

"I fucked up with Cory and Inez, baby, I really did," was all I said as she took care of me and I watched her in my pain.

An hour later, I sat downstairs, staring at Mama's picture again in my thoughts. My elbows rested on my knees. My hands pressed together resting against my lips. I stared at Mama's face, ready to speak to her until I heard someone enter the parlor. Looking toward him, I saw it was Uncle Snap. That hurt was still in his eyes.

I had my reasoning for what I did, in keeping the truth from him. I hoped he understood it when I shared it with him, but if he didn't, there wasn't shit I could do. I honestly loved the man like my father. Hell, he was the only father I knew. My real old man was so old and inactive there wasn't shit he could do for me as a child.

There was no love lost there. But if anything happened to Uncle Snap, especially with Mama gone, I'd be a broken man. People always thought Shanelle was my weakness, and she slightly was, but in reality my family as a whole was my weakness, with Uncle Snap at the lead.

"Uncle . . ." I started.

He stepped forward ready to talk but Jojo walked by and it stopped me.

"Later," I said to him and he bobbed his head taking a seat where I motioned. "Jojo, hol' up, baby brother. Come here for me please."

The sound of his kicks squeaking in the kitchen let me know he had heard me. I knew Naveen was in there as well, because I heard him mumbling to himself about someone eating all the grape jelly. It seemed to me that today would be a good moment to have my talk.

"Naveen, you too, bro," I yelled then sat back.

I could see Shanelle peeking on the steps. She looked good in her college-cut shorts, tank, hair pulled up in a bun, and barefoot. I gave her a nod and she sat on a step keeping herself inconspicuous.

Once my brothers walked in and saw Uncle Snap, I knew how they both shifted on their feet that they knew a major discussion was about to go down. Taking a seat in front of us, Uncle Snap set his Mason glass down, which had crushed ice and water in it this time, then gave both young men hugs and daps.

Shifting on the edge of my chair, I looked between the both of them with my fingers pressed against my lips. "We lost Cory and we lost Inez. I'm being real honest here for you both because I realized from what they said that I haven't been here for any of you all like I should have, like I thought I was. I was to start off by saying I've messed up deeply and I'm sorry. Their deaths are on me. I should have been more focused and kept them here, or at least kept them better protected."

Disappointed at myself, my gaze fell on Jojo and I exhaled. "See, I didn't hold up to my responsibility as a brother in that and I let the whole family down while sending Cory and Inez to their deaths. Mama wouldn't put up with how I acted, I know it."

I sat quietly swallowing down my pain, and when I saw Jojo open his mouth, I held up a hand. "One more thing. I want you all to know I'm here. I'm willing to open myself right now and show you all that I'm not perfect. Not in how I am individually as a man but also how I've handled my relationship with Shanelle. Cory was a good man, who had demons that just ate at him and seeped out. We all fall—"

"I was with my birth mom when Mama was killed," Jojo interrupted. He reached up to slide his glasses off and slid the palm of his hand over his face. "She had hit me up and asked to see me. So I was with her."

Naveen shifted to the side to stare at Jojo. Before I could even ask why, Naveen handled it for me. "Why? How y'all even link up, man? Where the hell did that come from?" he said incredulous. His fingers dug into his legs to keep his cool, as he usually did. Navy waited for a response shaking his head. "How she find you, bro?"

Water leaked from Jojo's dark eyes. He exhaled, shaken, and dropped his head back looking at the ceiling. "It happened about a year ago. I was working at Subway, right, and she came in. Said she'd been looking for me for years and that she just needed to see me. At first I didn't know it was her, didn't believe her, so I tried to ignore her. When she showed up at my school I got scared and decided to look up my file."

Damn, echoed in my mind. Our files were sealed. We all were wards of the state so getting into our files could be hard, but with talents like Jojo and Naveen it could be simple as one, two, three.

"That's what you had me breaking into? The state files of your background info?" Navy asked with wide eyes.

"Yeah. All I needed was Mama's info and I took that from her room and found out about her. Learned that woman was my birth mom. I decided to talk with her after that since she kept coming to my job. When I quit Subway, I used that time to spend it with her. She's my mom. I wanted to know why she . . ." Jojo broke off in his words.

I knew that he was reflecting on when we found him and it broke my heart. Standing I walked to him and pulled him into a hug. I understood that Navy didn't get what was going on and it wasn't my place to share that.

"I can't . . . I . . ." Jojo dropped his head and shook it. "Fuck. So that day, I was with her. She was sick, like, she kept asking me to get her some drugs, so I got it. I stole some from Cory and Inez and gave it to her with the stuff I was making, just so she would talk with me. That was the day Mama died. My birth mom was ODing and I had keep her chill; that's what took my time. I'm so sorry."

"All because you wanted to know what?" Navy asked standing. Pain made Navy's voice crack and he stepped back looking at us as if we were crazy. "Mama died so you could feed your junkie mama dope?"

"Hey, chill with that, Navy," I said. "You don't know the whole story."

"Fuck the whole story. Mama died so he could . . ."

I gave a quick glance at Jojo and he gave me a nod of the head letting me know it was time for Navy to know.

"So he could find out why the fuck she sold him to a pedophile old woman!" I shouted. "I found him in some bushes, covered in bruises and his own shit. Just like you, Navy. Just like you! He ran and I found him."

Navy's mouth fell open in shock. He stared at Jojo then dropped his head in shame.

It was then that Uncle Snap spoke up while I stood between both young dudes. "Chill out!" he shouted breathing in and out.

When I saw his Mason jar ready to fall, I dropped low to catch it from breaking, making it in time. As I held it like a football in my palm, being careful with it, I shifted on my knee where I kneeled and looked up at my uncle in confusion at his sudden rage.

The old man walked past me then stopped and abruptly turned to reach a hand out as a means to help me up. Though we all had been living in agony over Mama's death, it was clear that we forgot how close Uncle Snap was to Mama. I suddenly felt ashamed. Grief and agony made the whites of Uncle Snap's eyes turn red while he spoke.

"This house was a refuge for you all. Claudette had her reasons in shaping you all to step in her world, but the real reason why she chose you all was to help you all and heal you all. All of you came from the same types of backgrounds. She and I saw a lot of shit in the streets, but it was because her husband dealt with these very same demons that she chose you all." Taking the jar, he walked with it and gently set it near Mama's pictures.

"You all were just little boys and girls suffering physical, sexual, spiritual, emotional abuse. Scrapping and fighting. None of us, including you all, had a chance in life. Claudette, her old man, and I knew what that was like and chose to use our street smarts to pull us out of our hell. Claudette fought to do the same for you all so, Jojo, my boy, you started out with good intentions that turned a situation bad."

"I'm sorry, Uncle. She called me asking for help. I thought I'd make it to Mama on time. I'm sorry," Jojo said, hurt.

My palms ran down my face. "You did what you thought you should. It's not your fault, Jojo."

"If I had left her alone though—" he started.

"Then you'd be hurting over her dying and not getting your answers," Navy solemnly stated. He moved back to where Jojo was, pulled him up by his forearm, and wrapped his arms around him. "I'm sorry, baby brother. I'm sorry. I know how that goes, and I was just . . . I am just angry."

I watched Jojo slowly wrap his arms around Navy and they hugged it out.

"Claudette only wanted the best for you all. I know she's not mad at your choice, Jojo, not at all," Uncle Snap said.

Walking up to him, I whispered my own apology to him, and he gave me a nod of understanding. We moved to the side to give Jojo and Navy some minor privacy to patch things up and I exhaled.

"I know this isn't the time, but I need to move forward and hit up the next phase of my removal plan. We don't have time to be idle on that end. Mama wanted to be a force of nature; well, I gotta be that, Uncle. I know you think that I'm being reckless, but there's a method to the madness."

Bowing his head, Uncle Snap's jaw clenched then he blew out steam. "Yeah, I get that. Been in this game too long not to get that, but I still say in your force of action, keep smart. Not all the old ways are bad, nephew. Not all the old ways need to be erased; respect the past so you can do better in the future."

"I'm trying to do that. Trust in me, a'ight? We have to be moving, and remind them that Mama's legacy isn't gone. That's why I went after the Irish like I did. I had to for her, and I had to for Cory and Inez. Their deaths can't be in vain. None of this shit can be in vain. So we move on to the next phase. A'ight?" I clapped a hand on his shoulder and locked eyes on him.

"What did you do?" he asked me again.

My shoulders slumped in defeat as I gave in with a gentle sigh. "I used only what was owed us and it was given freely in honor of Mama's memory and what y'all lost in the past." Uncle Snap's eyes widened, and I gave him a hug like the son he always wanted. "I had to do it and do it without you. This was no disrespect to you, on my word. Everything I do, it's with reason and to be steps ahead of everyone else just like Mama. Trust that."

"Shit, nephew. Shit." He held me tight and stepped back so we could look at each other like the bosses we were.

Shit was hard, and the pain was real, but this needed to happen. We now had to share this with the family and prepare for more pain.

After our talk with Jojo, the week ticked by slowly when we spoke to everyone about Jojo's truth. It was hard for the rest of the family on top of our grief over Cory and Inez, but we all vowed to focus and give them honor. So it went like this: we all stood in the parlor dressed so clean that it would put many fashion houses to shame. I looked around my family. Emotion was high that I knew that any one of us could break down in tears at any second at mention of Mama, Inez, and Cory. I decided to talk around that and bring in some minor business beforehand.

I walked up to where Shanelle was fixing Jojo's outfit. Baby brother stood in all white from head to toe. The only color he wore was his red bow tie. Red was one of Mama's favorite colors. We all were readying for the memorial we had put together for Cory and Inez.

"Everyone. Before we head out, I want to lay out some clear guidelines, now that we're running the Syndicate. This is not perfect, again, I'm still learning our places, but for now, what I need from you is simple," I started, looking around at everyone's faces.

Uncle Snap, in his all white but wearing a red cap, came from where he stood on the stairway talking to one of the Forty Thieves on his cell phone. They were going to be our escorts to the memorial. He gave me a respectful nod of support and put his cell away.

"So everyone can know the roles I'm giving out is congruent with the Syndicate's growth and what I'm learning as leader. So, yeah. Melissa." I glanced at my sister.

She was off near the door, staring out of the window in thought. Standing with her ankles crossed leaning against the corridor wall, she wore a body-contouring white dress with red heels. Her hair fell over her shoulders in soft curls with a large brimmed hat upon her head.

When she looked my way, I continued. "Lissa. As we already told you, and we all know in this family, you're mad good with crunching numbers and money. We're going to be trusting in you to go over Mama's account info, insurance, and whatever else moneywise to make sure we are good financially. So, your office will be out of the club that we have you running as our clean cover. Good with that?"

Melissa pushed away from the door. "I got it. I mean, that's what I'm good for right? And you don't need any more problems so the family will be protected."

"Thank you, baby girl," I said watching how slightly off she sounded. "Whatever work you do, we will always come around and keep you safe as well. Which leads to security."

Exhaling, I turned my attention to Lamont. He sat on the armrest of one of the old, big wingback chairs in the parlor. His gaze seemed to be focused on Mama's picture, as I moved his way. He wore white jeans that were slightly baggy, held by a red belt with a big buckle that he tucked his white button-down shirt into.

"Monty," I said to get his attention while reaching out to rest my hand against his shoulder.

"Yeah, Von? What up?" He turned to look at me and I could almost view the ghosts that reflected from his eyes.

I understood it; today was a difficult day. "Monty. You've been this family's protection for years. You know how you love to fight right?"

He laughed as I did, then nodded. "What about it?"

"While you do your training to box, this is what I need from you. As of today, you are the manager of the Forty Thieves. Right now, I know I won't put it all on you. You have to learn the ropes of what it'll take as well as train with them. But check it, as you learn with me, I want you to eventually be my head of security. Cory would have shared that with you but . . ."

"Yeah, I get it and this is dope. I'll learn what I need to make sure you're secure and they learn my type of style of fighting, brah," Monty reassured me.

"I appreciate you, fam," I said, reaching out to give him a brotherly hug and squeeze of his shoulders.

"Naveen and Jojo." I let go of Monty then walked up to our two youngest members of the family. Navy stood on the opposite side of Shanelle.

He sported white kicks and a similar outfit to Jojo. His long hair was pulled up on his head in a bun, and the red he wore was the watch on his wrist. "You two are our hearts, the babies with gifts that can serve us well. But, for now, I just need you both to finish up school. Once that happens, I'll introduce you both to the rest of your roles okay? Just trust in me on that and I promise. I got you both."

"It's cool," Jojo said shrugging. "You got us on the Mist design anyway."

"Yeah, I have some mechanics to tweak with it anyway," Navy added with a slightly unsure tone to his voice.

"Much appreciated then," I said giving them a warm smile.

Shanelle came my way when I turned my attention to her. I took her outreached hand, then I leaned down to kiss her. "Baby, you know the deal. You're my right, but since you're mean with the guns, I'll need you to work with Monty in regard to weapon distribution. I also want you to look in on the other legal businesses Mama had like you did with the club. I want you to put your business savvy to good use and figure out how to take more of our illegal activity and make it legal. On top of that, I need you to pick up where Inez and Cory would have been, but we'll figure this shit out as we go. For now, everyone, just know, we are all we got. We can't keep breaking like we are; otherwise, the enemy comes in and destroys all that Mama worked for with us."

"Damn right," Uncle Snap chimed in from the back.

He signaled to me that it was time to go, and I turned to glance at Mama's pictures. "We lost so much. I haven't held us down like I should, but at the end of the day here we are. Let's go honor our family and show the love Inez and Cory needed."

As we finished handling our family business, it then led to our memorial for Cory and Inez. We all stood side by side in white staring at the smiling faces of Cory and Inez, next to Mama's picture. Uncle and Mama were right. Our intentions were good for all three of them, but in the end it had turned foul. As I laid my flowers out for my lost family, I wished that there were some Irish left so that I could personally pour their blood over the graves before me in revenge.

Chapter 24

Shanelle

Things weren't perfect in our lives, but we were getting better. There wasn't a day that went by I didn't think of Cory and Inez. I missed them both, but Inez's words that I only cared about Javon stung. There was a strong churning in my stomach each time I replayed her words because I was guilty. I was so in love with Javon that sometimes he was the only person who mattered and, in that sense, we'd failed our younger brothers and sisters. It would never happen again; that I was sure of.

"So how are you, sis?" Melissa asked me. She looked at her watch then glanced at her cell before looking back at me. She had been busy setting the club up and, I had to admit, she was doing the damn thing. The grand opening was in two weeks and she had shit set up so perfectly neither Javon nor I could find anything to complain about.

I was at the stove, cooking Mama's famous fried chicken. Jojo and Navy were off doing whatever teenage boys did. Monty had been seeing that chick from Rize heavily. Javon and Uncle Snap were out handling business with the Syndicate. We were getting back to business.

I smiled at Melissa. She was dressed in all white, looking like the business owner she was. Although she was smiling, there was something eerie about the moment. I got a strange sense of impending doom while looking at her and I didn't know why.

"I'm okay. Could be better. Missing Cory and Inez," I said.

She laid a hand on my shoulder. "Me too. Hey, remember the time Cory rubbed jalapeno peppers in Monty's underwear to pay him back for putting those grubs in his bed?"

I threw my head back and laughed. "I do. I do. That was the funniest shit! Monty thought some girl had burned him so he had Mama take him to the clinic."

Melissa laughed with me. We were cracking up when her phone buzzed.

"Oh my gosh, yes," she squealed. "Mama got in both their asses something good."

I may have been laughing, but I had always been one to pay attention to detail. So when her eyes darted around like she was expecting something or someone to jump out at her, I took note of it. I was about to ask her what was wrong when Jojo came running in the house.

There was panic in his eyes as Navy came falling in right behind him. "They got Monty," Navy cried.

My heart did a somersault and I tossed the towel I'd been holding then turned the chicken off. "Who?" I yelled. I grabbed my cell from the counter and dialed Javon. I'd been trying to reach him off and on all day. I needed to tell him something, but couldn't reach him. Anytime he was doing business with the Syndicate, he was hard to reach.

"The cops," Jojo yelled. "He was turning into the neighborhood when they pulled him over. Navy and I were watching and they found drugs in his car and a gun," he rushed out.

"What?" I yelled.

"And they coming here, big sis," Navy added in a rush.

I didn't even have time to question him. He wouldn't have been able to respond anyway. Cops and federal agents bum-rushed the house.

Guns and assault rifles were shoved into all our faces. "Get on the ground! Get on the ground," was shouted all around.

I yelled for Jojo and Navy to get down and do as told. Last thing I needed was a trigger-happy cop to kill one of them. I turned around to check on Melissa, only to find she was gone. All kinds of emotions overtook me in that moment. The main one being that she'd had something to do with this. I prayed I was wrong.

A cop had his knee in my back and it hurt like hell.

"Stand her up," a familiar voice said. I knew it was Detective Monroe. Once the agent stood me up, I spit in his face.

"Fucking asshole," I quipped. "I'm pregnant you piece of shit."

Monroe stopped the agent from retaliating against what I'd done. "Calm down, Shanelle," Monroe said. "That language isn't befitting of a lady."

"Yeah, well you just stormed into my mother's home and then your fuck boys threw me on the ground while I'm pregnant so pardon me if I left the lady in me somewhere else."

I was breathing hard. Jojo and Navy were yelling. Two agents snatched Jojo up and shoved him into a wall then stepped on his glasses. Jojo normally panicked when he couldn't see.

"Hey, you stepped on my fucking glass," he yelled.

Another agent had Navy cuffed but snatched him from the floor by a handful of his hair.

"Leave them alone," I said and tried to get away only for the agent who had me to snatch me back.

"Ms. McPhearson," Detective Monroe said to me as he pulled out a piece of paper, "this is a warrant to search this house."

I frowned. "A warrant to search . . . What the hell for?" I couldn't front like nervousness hadn't settled into the pit of my stomach. My mind thought about the secret bunker underneath the house.

"We have reason to believe this house has drugs in it," he answered calmly then pointed to the basement door then upstairs.

Agents immediately headed for the basement and upstairs. It sounded as if they were tearing up the place. I looked at Navy, who hung his head; then I looked at Jojo. He couldn't see me that well with his glasses off but I knew he was trying to search for me by the way his eyes squinted.

"Drugs. There are no drugs in here I can assure you," I said. I prayed that what I was saying was true. I knew Javon had already had all the drugs and money in the bunker removed from the house.

Monroe smiled a bit. "I'll be the judge of that. Oh and allow me to introduce myself properly. I'm Special Agent in charge, Andy Monroe. My partner is Special Agent Magoo Stillwaters and we've been investigating your little brother Jojo over there for quite some time now," the man said then chuckled. "Sorry we had to pretend to be local cops. Part of the job ya know."

I would say I was relieved to know it wasn't Mama or Javon being investigated, but my heart sank to the pit of my stomach knowing Jojo was the target.

"He has quite the operation set up," Stillwaters said.

I wanted to spit on the dog-faced man. He annoyed me way more than Monroe.

"We found something," an agent said.

Jojo groaned low against the wall. Tears were coming down his face. I knew when they had gone to the basement where his lab was that they would find something.

"No need to cry now, son," Monroe said.

"Leave him alone," I yelled.

"What is that?" Stillwaters asked the agent who had come from the basement.

"Looks like Ecstasy," the agent answered.

"Those are mine," I lied.

Monroe shook his head. "No, they aren't, Shanelle. Both you and I know that." He looked at the agent who had been holding Jojo. "Put him in the car."

"No, no," I screamed.

"Let him go," Navy screamed trying to move toward Jojo only to have an agent throw him to the floor.

"That makes two brothers arrested in one day," Monroe said. "Did you know Lamont was involved with Jojo's business?" he asked. I scowled at the man who only smiled. "This would be a good time to call Javon and let him know he can call his lawyer now."

Outro

Uncle Snap

Shit had gone way left. When Javon had told me he was going to remove seats and replace Syndicate members, I knew all hell would break loose and that was exactly what was happening. After losing Cory and Inez, Javon had been on a roll. I still had no idea just how the hell he had managed to make a move on the Irish as he did. Just like I didn't know how the fuck my nephew was going to pull this shit off.

"How the fuck is this possible?" Creed asked. He was the head of the MC Federation. All the motorcycle clubs in the South who were worth anything had to answer to him. He looked every bit of his role, too. Leather and denim from head to toe. Tattoos covered his arms and neck.

But if you had the eye and looked close enough, you would see that Lucky wasn't the only mixed breed at the table. Javon sat at the head of table in a pose that was reminiscent of the one Malcolm X made famous. He was dressed in all black. Lucky sat to the right of him quietly observing everything.

"You're taking my seat, kid?" Creed asked again.

"Six seats will be removed by choice or by force," Javon reiterated. "But, Creed, you can relax. We need you at the table. Now I have to be honest here, full disclosure. I was going to allow six chairs to stay, but have the older members removed; but I was going to allow those members to choose someone from their faction to replace them. I'm not so sure anymore."

Creed looked around with a frown still etched on his golden, tanned face.

"We need the MC Federation. You guys run a clean ship. Not to mention your pipelines to prison are precise. Also, the clubs have access to other pipelines overseas that bring in a shitload of guns, product, and money so it would be stupid of me to remove you from the table. The money you bring in alone is enough to secure your seat, Creed. My mother spoke well of you, although she didn't like your old lady or your father," Javon told the man honestly.

Creed chuckled, but kept his thoughts to himself.

I flanked Javon when he stood. He glanced at his phone again then looked at me. By the look on his face, I knew it was Shanelle. That would make the fourth time his phone had distracted him during the proceedings.

I laid a hand on his shoulder. "Ignore it until business is done," I whispered to him. He needed to be on his toes while around these men. One slip and he could make a mistake he couldn't come back from. Shanelle could wait. I'd talk to him about that later. Clearly she could pose a threat by being his weakness and I couldn't have that. I was happy when he nodded and kept to the business at hand.

"I know you're all wondering why I had the seats arranged as they are today. Normally everyone has a designated seat. Today is the start of change. The Syndicate is a big deal. We all know that. I also know that most of you think I'm just some shit-faced nigger who doesn't deserve to be here. And I give you that; however, I'm a businessman and before the Syndicate is anything else, we're a business, a conglomerate if you will. On my right side, we have Lucky, who speaks for the North. You know his stock. Know what bloodline he comes from. So I wouldn't suggest any of you try any stupid shit like taking him out."

Javon let his eyes linger on each man and woman at the table. He smiled.

"Next we have Ming Lee. She speaks for our Chinese friends and runs a damn clean organization."

Ming smiled coyly and gave Javon a slight nod.

"We have Miguel who runs the Mexicans in the South and West. He's also our connect to the Cartel across the border. His seat is solidified."

"Thank you, *amigo*," Miguel said.

"Nighthawk is our connect to the reservations all over the U.S. It would be foolish to get rid of him. Not to mention with the way we wash money using the casinos in some places, to cut him off would be a fatal mistake for many of us."

The big Seminole Indian nodded with a smirk on his face. I'd heard him speaking to Monty a few days before. It was good that Monty would have someone who would school him on the life he never knew.

"So," Javon continued, "we have Nighthawk, Creed, Lucky, Ming, and Miguel. The Natives, the MC Feds, the Italians, the Chinese, and the Mexicans. That leaves one more seat."

"This is bullshit!" shouted Rusev. "My family has been at this table for decades."

"And what exactly have you brought to the table within the last ten years?" Javon asked. "The money you bring in can be replaced ten times. The product you're having shipped from Russia is not top quality. You've been fucking over the Syndicate for years, but you and Cormac had a system, right? You let the Irish skim off the top as long as Cormac always voted against you losing your seat."

I could tell that everyone else at the table was stunned to silence.

"We're no longer running this fucking house as we once were and if you got a problem with that, you can join Cormac," Javon said, venom laced in his tongue. "I've made my choices."

"So we just get pushed out?" Roman, the head of the Romanian empire, asked. "We no longer get to eat?"

"Oh you eat. We all will eat, Roman. You just don't get to have a say in what goes on at this table anymore," Javon answered.

"This is . . . this is madness," Rusev blasted. "We're just going to stand for this?" he asked, eying the other members who had obviously been ousted just as he had.

"And who gets the last chair?" Delanna asked.

An easy smile covered Javon's features. It was a smile that said he knew something no one else did. Shit even I was curious to know who would be taking that seat.

Javon adjusted his suit jacket then his cufflinks and said with finality, "The last chair goes to a member of the Commission."

The room got so quiet you could hear a fly piss on cotton. My eyes were just as wide as everyone else's. Holy fuck, Javon had just called an audible that would change the entire game. My nephew had officially shut me the fuck up.

Lucky leaned forward and quirked a brow at Javon. "You can't be serious," he said.

Javon nodded once. "I am."

Just as Javon said that, the double doors opened and in walked an old but spirited Italian man. The man had so much power that it settled over the room like a blanket. We all knew who he was so there was no need for introductions. Lucky stood immediately and made his way over to the man. It was no secret that they both sported the same crested ring. The man was flanked by armed guards, both men and women, who looked like they wouldn't hesitate to kill anyone in the room who moved the wrong way. Lucky, who was much taller than the man, kneeled. The old man placed a kiss on the top of his head then on both his cheeks.

"They treating you well, *il nipote*?" the old man asked, his voice croaky, but stern. He reminded me of Marlon Brando from *The Godfather*.

"Yes, *lo zio*," Lucky said then stood. "Come, have my seat."

Lucky helped the old man over. It was odd to me to see Italians so accepting of a bastard offspring, especially one who had black in him. Javon didn't kneel, but he dipped his head so the old man could place a kiss there. He took Javon's hand in both of his and squeezed as he spoke.

"The Commission grants you with our protection from here until you step down from the Syndicate. The proposition you submitted could not be ignored and as long as it's in place you have the blessing of the Commission."

The old man held his hand out and one of his guards placed a small black box in it. He opened it and pulled out a ring. It was similar to the crested one Lucky and the old man wore, but it had the symbol for the Syndicate on there as well. He slipped it on Javon's left ring finger then grabbed his face to kiss both his cheeks.

Now it made sense how Javon was able to effectively take out the Irish. I was so gotdamned shocked that I didn't notice the old man give a hand signal to his guards. So when gunfire erupted, I immediately drew my weapon and shielded Javon, but there was no need to. The other six members of the Syndicate had been executed at the hands of the Commission. Javon's hands were clean so any backlash against him would mean backlash against the Commission.

The Commission consisted of the top five crime families in New York and Italy. Javon had just made himself a "made" man. No one saw that coming, not even me. The game had officially changed.

Stay tuned for *The Syndicate Part II*